Ac

*Time in a Tea Crate* by Donna Robinson

"This charming book tells of Donna Robinson's great-grandfather Louis Suzor as he realizes his dream of bringing automobiles to Japan. The stories related here are rich with historical detail and valuable cultural insights and include photographs of this bygone era in Japan. It's a time of gentle French manners and big events, and Donna writes a memorable story of love and ambition."
- Vickie Farmer EdD

"Having traveled extensively throughout France, and having spent time in Japan and North Africa, *Time in a Tea Crate* brought back the essence of these different cultures and allowed me to a have glimpse into the era when the onset of automobile travel changed the world in unpredictable ways. Take a ride with Louis Suzor as he navigates through financial gains and losses. Meet his family and other characters. Enjoy the photos and lyrical descriptions. Well done Donna Robinson!"
- J.R. (Janet) Bergstrom, author of
*Three Passions: Art, Adventure, Words*

"Donna Robinson combines Louis Suzor's 1955 memoir with family correspondence, oral tradition, and historical research to give her great-grandfather's adventures new life. A delightful story of a young boy born in France in 1873, then served in a Zouave battalion in Algiers in the 1890s. At the turn of the twentieth century, he and his family moved to Japan, where he was one of the first to import automobiles."
- Richard Pearce-Moses, *Fellow, Society of American Archivists*

# Time in a Tea Crate

By Donna Robinson

*Hold close your memories.*

*Donna Robinson*

ISBN: 978-0-578-76935-6

Contact
donnarobinson1900@gmail.com

Website Info
donnarobinsonwrites.com

Disclaimer: This is a work of creative nonfiction. Names, places, characters and incidents were viewed through my great-grandfather's eyes and then through mine. Some names are the product of the author's imagination, and any resemblance to actual persons, living or dead, is entirely coincidental.

Cover Photo by Hamilton Hayes

Printed and bound in the USA.

"Sometimes you will never know the true value

of a moment

until it becomes a memory."

THEODORE SEUSS GEISEL
WRITER, CARTOONIST, ANIMATOR

If there's a book that you want to read, but it hasn't
been written yet,
then you must write it.

# Preface

I met my great-grandfather, Louis Suzor, when he was 89 and I was eleven. My parents had sent me to live with my grandparents for a year in Paris. I had heard many stories about him and my great-grandmother, Henriette. I remember standing in his home watching how he walked carefully, holding onto his cane. Henriette kindly held onto his free arm as they came to greet me, their American great-granddaughter.

Louis Suzor was born in Anvin, France, in 1873, two years into what was later called La Belle Époque, an era of Western history spanning the end of the Franco-Prussian War in 1871 to the beginning of World War I in 1914. During this golden age, France experienced a surge in the Arts, culture, and most importantly for businessmen, industry that produced raw materials, some of which were used in fabricating automobile bodies. Then, in the 1890s, Edouard Michelin invented removable pneumatic tires for bicycles and automobiles. For my great-grandfather, a man fascinated with automobiles, anything seemed possible.

Simultaneously, on the other side of the world, Japan—a country that traditionally kept to itself—was suddenly open to the world. Yokohama grew from a small fishing village to a major import and export center. Manufacturing districts appeared and settlements of Chinese and Westerners were built to accommodate the expanding new commerce.

When an unforeseen event in 1900 sent Louis, and therefore his family, to Yokohama by steamship, my great-grandfather embraced the challenge. A visionary with unrelenting enthusiasm, Louis jumped at the opportunity to travel half-way around the world and take part in a new era of economic prosperity—introducing the automobile in its many forms and uses to Japan. Of course, this was possible because he came from wealth and high social standing, and he was therefore able to take this economic risk with his wife and of his five children. However, his daughter Andree was forced to stay behind in Paris, due to asthma. I spent a week in Nice in 1973 with my aunt, Andree, and she said that although she was raised by Louis' and Henriette's mothers, she was never able to get over being left behind

Louis's story is about risk, adaptability and resiliency, family, and what we hold close when it appears that we have lost everything.

When my mother, a French war bride, passed away, I became the keeper of my great-grandfather's written memories of the debut of the automobile in Yokohama, complete with historical photographs. The photos of family, automobiles, and stunning mountain scenery, postcards and letters recording his twenty-five years in Japan lured me into the museum of his family's memories.

For three years, I researched his life, examining his Japanese postcards and identifying the postal dates by the year of the emperor's reign. I pored over one-hundred-year old photographs—miniature mysteries—that held details waiting to be understood. For hours I delved into the history of Yokohama and I learned about French automobiles. My research led me to Siberian fur trappers, ocean liners, caviar merchants, and finally the natural disaster that changed Japan's history and a family's life forever.

As a child, I remember hearing stories from my grandmother, Edith, Louis' oldest child. She told me Japanese stories and sang Japanese children's songs. Sharing her memories of living in Japan helped me appreciate the way Louis' children felt about being raised in Yokohama.

I listened to other relatives' accounts of the Suzor family's experiences and tried to stay true to the stories. My cousin in France, Gilbert Viel, Louis's grandson, filled in the blanks when I couldn't find my way out of a rabbit hole. Gilbert's memory of his grandfather's stories and his sense of humor helped me see events from Louis' point of view. I researched turn-of-the-century Japanese newspapers archived on-line to support Louis' stories with authentic details.

Originally, I wanted to focus on Louis's business dealings as the main thrust of my writing. However, in working with my editor, we realized that Louis's stories held so much more. After strategizing with her about how to best connect and tell these fragments of stories as a unified whole—and after many hours mulling over my various options—I ultimately decided to frame these snapshots of history when Louis was writing his memoir in the years after he left Yokohama. And when I found a tea crate in an antique store — the one pictured on the cover — the pieces all fell into place.

I also chose to have Louis be the narrator in all but three stories because I felt an uncanny connection to him. When writing in first person the story fell out of my proverbial pen. When the Muses offer, I figure I might as well accept.

I strove to portray sensitivity to Japanese citizens struggling to adapt to the challenges of new Western influences as well as Europeans immersed in a strange culture. Because these events took place over 100 years ago and memory can change the shape of stories, some facts may have been omitted. I have no way of verifying what happened for sure. I may have inadvertently changed some names and details. I strove to reimagine scenes with as many factual details as possible — many coming from artifacts that I own — to point towards the essence of the story and to do my best to capture the truth.

Writing this book has made my memory of that moment when my great-grandfather and great-grandmother gingerly walked down the hallway to greet me, so much sweeter. I feel an indescribable kinship with this man, as well as a new closeness to my family and the generations that came before. I also write this for my children and grandchildren, so they may know about their ancestors. And, of course, I hope my efforts offer new details to the historical world.

If I could see him now, I hope he would remember me and be pleased with how I reconstructed these stories. I would love to show these stories to him and learn even more details that only he would truly know. And I hope that he would understand the love and care with which I hold close his museum of paper memories.

In loving memory of my great-grandfather
Louis Marie Suzor Malet de Graville
1873-1967

# Chapter One

Camille Jenatzy (in the driver's seat) and his wife riding the *Jamais Contente* celebrate another win in 1899. He was the first driver to exceed 100km/h. Paris, France

*Photograph Hulton Archive/Getty Images*

# Chapter One
## The Drawing Room
## Chateau de Rilly, France, 1947

*Jenatzy Shot Dead* reads the New York Times headline.

Thirty-four years later, the yellow tinged crumpling newsprint, dated December 8, 1913, still brings back memories of watching Camille Jenatzy, the famous Belgian auto racer, in the streets of Paris. I believe now that is where my fascination with automobiles began.

I sit in my armchair in the drawing room of our chateau, pulling old photographs, postcards, newspaper articles, and letters from a Japanese tea crate nestled close to my desk. The crate's tin lining has kept everything dry all these years.

I pick up the Jenatzy story. The article reads he was rushed to the nearest doctor by motorcar after a tragic hunting accident in the Belgium Ardennes. A mutual acquaintance at the time told me that he had been pretending to be an animal in the bushes, another hunter shot him by accident, and he died on the way to medical help. What a shocking ending for one of Europe's most wild and daring racers. And even more staggering because my father died from a similar hunting accident when I was a young boy. He was leading a friend on a hunt through the brush and that friend tripped and fired his gun, a fatal accident for my father. A shocking loss for our family, too.

Followers at the racetracks and fanatics on the streets knew Jenatzy as an enthusiastic motorist and a successful businessman. I close my eyes and lean my head back against my chair, the late-morning sun warms my cheek, remembering how even I wanted to be *Le Diable Rouge*.

## Le Diable Rouge — The Red Devil
## Paris, France, 1900

I feel cool morning air against my face as I fold back the metal shutters and close the windows to our Parisian apartment by the Seine River. My lovely wife, Henriette, puts on a warmer sweater and pours two steaming cups of *café au lait* and hands one toward me. Before taking the cup from Henriette, I move several disorganized stacks of papers and pull out the writing shelf of my bureau. Then, I take the *café* from her, take a sip, and savor the flavor. I settle into my chair and take a minute to enjoy the warmth and aroma rising from the cup before I set it on the desk and start the task at hand.

"So, another day of champagne rain," Henriette mutters as she attempts to wrap our infant daughter, Edith, in warmer blankets. The last two months have left Henriette fatigued, so a day of sunshine would be much appreciated.

Mounds of transport documents have been accumulating for my new import and export business. Because of shipping schedules, arrangements for cargo deliveries can take weeks and are often complicated, let alone expensive. I need to raise capital. I have decided to offer fire insurance as part of my company's services, but the more services, the more paperwork. I am aware some plans and risks are sizable, but my wife and I are young, and I feel eager for the challenge. I remove my cufflinks, roll up my sleeves, and begin to sort the insistent heaps of paper on the shelves, reaching for the ones from Japan.

A loud commotion on the street below interrupts the tranquil morning on the picturesque Quai Billancourt once again. I startle, yet the sounds are now familiar since Paris became an essential part of three principal automobile races: The Tour de France, The Paris-St. Malo, and the Paris-Ostend. The baker down the street told me there would be practice time trials today. I forgot! I drop my papers, rise, and dash to the apartment window. Never mind the paperwork for now. My eyes focus on the magnificent machines.

"It's that crazy Belgian race car driver, Camille Jenatzy again," I say to Henriette. "Did you know the other drivers call him *Le Diable Rouge*? You can always tell it's him driving by his fiery red beard." My wife purses her lips in disdain as she lays Edith in her bassinette. "Henriette, this could be the beginning of a whole new industry in France. Come look! The vehicle is shaped like a cigar with tiny wheels! His speed is *formidable*."

Baby Edith has been roused by the noise, so Henriette is not impressed. She picks Edith back up, stands, and begins to bounce our baby, trying to soothe her. "The Red Devil? Is that what they're calling him these days? Well, it's unfortunate he has chosen to use our street as a speedway. He and his friends are always striving for higher speed. He has become a terror to the neighborhood and he's a dangerous driver, too."

"Oh, Henriette, he is young like us, and passionate about driving. Do you know that he has been whizzing by at the dazzling speed of 26 miles per hour? He wants more speed, always pushing to go faster and faster! It's not a coincidence that the name of his car is *La Jamais Contente*!" I pace the room, finding it impossible to disguise my exhilaration. "More and more people are lining the streets. Come and look!"

"His car is named the *Never Satisfied*? That's what I should call you." She usually loves my passion, but this new obsession has become a challenge. "Do you forget so quickly that our poor dog, Fidel, was run over two weeks ago? And we are not the only ones to have lost our pets. Jenatzy is indeed the reckless *Diable Rouge*." She walks back and puts down the now calm Edith and takes a grateful sip of *café*.

"Ma Henriette, I'm so sorry about *le petit chien*," I know these are the words to say right now, but my honest attention is on the car outside. "And I realize the uproar from the automobile motors keeps waking up the baby and it is difficult for you, too. *Eh bien,* I'll go outside to see what is going on," I propose, attempting to look apologetic, while anxious not to miss anything happening on the streets. I cross to the front door and open it, while at the same time taking my hat from the stand. "The rain has stopped for now," I add, flashing a smile before closing the door behind me.

Once standing on the street, the commotion draws me like a magnet. I make my way over to the other enthusiasts, eager to learn more about this car. "What is going on?" I ask a gentleman in a bowler hat standing next to me on the *quai*. He holds a stopwatch.

"Genatzy's torpedo-shaped car has two 25-kilowatt electric motors run by batteries, and it weighs 3,200 pounds," the man states. "Last year in April he reached 49 mph on the racing course. I'm convinced he will break his own record in the next race!"

Impressed and energized, I readily join conversations with the onlookers. "Look at the number of people viewing this spectacle. We are part of these new possibilities!" People nod their heads in agreement. "Just think," I say to the gentleman beside me. "As we're here watching, motor racing is exploding in popularity here in France. This upsurge in interest can only mean opportunity for automobile enthusiasts like us." He continues to nod, but I can tell he, like the others around us, are just looking at the car. They, I realize, do not see the implications—with more cars, more novelty.

With more novelty, more readiness to invest. More readiness to invest, more opportunities for profit. The link between the future and my pocketbook becomes clear. The men around me banter, and I hold my new knowledge to myself while joining them in the pure fun.

After 30 minutes, I walk away from the crowd, my head buzzing with my new notions. I want to celebrate with Henriette. I go to the *boulangerie* around the corner for a *baguette* and some special *chocolat*. I head home, purchase a bottle of *vin ordinaire* on the way, and sprint up the cobblestone stairs two at a time. I pause to wipe my feet on the mat, and then I open the door to the apartment and place the bread, chocolate, and wine on the living room table. Before I cross the red Persian carpet, I kiss Henriette on the cheek.

"You should have seen that car, Henriette!" I exclaim. She raises one eyebrow, and I bend over the white bassinette to pick up my *bébé* Edith. "Edith, our little family is going to have many challenges, but I have made up my mind that we will be happy here—or wherever we go," I say. "I promise you and Mama that my business will be a success, and you both will be proud of me."

"What are you talking about?" Henriette looks confused. "And take off your hat, please."

"Ma Henriette, you will be proud, too, riding in our new automobile if our business takes us to Japan," I say with a self-assured grin.

"*Alors!* When do you think this will happen? Next week, in a few years, or ten years from now? I have no interest in waking babies or killing dogs in any wild extravagance, let alone leaving my home."

I place a second reassuring kiss on her cheek, despite her short temper today, and reply, "I don't know. It depends on the business. We will go when the time is right. Now, if we want to go at all, I must look over these papers on my desk," I say, taking my hat off, placing it on the stand next to the door and returning to my desk for the afternoon.

# Chapter Two

Louis Suzor at boarding school in Normandy, France.
He was born in 1873 in Anvin, France.

# Chapter Two
## The Drawing Room
## Chateau de Rilly, France, July 1947

Henriette bustles into the salon. "Louis," she says, "please help me by putting your photos and letters in these boxes. The maid will be coming in to clean for our party, and I wouldn't want to interfere with your organization." She looks at me and smiles.

The aroma of freshly sautéed onions floats into the room after Henriette. "Ah. *Soupe aux oignons*. And fresh baguettes. Gruyere cheese from the village market?" I ask, savoring each scent.

"Yes, for lunch this afternoon. I knew you'd be pleased. You have a few hours, so you should have time to put some of this away," she says, motioning towards my envelopes overflowing with pictures. I look down at sepia photos of myself at five years old at boarding school, and a photo from my wedding day. I stand as a young man in suit and tails with my 18-year-old bride in Paris. Has it already been 50 years?

I have kept my photos, newspaper clippings and postcards for the day I finally start writing my memoirs. Perhaps today is that day. Yes. I will start after lunch. The process feels daunting, but I have the time and the memories here in my tea crate.

"I will come and get you when your favorite soup is ready," she says, arranging three pillows on the sofa before leaving to do other tasks. I smile, as the scent of garlic makes its way from the kitchen.

*Soupe du Jour*
**Normandy, France, 1879**

I am small, but I can think big. My brothers Paul, Georges, and I go to a Catholic boy's boarding school in Normandy. I am five years old. My father died in a hunting accident a few years ago. My mother won't hear me if I have a problem. She is far away in Paris. She has left us with the nuns, and they don't really care if any of us get homesick. I usually sing myself to sleep. I try to bring food back from the kitchen and hide it under my mattress, in case I get hungry.

I always wake up early and hungry. Breakfast is bread and *café au lait*. Sometimes, instead, we get a bowl of awful thin and watery onion soup. It's cold and has grease floating in circles on top. My stomach flops whenever I inhale that onion and oil odor. But I have to eat it. The nuns in long white robes pace through the dark dining hall and watch us until we finish.

I have thought of a way to fix this. Two weeks ago, I sent our cook a letter asking for her soup recipe. She lives in Paris and has one cat. I like her cat, but don't like the mice it brings inside at night.

So, I am bringing the recipe to Soeur Emmanuelle, the school cook. She will be happy, I am sure. I'm wearing my middy shirt and shorts just like I should. When I get to the doorway of the kitchen, I stop and wave my arms and get her attention. She walks over to me and looks down at me from under her floppy hat.

I smile politely and say in a quiet tone, "Excuse me. Our cook in Paris makes our soup with more salt. With extra beef bones and lots of cheese, too. Maman lets me put extra Gruyere cheese on top." I try to read the nun's face, but I can't tell if she is happy. "We dip fresh baguettes into the *potage* and soak up the broth. It's delicious!" I say, proud of my big word. "Here is the recipe." I feel shy, handing her the paper.

She takes the paper from me. "Merci, Monsieur Suzor," she says without a smile. My eyes get big as I see her tear the recipe in half. I feel confused. Why is she being so mean? She turns and heads to the kitchen. I stand there, not sure what to do, but she comes back right away and says, "I will trade you the recipe for four washcloths and a tub of water for cleaning up after breakfast. Bring the towels back when you finish."

I take the bucket and hang my head and go to look for my two brothers in the dining hall. As I walk, I accidentally splash the water on my shoes. I tell them what happened, and they laugh at me which doesn't feel good. Paul pats me on the back, which does feel good, and says, "Louis, life is full of surprises. You might as well get used to it." They leave me without offering to help. I feel more alone without them than I ever have without my Mama.

I learn that day that washing all the tables takes about an hour. As I scrub, I think of another plan. I won't give up. Next time when I have onion soup, I will fill my mouth with it and then spit it into a napkin and put it in my pocket. Every…bite. Anything other than eating that yucky soup. The boys might laugh. My shorts might drip with water, but I won't care.

I feel very smart. And I decide that I am on my own. I will always find my own way.

*An Impulsive Marriage Proposal*
**Normandy and Paris, 1880-1981**

I'm seven now. One day while at home in Paris for the weekend, Maman and I pay a special visit to mother's best friend Fanny Boutard, and her new baby, Henri. They don't live too far away and are our close neighbors, just a short buggy ride away.

When we knock on the door, the maid in a grey and white striped dress opens the door and smiles. She announces as she opens the big wooden door, "Madame Suzor Malet de Graville and her son, Louis, have arrived." I always feel special when she says that

The maid's name is Helene. She has dimples and makes me feel welcome. She leads us to the drawing room. Their apartment is a lot like ours. Tall windows with shutters look out on the street below. Green and gold curtains hug the windows trying to keep the heat in. Antique gold damask chairs add color to a gray day in the city. A basket full of baby blankets nestle close to Madame Boutard who is resting on a jade green settee.

"Fanny, please don't get up," Maman says. "I'm sure you are very tired. We are so happy to be here and meet your little one!" She sits on a brocade love seat and coos at the baby.

I take my seat in front of an elaborate tea table with an ornate silver teapot. I hope for lemon biscuits, my favorite. Maybe I can go into the kitchen and have some pumpkin soup with butter and cream. I could smell it cooking when we walked by the kitchen.

Turning to me, Madame Boutard says, "Louis, you are getting so handsome, just like your brothers. Where are they today?"

"They are taking our dog, Petit Pierre, to the Bois de Boulogne for a walk. Georges and Paul stayed homne to study. But I finished my schoolwork yesterday, so I could come and visit with Maman."

"When do you go back to school, Louis?"

"We have to go back Tuesday to Normandy."

"Helene, could you bring us some tea and biscuits, please?" The maid nods and retreats to the kitchen. The aroma of freshly baked bread escapes the pantry and tickles my nose.

"Maman, can I go and get the toys under the stairs?" I ask after we have waited a few minutes, hoping to spend the afternoon playing instead of visiting with the adults.

"No, not yet, Louis. We are here to meet someone very special, the new petite Parisienne."

I stop what I am doing. "Ah no," I think to myself. La Petite Parisienne means it is a girl. The baby's is not a Henri. I shrug my shoulders and remove my school beret, turning it with my hands. Trying unsuccessfully to hide my disappointment, I admit, "Madame Boutard, I was hoping for a baby boy. I would have taught him how to build a chateau with all the castle blocks and bricks behind the curtain under the stairs. And I could have shown him how to make a wagon out of wood. I'm getting good at making coaches and carriages. Maybe I will build Maman a new coach when I get older. I have some great ideas."

Madame Boutard smiles and leans over, patting the settee next to her. "Come close, Louis. Her name is Henreitte. It's too late to change her name to Henri. I am so sorry," she grins, ruffling my hair, and glances at my mother. Then she gently hands me the bundle swaddled in lace-trimmed white baby blankets. I think her head is under this lacey cap. I pull the bonnet back, and peek at her cheeks. They're rosy.

"I'm glad she is asleep. If I do something wrong, she won't know it was me!" I look at the baby and feel nervous. "I'm afraid I might drop her." I look at her again and notice curls framing her tiny face. "Maybe a little girl isn't so bad," I say with good manners. I do like babies. But the longer I hold her, the more tired my arms get. I'm ready to go play. "She may even become charming when she grows older. Like me." I add with confidence.

Mama and Madame Boutard laugh.

I don't know what to say next. I want to go play, but I do not want to upset my mother's best friend, or my mother. So, I say what I hear good boys are supposed to say. "I've been thinking. Since la petite Parisienne is not a boy, but a nice little girl, I will ask her to marry me, but I don't expect an answer now since she is just a baby. Now, may I go play under the stairs?" I hope the plan will work.

Mama laughs and replies, "Of course, Louis. Today is a day for playing. Now return your bride to be, la petite Parisienne, to Madame Boutard. I will get to know my future daughter-in-law while you amuse yourself building a marvelous chateau. Maybe you can build one for you and Henriette to live in."

"Can I have lemonade and biscuits?"

"Yes. Helene is in the kitchen and she has some pumpkin soup for you too.

# Chapter Three

Louis Suzor in full Zouave uniform. He was in a class of light
infantry of the French Army in North Africa.
He is wearing traditional white summer sarouel trousers. Algiers,
Algeria

.

## Chapter Three
## The Drawing Room
## Chateau de Rilly, France, 1947

The drawing room has become a retreat where pictures and postcards spark old memories. Each one unlocks a different room, summoning up even more stories from my life.

I am brought back to the present as Henriette enters the room. "Louis, I have good news for you. Michel went to London and stopped in at The Algerian Coffee Store. I brought the package in for you to breathe in the aroma," she smiles and hands me a fragrant cloth bag of coffee beans.

"Do we have some cardamom in the pantry?"

"Yes, I believe we do."

"Oh, please ask the maid to fix me a cup," I say, handing the bag back to her. Henriette winks, and leaves the room.

Our maid, Jeanne Marie, returns with my coffee, cream and sugar on an ornate silver tray. She places it on my coffee table, careful to move a framed photo of me in my military uniform.

Algerian coffee can be bitter, so I like it with brewed cardamom. I add three cubes of sugar and rich cream from the neighbor's cows. I breathe in the strong aroma and take a sip from the small white and gold cup. The flavor unlocks the door to Algeria, ten years before my journey to Japan. I reach across the table and gaze at the sepia-tone photograph. In the photo, I am 18 years old and wearing the traditional Zouave clothing of the time.

## A Zouave, A Gentleman, and Cabaret Pasha
### Algiers, Circa 1893

I transferred to this Zouave battalion in Algiers three years ago after two years in the military serving in France. I was restless and ready for something new. Now I am stationed here to support the French conquest of Algeria. The European population now in 1880 is more than 350,000. Some soldiers take the opportunity to socialize and some get into mischief after work.

As a rule, the days in Northern Algiers are warm and breezy. The military infirmary is humid today, but comfortable since the windows are open. The marine breezes wander through the rooms. In the infirmary, I wipe every remaining trace of blood off my dental instruments and my hands as I finish my cleanup for the day. After I wash my hands in a basin of warm water, I run my wet fingers through my hair, and twist my mustache. I notice the dust from passing trains has built up again on the wood and tile window ledges.

I bring a few pieces of ice in a sterile bowl with me as I cross to the back of the infirmary where our small kitchenette is installed. I take a tall glass from the shelf and pour in a bit of coffee syrup and add some sugar. We are out of cream again, so I fill it halfway with cold water. The finishing touch is the ice. Finally, I take a big swallow of my strong Café Mazagran and feel instantly refreshed.

I call across the room to my last three patients, who rest comfortably in red velvet chairs, legs supported by ottomans, in front of a white stucco wall. "Keep replacing the cotton gauzes. You may go when there is no more bleeding. If you feel light-headed, sit down again for five minutes. I will be outside on the porch if there is a problem."

One patient asks another in a muffled voice, "Did he pull the tooth already? I feel fine."

"I believe so. The gas relaxed me a lot. I guess it wasn't so bad if I feel this good!"

The first mumbles, "I thought I would feel terrible. He really took the pain away when he pulled my offending tooth!"

An older gentleman who had a more serious extraction remains asleep under the peaceful rest of ether.

"You should be a dentist when your military service is completed," the first patient says to me, as I cross the room and go onto the porch, the cool sea breezes greeting me. I notice the boards already need sweeping again.

I sit next to Hakim, my new assistant and fellow Zouave, who smiles as he listens in on the clients' barely intelligible discussions from his perch on an old leather-topped camel saddle. I sit next to him and stretch my legs to the steps below. The saddles are more comfortable than the stools patients usually sit on as they wait for their dreaded turn. I watch as dust devils dance down the sandy roadway. Another day of work behind me.

"Did you want this job in the infirmary?" Hakim asks me. "Are you thinking about becoming a doctor?" Hakim is shorter than I am, but has a much sturdier physique, as well as the traditional olive skin and wavy dark hair of local Algerians. His father is a high-ranking commander in the elite Spahi cavalry, and, thus, Hakim is a young product of our French colonial system. He has been taught under the French education structure, learning to read and write in French from an early age.

"Well," I reply, taking another sip of my cold coffee. "I'm embarrassed to say this, but when the commanding officer asked me what skills I had, I didn't have a good answer, so he assigned me to the infirmary. He said that this job didn't require any skills, but I disagree." Hakim nods. "Did you know," I continue, "that until recently, people always went to a barber to get their teeth pulled? They sat on the floor, and the barber pulled until the tooth came out. The pain must have been excruciating. No, I'm glad we use comfortable chairs, the newest instruments, and this new cocaine treatment to numb the gums. I have become quite proficient, if I say so myself, and I can pull more teeth in one afternoon than you can in two days!"

Hakim grins. "Well, thank you for letting me learn by working on easy patients."

"What about you?" I ask. "Did you want to work in the infirmary?"

"No. I wasn't skilled in this area, either, but I'm willing to learn. I'm glad you're my teacher—you have a reputation for being quick and almost painless." He smiles as he adds, "A true gentleman with pincers and forceps."

I laugh at Hakim's comments. "Since you are my student, I'll share a secret with you," I say. "I give my patients extra laughing gas to make the extraction more bearable. As you heard in the other room, most of them barely know that their teeth have been removed. Nitrous oxide is a remarkable invention! But, don't give them too much—oh the stories I could tell."

We are distracted by a familiar voice coming from inside the infirmary. Through the doors walks Bastien, the son of local French settlers, who is completing his required military service in Africa. He is blonde, and his skin is tanned from the desert sun. He was born in Algeria to a French blacksmithing family. They have been through the colonialization of Algeria first-hand, and I find their stories most interesting.

Bastien seems jumpy as usual. Fidgeting with his shirt collar with his right hand, he says with eyebrows furrowed and left hand pressed to his left cheek, "I woke up this morning with a sore tooth—the same one as last week. I couldn't sleep at all. How about some laughing gas to get rid of the pain and I can enjoy the evening?" he asks. I have heard this story before.

"No, Bastien. I believe it was your right cheek last week. You know the rules, and I'm not going to break them for you. You only get the gas if I pull your tooth out—would you like me to pull a tooth now?"

"No. Of course not! What about some cocaine? Can I get some before you leave the shop?"

"Cocaine is out of the question."

"I thought we were friends," mumbles Bastien.

"Bastien, no!" I say, half-laughing and not really sorry at all. "It is under lock and key for a good reason! Why don't you have a seat on the porch? I'll get a bottle of wine for us to share."

Bastien sits on a wooden stool next to an old well-worn chess board. I grab a bottle of wine and three goblets from inside and return to the porch. Bastien fumbles with his match case and starts to light matches, aimlessly flicking them over the railing into the street.

I uncork the bottle and pour aromatic red wine into three glass goblets. The French have brought vines from France successfully making good wine in Africa. We watch Algerians in white robes and scarves walk by, on their way home from the outdoor markets. The steam whistle of another long train announces its arrival in town. Even edgy Bastien relaxes after a few glasses of wine.

I am amazed at the cargo on these trains. No one suspected esparto, a fiber produced from an African grass, could be in such demand for export in Europe and Asia. The train cars are overflowing with bales of these plants, esparto rope and cotton. Miracle plants, indeed. Every market in town has a large display of esparto baskets for sale along with their main merchandise.

Hakim looks at the trains and says, "Every day I see more of Africa's products exported to other places. Our vibrantly colored cotton fabrics are becoming very popular here and overseas. Africa's lead and copper are highly marketable in newly developed areas, and leather from hides and skins is in great fashion demand from New York to Paris. We are living in a time of seemingly endless progress." He turns to me. "Do you think you will become part of these new commercial prospects? Or, when you return to France, will you become a magician-physician in an infirmary pulling teeth?"

I chuckle at his compliment. "A doctor's office would be too small for me. I could not work in the same place day after day. I would suffer, and so would my future family." I take another sip of wine. "I see the ships in the harbor, going to ports I have never seen, in countries and cities with names I have never heard before. The marine air fills me with curiosity. No, pulling teeth isn't my dream career, but I must make the best of it for now." Hakim nods his agreement as I continue. "I am trying to learn as much as I can about this country and the people. Algiers is a port city alive with challenges, but I know there are many other intriguing ports and places to explore. I think the military is a good training ground for us. And I've learned that taking a risk makes a situation more appealing to me. But I think understanding how to adapt to different cultures will help anyone with aspirations to do business overseas. I am intrigued by the electric trolleys in Paris and Algiers. Electric automobiles are developing rapidly in Europe, so quickly that horses and carts will go back to the farms. I am excited to try to become a part of this new commerce. Who knows? Maybe I'll even get a car of my own!"

But Bastien is not listening. After serving himself another glass, he gulps it down. "It's too warm to just sit here in the heat," he says, wiping his mouth on his sleeve. "I'm off to the piers, and I'll hopefully see you later at Cabaret Pasha." He puts his matches away, clicks his new cap lighter shut, stands up, and leaves the porch, almost all in one motion. Hakim and I gaze at his skinny frame and baggy pants strutting down the street towards the port.

"And what about your future?" I ask Hakim.

"I enjoy working in the infirmary, and I plan on helping the people of Algeria. I think I will go to Paris, get my medical credentials, and return to my country and start a family. I have always been a good student, so I think it's a reasonable goal."

"Sounds well thought out, my friend. Well, while we are completing our military service, we will have lots of time to think about our future. Shall we head to the port? There is an ocean liner arriving from Paris tonight. It's always good entertainment to watch the looks on the passengers' faces when they see Algiers for the first time. Passengers anticipate what they have seen in postcards, which tend to give a brighter picture as a method of advertising for cities. But often the photos are staged to look wonderful, and passengers disembarking the boat are consistently overwhelmed by the local people and activities not shown in the picture postcards."

Hakim agrees. We go back to the *réfectoire* and get cleaned up. As we reemerge and descend the stairs, Hakim asks, "Louis, are you going to the Cabaret Pasha on the waterfront? Remember the last time you were there? And the dancers left early because the French soldiers got so drunk on too much German beer?"

"Oh, what a disaster. Hopefully tonight will be a different story," I reply, as we make our way down the road to the waterfront. The wind has died down, and there is a calmness in the streets. Most of the traders and peddlers have already gone home to be with their families, before the waterfront community revs itself up for the European evening crowds. A tired vendor along the street packs up the remains of her once vibrant yellow daffodils and purple irises, placing them in esparto grass baskets on her wooden cart, ready to lug them home. A dusty scent of cinnamon and saffron from the markets lingers as the sun slowly sinks toward the horizon. The discordant voice of a *muezzin* high up on a mosque minaret recites a call to prayer. The contrasts of religion and culture in this city are at times astonishing. A cathedral full of Catholic relics and statues of the Holy Family sits right across the street from the white Great Mosque. The decorative blue and yellow mosque tiles, white pillars, balconies, and walls on the outside impress the eye, but Hakim says that it is very sparse and plain inside.

"Do you still go to the mosque, Hakim?"

I have seen the effect of colonialization on other native Algerian soldiers. The French government has turned Hakim into a Colonial Frenchman in many ways, especially through the education system.

Hakim responds, kicking sand covered stones as we walk towards the port. "I went to Quranic schools until I was six, and I hold on to some Muslim customs, like going to the Mosque. But because of my Muslim culture, I still have a problem understanding separation of state and religion." He looks up at the blue evening sky. "Depending on the situation, I can see the value of both government positions. You know that to become French citizens, my family and I had to renounce Sharia law, and adopt the French cultural code? Only one wife and adherence to inheritance customs. We are letting go of the ways of our forebears in exchange for progress."

I consider what he says, and I decide one wife would be quite enough for me.

"Hey, look!" he says. A flock of gliding white storks, calling like the *muezzin*, are announcing that we are nearing the port. Breathe in! The cooler marine air feels quite refreshing in my lungs.

We turn left at a corner café and are greeted by some of Hakim's countrymen and fellow Arab soldiers who have gathered on the porch. The aroma of strong brewed coffee with cardamom drifts through the open doors.

The communities in Algeria are selective. While Europeans and Africans work side by side during the day, at night we gather with our own. The Algerian-born Zouaves socialize with fellow countrymen; the French

Zouaves mix with their own, with a few other Europeans thrown into the mix.

"*As-salam alaykom,*" Hakim says, greeting his friends. "La Palmeraie is a busy place this evening. Good coffee and good food today?" I observe the usual group of Bedouin men in long white robes seated on dusty stools on the porch. The men inhale from a hookah and pause, holding the smoke in their lungs as they take in the camaraderie. One man nods his head, exhales, and replies, "Undeniably, the best bakery in town. Come join us, Hakim." Hakim waves goodbye to me and joins his friends at the café.

"Hakim, *à demain!* See you tomorrow," I call out as I continue towards the *café chantant,* a favorite cabaret for Frenchmen and other Europeans. I don't worry about Hakim since there is no alcohol involved at the café or when he is with his Muslim friends. Cabaret Pasha, however, is another story.

As I near the building, I see elaborate Zelig blue tiles adorning the white stucco pillars. Several enameled tile archways await and greet the evening crowd at Cabaret Pasha. On the tile roof above, long legged white storks with elongated yellow bills stand guard like soldiers. Perhaps they are the same ones we saw on our walk over.

As I enter, three friends call to me, pulling another chair up to the rustic wooden board table. Behind them hammered copper plates embellished with stones cover the wall. I notice movement behind a platter: two native geckos. I laugh and compliment the German owner on the live gecko décor.

"*Ja.* We hire the gecko to work here, then give them plates of good German food after work if they do good job. *Es ist wahr!* True story," he laughs, as he turns back to drying beer steins with a worn linen cloth as the band from Paris begins to warm up.

As I sit down, I recognize a voice through the din. Looking over, I see Bastien standing in the doorway. My friends Marcel and Victor hail him over to join us. Grabbing another chair to join our group, Bastien says, "I'm just in time for the dancers." He sees something skitter under the table. He puts his chair down and crushes a gecko's tail with his chair leg. The gecko runs off without its tail.

Bastien looks down maliciously and laughs. "He'll grow a new one, if he is lucky. Maybe I could burn it to seal it. Anyways, I saw the dancers last night. Their skirts catch at the ankles, and their blouses are decorated with clinking copper bangles. There's a blonde girl who works here, too, and I've been trying to get her attention. Maybe tonight is my night," he says, craning his neck, trying to see her over the crowd.

I'm thirsty, and I use it as an excuse to get up and away from Bastien for a moment. I'm annoyed by his inhumane treatment of the gecko, and I can't help but wonder if he was here last night—and was one of the men who got themselves kicked out. I cross the dusty floor to the bar and get several glasses and a bottle of wine to share.

When I return to the noisy table, I pour the rich red wine into our glasses. Sitting, I can't help but feel a bit concerned about his increasingly nervous behavior.

"Hakim and I were discussing our futures this afternoon after you left, Bastien. What are your plans after your military service?"

"Oh, you know," he says, looking down at the table his eyes shining a bit. "I'm going to be a blacksmith in Africa or France. There is a lot of work on the trans-Sahara railroad, too much for my father to do by himself. He has made a good life, so it seems like a good choice for me."

"Oh? What intrigues you about that job?"

"Well, when I was small, I would watch the forge as my father heated the coals and bent metal bars. He would let me work the bellows. The fire got so hot you couldn't look at it."

"Too bad camels don't need shoes. Your father would be rich," I say.

"When I was a child," Bastien says, leaning back in his chair, "my father told me horses wear shoes, but giraffes wear high heels!" He laughs at his joke. "Let's have a toast for the beautiful women about to dance!" he says, as the music rises in volume.

His toast is interrupted by the daughter of the owner, Angela, approaching our table. This must be the blonde woman Bastien mentioned. As she places a bottle of water on the table, she asks, "And what would the brave and fierce Zouaves like to order tonight? Sausages from Portugal? *Coq au Vin* from our garden?"

Bastien fidgets and lights his silver lighter. He lights the flame, holds it for a while, then flips the top down. He has always been a bit vulgar, and tells her, "You'll have to sit in my lap to know my order."

Angela is used to the coarse talk of soldiers, but this time she is not amused. She glares at him with her bright blue eyes and turns around with such speed that her blonde tresses sweep over the flame from Bastien's lighter. I can smell singed hair, and I notice that the momentum from her turn has pushed her smoking hair against her cotton skirt, scorching it as well. I bolt to my feet, grab a pitcher of water from the table, and douse her shirt as quickly as I can. She shrieks as I grab her arm, trying to keep her sudden movements from starting a flame. But Angela jerks her arm away from me and runs across the room to her father. I watch, embarrassed. She appears to be all right, spared of burns. Some customers eye us and stand, deciding to end their night before the situation gets worse.

Marcel and Victor laugh nervously, but I begin to clean up the mess on our table. I feel terrible for her and irritated with Bastien's behavior. From the corner of the room emerges the burly cabaret owner. He approaches our table, enraged.

"Let's get out of here, quick," says Bastien as he rises and bolts out the door. Marcel and Victor, no longer laughing, stand to address the owner, taking turns to sincerely apologize.

"I am so sorry for what our fellow infantryman did. What can we do to help you?" my friend asks. But Angela's father has nothing but rage and foul words for us. I raise my eyebrows and look at my friends who are still standing around the table—I didn't know the Germans could speak French so well, especially foul slang.

A red-faced Mr. Van Dyken closes in on us, grabs Marcel and Victor by their shirts, and drags them to the door. I follow them closely. Mr. Van Dyken throws them into the street, turns around and grabs my right arm, and sends me to join my friends. I trip and my breath is knocked out of me. "Don't ever cross the threshold of Cabaret Pasha again. I will contact your commanding officer tomorrow!"

Moments later, the rest of the men from our table run out into the street, and Mr. Van Dyken slams the door. My friends and I pick ourselves up.

"I believe," I say, wincing at the pain, "that the lesson here is to somehow get around socializing with Bastien."

The other Zouaves agree. "I'm in no hurry to see him again either," adds Marcel who has been in Algeria for six years. "What happened tonight is inexcusable and makes the military Zouaves look irresponsible. I would prefer not to cross paths with him again. I would rather be remembered as a gentleman."

Dusting off my pants and tucking in my shirt in again, I notice a charred hole on my sleeve, and my ankle is sore. We start walking home to our military barracks in the obscure light.

# Chapter Four

Newspaper headlines report how an annual charity organized by
French Catholic aristocracy in Paris
turned to fire and tragedy in May 1897.

# Chapter Four
The Patio
Chateau de Rilly, France, May 1947

The cobblestone patio is the perfect place to relax and watch horses and cows grazing in the fields. A local farmer, Michel, grows hay on our property to feed his gentle brown Guernsey dairy cows.

Jeanne Marie comes outside to the patio. "*Voilà,* Monsieur. Your coffee and golden cream from Michel's happy cows."

I quickly clear the timeworn newspapers I have been rereading from my coffee table. Receiving the café, I breathe in the strong aroma, but I smell smoke instead. I put my cup down, splashing a bit over the lip. I stand and look around the outside of the house. My heart beats faster and I feel panic coming on.

I see my grandson Gilbert come around the corner of the front porch. He looks calm, so I relax a little.

"Gilbert, do you know where the smoke is coming from?" I ask, hoping for good news.

"*Bien sur, Grand-père.* It is Michel burning our hay field before a new planting in order to get rid of insects, and so the weeds won't have a chance to multiply. I've heard it adds nutrition to the soil and makes better hay. He told me about it yesterday so we wouldn't be alarmed."

"Well, it is a little late for that," I say. "The scent of burning wood always reminds me of the first fire I witnessed in Paris. At least these flames are under control and no one will die. Here, look at this old newspaper article," I say, handing him the time-yellowed front page of Le Petit Journal, Sunday May 16, 1897.

*Tragedy at the Bazaar de la Charité*
**Paris, France, 1897**

The air smells sweet as I open the buggy's door at Henriette's apartment. She opens a window to greet me. "Cinderella, your carriage is here," I call up, teasing my lovely fiancée.

"I'll be right down," she says, and closes the window. The horses exhale and shift their weight. When Henriette comes out, pausing at the top of the stairs, I can't help but notice how striking she looks wearing the newest style, a frilly puffed baby blue blouse and a blue striped tunic worn over it with an ankle length hobble skirt.

"Louis, come and hold my arm. The stairs are difficult with the skirt so narrow at my ankles. You may have to help me into the carriage as well."

"Of course. I had the driver put out the lowest steps for you," I say as I lead her down the stairs and help her into the carriage. "You look lovely," I say, climbing in after her. She smiles as the driver chirps to the horses to start.

Looking out the window, I am grateful that the fall and winter rains have left the city, making way for flowers and new greenery in the parks. The streets are especially busy today with people from our city as well as neighboring towns and villages. I am taking Henriette to the Bazaar de la *Charité*.

We arrive and join the bustle of the Bazaar. Henriette descends the carriage carefully, with a small sigh of relief when she lands on steady ground. We carefully weave in and out of the crowd, Henriette holding onto my left arm.

"Louis, look at the decorations. The street looks like Paris in Medieval times! The wooden walkways look just like a painting in our hallway! Look, the fronts of those buildings are painted a bit too bright for old Paris, but they do give a festival feeling. Oh, the costumes and dresses are magnificent, don't you th— Oh! look at that woman dressed like Marie Antoinette!" Henriette says, pointing to a woman in a tall white wig and blue gown.

Many of our mothers' friends have worked hard to attract as many well-to-do patrons as possible to this bazaar. I hope the wealthy guests will empty their pockets in generosity, helping the shops to raise a lot of money for children and poor families.

"Come with me to look at the fashion stalls," Henriette says. "Parisian designers have donated garments to be sold at high prices to benefit the charity. I could use a new short linen jacket this spring." We turn and cross through the crowd to the stall, Henriette hobbling a bit. When we get there,

Henriette immediately reaches out and fingers a light blue linen jacket with navy trim.

"Ah, Louis, it is perfect," she says, leaning over the counter to feel the soft fabric. "What do you think?"

"I think you should get it and the skirt that goes with it. It's not so tight at the ankles," I suggest, winking.

"Louis, look at the shoes," she says ignoring me. "The short black boots with the buttons would be perfect. Can we get them, too, if they have my size?"

"Of course. You decide what you want, and I will pay," I say as I glance around the other boutiques in the warehouse. After a few minutes, Henriette hands me her wrapped packages and points towards the stall where we pay.

As we finish our transaction, I hear a group of men and women laughing out loud. I take Henriette's arm and, juggling our packages, move towards the commotion. As I get closer, I see it is the Lumiere Brothers' film stall and a long line of people waiting to get in.

"Henriette, would you like to sit with me to see the cinemas?"

"*Bien sûr.* You shopped with me, now I can watch with you."

Parisians love to watch other Parisians, so we stay entertained while we wait in line.

I breathe a sigh of relief as we are just able to join the next showing. "Henriette, you sit on the last bench and I will stand behind you." She sits on a crowded bench.

I take in a breath, eager to see the films. I have seen films on a kinetoscope, but only one person can see them at a time. This first film camera, the cinematograph, allows all of us to watch the film on a screen at the same time.

The first of the three movies shows people getting off and onto a train in a station.

I shift her packages to my right hand and take her hand with my left. "I have so many questions, Henriette. Isn't it fascinating?'

"A train station? The only good thing is that the film only lasted a minute," she says, smiling.

"Just wait for the next one!"

The film starts, showing Lumiere factory employees leaving a warehouse at the end of the day. Dogs run across the screen. Horses and a wagon leave the factory. This film is longer than the first one by one minute.

"I hope the next one is more interesting," says Henriette, arranging her skirt and blouse, careful not to nudge the lady beside her.

The film starts. "Ah. This one looks interesting. The Sprinkler Sprinkled," I read out loud.

A gardener waters his plants with a hose. A boy behind him steps on the hose. The water stops, and the gardener peers into the hose. The boy removes his foot and the water comes on again, spraying and knocking off the gardener's hat. The gardener turns around and sees the boy run off.

Laughing, Henriette says, "That film was the shortest, less than a minute, but the best."

"Shall we pay and watch it again?"

"I think it is time to go outside. It is awfully crowded, and the man cranking the camera looks tired. Good thing for him that the films are very short."

Once outside, Henriette continues holding my arm, drawing closer as the crowd flows into the bazaar. She directs me to look at an ornate carriage. "Look, Louis. The Duchess d'Alencon just arrived. I'm glad your mother convinced her to come. She cares about children so much! Her popularity will bring in a lot of money for orphans."

I nod as Henriette grabs onto me again, bumped by another woman carrying sacks of what smell like delicious baked goods. There are several hundred people now in the bazaar, and we can see that the crowd is still growing.

"The crush is too much for me. Let's go and sit down the street a bit," my *fiancée* suggests. "I would like a café and a *gateau*. Would you?"

"Of course. I am always hungry. We can watch high society from our table as they come and go. Look at those three ladies in the pink hats!" I nod towards three women laughing at a juggler in the street who just tripped over a pine log.

We enter a café, and the waiter leads us to a table on the patio. "All of these people. It's a kind of contest to see who can be most generous to help the poor. Quite admirable, no?" asks Henriette as I pull out a chair for her at our cast iron and wood table.

"Not as admirable as you, my love," I say, leaning down to give her a peck on the cheek. But my attention is interrupted by a whiff of what smells like smoke. "Henriette, I think I smell something burning." I look around but cannot find a source. "I guess it's just the ether and oxygen lamps being used by the bazar."

"I smell it, too," Henriette says, looking towards the crowd. "Louis, look over there!" she cries, pointing towards smoke curling out of a wooden building a block away.

"That is more than cinema equipment. Look at the rue Jean-Goujon! Flames are coming out of the windows!"

"People are starting to run into the street. No, Louis! There is a woman whose dress is on fire! Oh, and she is carrying a baby." We stand frozen by fear. Flames shoot through the window towards the street. We watch as some women run back into the fire. "Why are they going back in, Louis?"

"I don't know, my love," I clutch her package to my chest and pull Henriette towards the door. "We need to get out of here. Right now."

"Oh, Louis, my skirt! I can't run!"

"Henriette, you must," I say. But just then we hear her skirt tear.

"Oh, never mind," she says. "Let's go." We join other customers running out of the café and down the cobblestone road a few blocks. When we can finally stop, we turn and watch in horror as the tragedy unfolds down the street. The elaborate scene of charity and goodwill only took a few minutes to transform into blazing devastation.

Police and firemen arrive on horses and in wagons. As I watch the madness around us, I see someone running out of a fiery doorway. He has a familiar face. "*Mon Dieu,* Henriette. It's Bastien, from my military service in Algeria. After all these years." I recognize my fellow Zouave and his blonde hair immediately despite the smoke. We make eye contact, and I feel a bolt of unexplainable panic as he turns and runs away from the heart-rending scene.

"Is he the one you told me about at the Cabaret Pasha? The one who was always playing with matches and lit a girl's hair on fire?" my fiancée asks.

Coughing from the smoke and ashes around us, I nod my head.

"What is he doing here?"

"I don't know. But we should go home to safety. Your mother will have heard the fire trucks and will be worried about you."

We leave the bazaar, navigating the crowds until we turn onto a quieter side-street. "Shall I find a buggy for you?"

"No, let's walk. I'd prefer some quiet," Henriette responds. Tucking her hands closer into the bend of my arm, we walk in silence until we are away from the smoke. Then, nervously, she asks me, "Do you think Bastien set the fire?

"I don't know. Maybe. Or the gaslights could have started the fire. Or perhaps the wooden buildings and floors were dry, a perfect place for a cigar end to reignite. A person like Bastien, who liked to play with flames, may have started it, perhaps by accident. Sometimes we don't know all the parts of a story. This one is sure to be a wretched one however it ends." But I couldn't help but wonder, had I seen guilt or shame in his eyes?

# Chapter Five

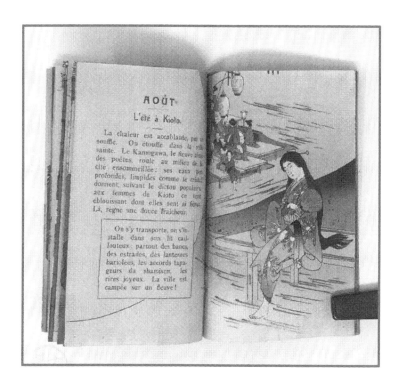

Les Douze Mois de l'Annee translated by Jules Adam. Jules shared these small silk and crepe paper books with Adrienne.
Paris, France 1900

# Chapter Five
## The Drawing Room
## Chateau de Rilly, France, 1947

*"Je vois la vie en rose,"* sings my sister-in-law, Adrienne, at the threshold to the drawing room, her arms open as she makes her entrance. Henriette enters right behind, tucking wisps of her grey-streaked soft curls into silver hair pins. Adrienne walks to my desk, continuing to hum, and interrupts my quiet morning task of sorting old letters and postcards.

"Louis, my friends bought a new Citroen *Traction Avant* without tires. They were wondering if you have a few they could purchase from you. I have seen piles of them in the old barn."

I unroll my sleeves and arrange my tie. "Without tires? Yes, I will have a look after lunch and see if I can be of some help."

"Why in the world would they purchase a car without tires?" questions Henriette.

"I read in the newspaper that some automobiles are sold at a lower price if a customer has their own tires. Since the end of the war, there has been a terrible rubber shortage. Perhaps in exchange they will let me take the auto for a drive," I suggest, and wink at Henriette. "Imagine going 60 miles per hour on the country roads!"

Henriette catches my eye and presses her lips together. She doesn't think I should be driving, but I know she will give in. I smile and turn back to my letters and photographs.

Henriette takes Adrienne by the arm and guides her out of the room to work on their party plans. I sit back and hear Adrienne sing, again, a refrain about regrets, *'Non, je ne regrette rien.'* Humming along, I ask myself if I regret anything. The pictures bring back such memories—do I regret anything? Not at all.

*Henriette's Intuition*
**Paris, France, Spring 1900**
— Henriette Speaks —

Adrienne's young soprano voice can be heard from outside the apartment. The windows are open so the neighbors will have to endure her songs as we do. My younger sister has just finished her studies in art, receiving an honorable mention for several of her landscape paintings. I have arranged for a little dinner party this evening to both recognize her graduation and to say farewell to my husband's business friend, Jules Adam. He is the Senior Interpreter for the French Legation in Tokyo and will be an important business liaison with Louis' brother, Paul, in Japan.

I am looking forward to the socializing, and I am relieved that we have Madeleine, a new cook, in addition to our maid, Jeanne Marie, as I am pregnant with our second child. I would not be able to host without the blessed women, as I tire too easily.

I must admit that I feel a little nervous about this evening. At our last get together, I noticed Adrienne seemed to show an interest in Jules. She is only fifteen and he is in his late thirties — too far apart for a marriage, if you ask me. I almost threw two separate parties, but I feel too tired with my pregnancy. I assure my nerves that it is just his art that charms her.

I enter the drawing room and tidy some pillows on the sofa. Mother is holding my wiggling one-year-old Edith. She holds her arms out to Adrienne and my sister welcomes her, lifting her off my mother's lap. My mother is happy to share her granddaughter after taking her to the park for the afternoon.

Adrienne looks striking in her light green and gold dress. Her long auburn curls fall down her back, controlled with a silk ribbon. Always full of energy, she picks Edith up to waltz around the living room with the baby. Her ankle length dress follows her every turn.

"Petite Edith, my little niece," she says, "Do you know the popular French singer, Mistinguett? She sings beautiful songs. My classmates went to see her and taught us this so —"

I interrupt Adrienne, raising my eyebrow. "Be sure it isn't one of her naughty songs," I say, adjusting several china plates on the wall.

"But of course not! Baby Edith, let's sing one about our city, Paris?" says Adrienne, as she hums and starts to sing. *"Ça c'est Paris, Ohé Paris. Ohé Paris, merveille de chez nous, Ohé Paris, les amis, Comment allez-vous?"* The baby giggles as Adrienne twirls in front of the ornate white fireplace, and Edith reaches for the prisms in the chandelier. After several rounds, my sister sits in the baby blue Louis the Sixteenth chair, clapping hands with her niece.

My mother sits on the sofa and watches her girls. "Adrienne, you have so much energy. I wish I could dance and sing all day. One of these days you will have your own family and settle down."

Adrienne insists, "I may decide to have a family, but I don't think I will ever settle down!"

I hear footsteps coming to the door—my handsome Louis has arrived from the office. I meet him at the door.

"Bonjour, *Chérie,*" he says out of breath, and kisses me on both cheeks. "Running on cobblestone streets isn't easy, but I ran faster than the little river ferry, even though it was only two streets."

Louis greets my mother and sister. "Are you ready for a special dinner? I can smell the guinea hens and onions. Oh! Henriette, here are the baguettes I promised to pick up."

As I adjust an oil painting of a sailboat in Italy, I tell Louis, "Give the baguette to the cook, and then go get ready. Come down and join us as soon as you can."

"When will Monsieur Adam be here, Henriette?" Adrienne asks. "I have my portfolio from school, and I would like to know what he thinks about my work." She keeps clapping with Edith. "He said he would bring his Japanese Storyteller Books he is working on. He is translating them from Japanese into French. He knows so much and has been around the world… It must be a superb life," she says with an exhale.

"He will be here soon, Adrienne," I reply. Why is she so interested in this man?

Louis returns, looking handsome in his grey trousers, baby blue shirt and waistcoat.

"Henriette," he says, "after dinner, Jules and I will need to take care of some business matters."

"What business matters?" Adrienne asks.

"Jules leaves for Japan in two weeks. He is setting up some business opportunities for me in Yokohama. We will perhaps move there in a few years, if all goes well," he tells her. My concerns are quieted when Louis says Jules will be leaving Paris. I'm sure I am being an overprotective sister and Adrienne is just being her usual gregarious and genial self.

A few minutes later we hear a knock on the door, and Jeanne Marie welcomes Jules. I hear her ask for his hat. From where I am standing, I can see him reflected in the hallway mirror as he adjusts his herringbone silk tie, makes sure it is tucked into his vest, and comes to join us in the drawing room.

Adrienne jumps to her feet, nervously patting down the ruffles on her dress. After greeting the rest of us, he kisses her flushed cheeks in a hello.

"Monsieur Adam, did you bring your fairytale books? I hope so. And I brought my portfolio from school. I would like to hear what you think about my drawings. Please, come sit next to me."

I look at my husband again, finding it difficult to disregard my persisting uneasiness. He winks at me, as if to say, don't worry. I tell Adrienne, "Go ahead and show Jules your pictures if he doesn't mind. Louis, please make us a drink or two." I rise and offer my mother an aperitif.

After drinks and amicable conversation with our guest, we move to the dinner table, a carved dark walnut beauty that has been in the family for years. The places are set with our wedding china, faience with butterflies and flowers decorating the plates. My mother embroidered the napkins to match the dishes.

I ask Adrienne to sit next to our mother. Jules will sit across from her. He quickly crosses the room to hold her chair for her as she sits down, gently lifting her hair off her shoulders.

Jean Marie serves Madeleine's delicious meal and we are all entertained by stories from the Orient, as Jules has spent several years overseas.

"You must have an open mind to go to the Orient," Jules explains. "There are many Europeans, but it is not a Western culture; however, the progress is amazing. They have Western style parks, bandstands, and boulevards with sidewalks. Soon Yokohama will be a modern city, maybe like Paris."

Adrienne twists strands of her brown hair around her fingers. "Jules, are there theatres and beautiful hotels? Are there automobiles?"

"Yes, there are beautiful theatres and Western style hotels. But no automobiles. Instead there are rickshaws pulled by young strong men as well as horses and carriages to get you from place to place," says Jules.

"Would a person have to know Japanese to live in Japan?" she asks.

"It certainly helps," Jules replies.

"Monsieur Adam, how did you learn Japanese?" she asks, and as she does so her napkin drops to the floor. I swear she dropped it on purpose.

Jules rises and walks around the table to pick it up for her, handing it to her as he says, "I learned Japanese at home. We had a Japanese amah who helped raise us. My parents insisted that we speak Japanese with her and told us it would be like having an open door to other countries. Because of her, I am especially fond of the Asian cultures I have visited," he continues. "Their kindness and openness to new ideas is always calling me to go back. I am taken with their passion for art and enjoy working with the crepe paper artists. I will bring you a book when I return from Japan. I'll be leaving in two weeks."

Adrienne looks at me and frowns. "What will I do if you and Louis go to live in a new country? I will be left with Mama and will have to get a job singing in a cabaret!"

Accustomed to her dramatic outbursts, I reply, "Don't fret, Adrienne. We will be here for at least another year or two. A lot can happen in that time. You can go to a music school, sing at parties, and, if we move, you can even come and visit us."

Adrienne looks over and asks, "Monsieur Adam, could you please let me look at your picture books until you leave for Japan? I promise to return them to you before you go."

"Yes, of course, Adrienne. Come into the drawing room and I'll let you choose a few. Then, your brother-in-law and I must discuss some business matters. Henriette, thank you for the delicious meal," Jules says, nodding his head to me, before rising and escorting Adrienne to the drawing room.

My mother, Louis, and I are still at the table. I sit still and blink. "I think we have a problem on our hands."

"Don't worry, Henriette," Louis says again. "It is just a young girl's crush. He is leaving in two weeks, and she will find someone else more her age. She is only fifteen and, remember, he is thirty-nine." I don't say anything, but I can't get rid of my suspicion about Adrienne's intentions.


Two weeks later, Louis and I return to our house after being gone all morning. When we arrive, my mother is waiting for us in the salon, working on her embroidery.

"*Maman*, what a pleasant surprise! Have you been waiting long?"

"I came by to check on Adrienne. I was expecting her to come home this evening."

"She's not with us," Louis says.

Maman's face blanches. "She told me a few days ago that she was coming to stay with you to watch Edith while you prepare the nursery. Are you sure she's not with you?"

"Of course, I'm sure!" I respond in shock, dropping my handbag. "When did you last see her?" I ask, my suspicions slowly forming into a knot in my stomach as I bend over to pick up my handbag.

"She went a few days ago to meet Monsieur Adam to return his books before his departure. She told me she was coming here afterwards."

We pause as a new reality sets in. "Is she with Jules?" I ask, my voice raising. "He was supposed to take a train to Marseilles, and then the steamer from the harbor for two or three months to Japan!"

"Oh Henriette," Louis says. "I believe we have overlooked your suspicions."

"Come sit in the drawing room," my mother says. "We need to talk about this. Adrienne must get married as soon as she gets to shore. What will our friends and family say?"

"*Mon Dieu!* Louis, what are we going to do?" I ask, sitting down next to him on the velvet sofa.

"We will have to follow her. Make sure she gets married and is safe."

"Louis, we can't do that. We have a small child and another on the way. A trip on a steamship for eight weeks would be impossibly uncomfortable. Do you even know if there are doctors on board? How can we get our belongings together and move on such short notice? Besides, your business is doing so well right now, we can't leave."

"*Ma Henriette*, please, listen to me. I say we tie up our affairs here and go to Japan for a short trip, maybe six months. We will make sure Adrienne and Jules get married. Jules will be family, and he will be more inclined to help us get started in Japan. My brother can help us find a place in Yokohama, and we can see if we like it there. We can leave our things here and ship them over later if we decide to stay."


Three days later, I hear Louis humming a song, *Au revoir Paris*, as he sprints up the stairs. He enters the salon dramatically fanning his face to cool off with what appears to be a Japanese fan. He sits on the sofa next to me.

"Come close, *chérie*, and I will show you my new fan."

I put down Edith in her bassinet and turn towards him.

"These are our tickets to Japan. One for me, one for you and Edith, one for your mother, and one for Madeleine. We need a cook. Who knows what the food will be like over there?"

I stare at him in shock. "When do we leave?"

"In two weeks, my love. In two weeks."

I look around me at my beautiful home. Everything I know is about to change.

# Chapter Six

A new home in Honmoku near Yokohama. ca. 1905 Japan

# Chapter Six
## Chateau de Rilly, France, 1948

"It's a good thing I didn't unpack the boxes of photographs after our anniversary party. I will leave them stored since we are moving in a few weeks," I tell Henriette as I arrange the boxes by the door leading into the drawing room. I pick up a Japanese fisherman statue made of old tree roots, a souvenir from Yokohama, and wrap it in towels for his trip to our new home. We sold our beautiful chateau and are moving to a smaller home about 30 miles away, closer to Tours. I am 75 now and don't need the extra space and cost of running a huge home. I place the statue into the box before resting for a moment.

Using my cane, I walk into a chaotic kitchen hoping someone will make me coffee. I sit down at the table and watch the busy maids and Henriette working like bees in a hive. Henriette brings me my café, and I see our wedding dishes, matching faience terrine and tray with butterflies and magenta flowers, stacked by empty boxes in the middle of the table. Looking closely at a soup bowl, I see birds and a mosquito painted in yellow and blue.

"Look Henriette. We have had these dishes for fifty years and still have a service for a crowd," I say. "Do you remember when we unpacked the dishes in Japan, and none were broken?"

"Yes, a minor miracle! I still love these plates. It was a shame we lost a few when they were shipped back again."

"Oh, Henriette. It was easy enough to replace them once we were back in Paris."

"Yes, but we have cracked a few platters, too."

"But we have new ones in different patterns!"

"Edith has been asking me for these dishes to give to her daughter, Nickie, in America, since her trunk was stolen from the pier with her set of wedding dishes inside," Henriette continues, without skipping a beat.

I look at the boxes and packing frenzy in front of us, exhale, and recall that I have been here before.

## Precious Cargo
### Yokohama, Japan, Circa 1900

It is Tuesday morning, the day the cargo ship from France is scheduled to arrive. I have spent a restless night, anxious for my new crates to arrive. Sitting on the edge of our bed, I tell Henriette, "Today is the day! Ever since I saw Mr. Jenatzy in Paris, I have wanted to have a motorcar. You remember when I drove the Clement Bayard? How I made friends with the owner and got myself invited to drive? Remember how I showered the new owner with adulation mixed with a polite suggestion?

"How could I forget?"

"I told him, 'You are a marvelous driver, but perhaps a little overly anxious,' after he completed that harrowing 45 degree turn with me only mostly in my seat. But after catching my breath, the next thing I knew, he turned to me and suggested we change seats, and *voilà*, he put me behind the wheel. Flattery always works!" I love telling this story, reliving my first moments behind the wheel.

Henriette sits up and pulls her wavy chestnut hair into a chignon. "*Oui, mon cheri*," she remarks. "I know you have been consumed with the idea of branching into motorcars, adding to your growing business. When you get them, though, have you thought about who will put them together and take them apart when they need repairs?"

"Of course! I ordered some brochures on several makes of cars and chose the ones that come with the best instructions," I say with a grin. Henriette puts her finger to her lips, reminding me to speak quietly so as not to wake the little girls. "You know I love a challenge, and many have already crossed our path." I kiss her cheek before I rise to dress.

"Yes, Louis. Don't remind me."

Henriette contemplates my comments, and I can tell by her expression that she is thinking about the risks. A new business venture can be chancy. In truth, she knows my import and export business has been thriving, our insurance venture has been productive, and my home construction material dealings have been flourishing. All of this in only four years in Yokohama. Our six-month trial period quickly made itself permanent, and we are still living in Japan.

Henriette raises one eyebrow, returns my smile, and says, "*Allez-y, Louis!* I know better than to try to change your mind. Your ability to see potential and opportunity has mostly been golden. Go ahead. It's cold outside. Don't forget your woolen scarf that Mother made for you. Give my love to Jules when you see him."

I kiss our sleeping children and my wife one last time and then leave our room. I walk across the red and green Persian rugs to the front door where I pause to put on my jacket and hat. I open the door to red and pink azaleas lining the gardens on the winding steps down to the harbor.

We packed up and left Paris in two weeks. We took what we needed immediately and left the rest. On the long trip at sea we had ample time to discuss the situation and determined that a hasty wedding for Jules and Adrienne in the Catholic church in town was the only acceptable resolution.


The ship took seven weeks to steam to Yokohama, and after the wedding, which was small and simple as we didn't have any friends or family in Japan to invite, it took us another seven weeks to finally move out of a hotel and into a rental house. But with three children and grandmother, the rental house is quickly becoming too small. We need rooms for business affairs. So, I am having a European style home built for us in Honmoku, complete with a cottage for the staff.

The house is in a neighborhood with other European style homes in a popular international settlement called the Bluff. Our home will be a marvelous white two-story stick-style Victorian home. The lines are simple and reflect the popular European and American influence on local architecture. Foreigners compete for these houses, and I am so glad we will have one.

I walk at a leisurely pace to the waterfront, since the cargo ships may be delayed due to unpredictable wind and weather. When I finally arrive at Yokohama harbor, the docks are full of activity. Ships arrive with cotton and woolen goods as well as metal for the booming port. Men load other ships with raw silk, tea, and copper. The Red Brick Warehouse appears under a blanket of fog and smoke. It is three stories tall, complete with cargo elevators, sprinklers, and fire doors. It is all new, a necessity for the thriving import and export business. Japan is responding to the sharp rise in cargo and foreign trade. The Yokohama Customs Shinko Wharf Warehouse includes a transit shed, cranes, and a railway.

Turning left at the end of the steel wharf, I look to see if I can find my brother-in-law. Jules is a Consul of France and has become one of the first interpreters of the Japanese language. He comes to the docks frequently as his skills are invaluable in the import/export "goldrush" in Yokohama. Perhaps Adrienne's choice in husband was a good one after all.

Packing and unpacking boxes and trunks, and waiting for other cargo became a normal part of our lives when we followed Adrienne to Japan.

After the wedding, Adrienne would go to the docks every day to see if the ship from Paris had come in. "Louis," she would ask me upon arriving home again, "When will our trunks arrive from Paris? I can't wait to see what my wedding dishes look like."

One day, Henriette answered with a sting. "Adrienne. Be patient. You are a married woman now. You must practice the art of patience. Your dishes are from Bosch Frères in Belgium. Maman got you blue and white floral plates, bowls, and serving pieces. Nobody knows when they will arrive."

Eventually the dishes reached their destination, and Adrienne quieted down about the tableware, instead turning her attention to using them to serve her husband their daily meals. As I remember those first days of having Jules as a brother-in-law, I spy him coming towards me through the crowds.

"*Bonjour* Jules!" I call to him. "I had a feeling I would find you here." I extend my hand to him as he approaches. "Henriette sends her love to you and Adrienne. Have you seen my young cousin and assistant, Adhemar?"

"Good to see you, too, Louis," he says shaking my hand. "You mean that busy, adventurous chap who came here from Belgium when he was only 13?"

"Yes, him. Adhemar offered to come and help me uncrate the parts of motorcars if they arrive today."

"No, I haven't seen him. While we are waiting for him, tell me what happened when you spoke with the bank in Paris. Did you have any luck?"

I scowl. "As expected, they said no, and everyone else has advised against the motorcars. They haven't seen a motorcar and don't understand the potential for Japan; however, I can see the merit of importing the first automobiles from France to Yokohama. So, I have decided to finance them myself. I only ordered two Werners to start with."

"Which ones are those?" Jules asks.

"They are small, rather average cars without special characteristics: two front bucket seats, a small trunk in the back, and a cloth hood. They should be perfect for our needs for now. This new venture will be like planting a bamboo shoot and watching it grow. Thanks to you," I say, nodding, "the cars are being sent quickly through the diplomatic corps. They should be here today, though unfortunately, they will arrive in pieces."

Above the noise of the busy port, Jules and I hear our names. We turn and see Adhemar running towards us. He takes several steps to the side to avoid a rickshaw, then sprints towards the pier.

"Bonjour! Today is the day! I saw the French cargo ship coming into the bay and ran all the way here to tell you. Is the shop ready?" he asks, bending over, trying to catch his breath.

"Goodness! No! We still need to clear some room. I suppose we will have time since the crates will need to clear customs. Jules, could you please go to the Shinko Warehouse and use your influence to make sure we get the correct crates in a timely manner?"

Jules nods and leaves. Adhemar and I walk as quickly as we can to the shop. We work for two hours, clearing enough space. Jules arrives at the shop.

"Louis, you need to return to the harbor office to complete the final paperwork. While you do that, I will instruct the dock workers to deliver the crates."

"I'll stay here and finish the last of the organizing," Adhemar says. I nod and leave to sign the paperwork. When I return 45 minutes later, the workers are already transferring the crates from horse drawn carts.

I ask the three workers, pointing, "Please. Carefully place the crates on those hardwood dollies and wheel them into the shop, over there. I will be in to make sure we have all the crates we ordered."

I give orders to Adhemar and the other employees. "You open the crates marked *Frames* and *Bodies*. I will open the bulkier engine crate. Adhemar! These are the very first cars to touch the soil of Japan! Truly a day to remember."

Adhemar opens a crate and pulls the wood wool apart to get to the package underneath. The wood slivers and shavings from logs have kept the packages and boxes from moving or being damaged as they crossed the seas. He beckons me over to see a tea crate inside the larger packing crate.

"What's this, Louis?"

"Ah! I think I know what this is. Help me lift it out and we can put it on the floor next to my desk. Thank you for the help," I say as we place it on the floor.

"Keep unpacking the parts, Adhemar. I can deal with this."

I draw a chair up to the tea crate, sit down, and I admire its dovetail corners. I pull the top off, lean it against my desk and start pulling and dropping handfuls of wood wool onto the floor. Ah, yes. This is what I hoped it would be. I open another box within the crate and see six Swiss coach clocks. We use them on the dashboard of our automobiles and take them with us when we arrive at our destinations, so they are not stolen while we are away. I am pleased to see that the tin lining has kept the clocks dry. I put the box of clocks back in the tea crate and push it to a safe place under my desk, and I return to the workers.

Three employees carefully place the unpacked parts on newly fabricated elm work benches. Adhemar says with concern, "There are so many parts, if I lose one piece, I'm afraid we will only have one car!"

Laughing, I pat my young cousin on the back. "Here is your manual, young man," I say, handing him a booklet. "We must be extremely precise with this task of getting the cars operating. Follow the instruction book exactly. Above all, it's critical that we get the water, oil, and grease in the right places. Of course, the fuel must go in the correct place, too. Oh, I see you put air in the tires," I observe with satisfaction. "Better to have them filled before we take the automobiles off the jacks."

After several days of giddy anticipation, I step back to admire Adhemar's work. I take a deep breath. In front of us are two remarkable motorcars; the fruits of our labor.

"What should we do first?" Adhemar asks.

I walk to the front of one motorcar, which is near the warehouse's open sliding door. "I think this is how to turn the crank." After several attempts the vehicle begins to vibrate. "Oh, my goodness. Hear the lovely music of the engine! It works! Let's see if they both work! They are noisy and coughing, but I think that is a good sign." With a bit of work, the second car rumbles to life as well. "Come on, Adhemar. It's time to reward ourselves for all our hard work."

We climb into our new four-wheel vehicles. I shift mine into first gear, and with a few frog leaps, slowly drive forward and out into the sunlight.

"I think the gears balk more than they should, Louis. But it won't hurt to use them," yells Adhemar, encouraging me over the noise.

We drive out of the warehouse and turn left between a row of warehouses and continue onto the narrow roads. As we travel down the dusty rickshaw-lined streets, the locals turn, expressions of utter disbelief on their faces. Their looks change to panic and even fear when they see two strange vehicles moving without the help of horses.

I yell to Adhemar, "Let's drive to my office downtown, then follow me back home for lunch to my house. Its only about five miles. Henriette and the children will be excited and ready for a ride."

I see my young assistant motioning for me in his rearview mirror to pull over. "Louis. The road to the Bluff has such a steep hill. What if the cars can't make it up the steep grade?"

After thinking things through, I agree. "I was wondering about the hill as well. Let's take a safer route for our first trip." The new route I map for him will add a mile or two to our trip, but the experience will be good for us and the motorcars. I can't wait to see Henriette's face! All these years of dreaming, and the day has finally come.

# Chapter Seven

Louis and others get out of the car and are met by a curious group of
children and other bystanders.
Mountain drive outside of Yokohama

# Chapter Seven
## Manor de la Noue, France 1948

"Paule, where is your son? I thought he was coming with you," I call, leaning to the right on my overstuffed chair, trying to get a glimpse of my grandson. Gilbert and his mother are here to visit for a week. He is almost seventeen, turning into an adult right before our eyes. I always enjoy hearing about his adventures, wishing I were young again.

Paule walks into the room, bends over and kisses me on both cheeks. We have a surprise for you."

Gilbert walks in carrying a heavy cardboard box. He bends over and attempts to place it on the corner of my desk. He turns towards me for a kiss on the cheek, and says, "*Grand-père,* we have something for you, but we will need some room on your desk." Curious, I stand and cross to my desk. I pick up a stack of postcards and move them to my Japanese tea crate, but the box is full.

Paule looks around the room, finds a bamboo tray, and moves the bulk of my remaining papers onto it. Only then does Gilbert edge the box onto my desk. I look in the box, pause, and look at Gilbert and Paule. They are both beaming, waiting for a response. I read the side of the box out loud.

"Noiseless Portable Remington Typewriter. Made in the USA." I sit back down, grinning.

Gilbert lifts the typewriter out of the box as his mother pulls the packaging away and places it in a nearby straw wastebasket. Then she takes the cardboard box and sets it on the overstuffed chair.

"*Grand-père,* it's very lightweight. Try writing something," he says after he sets the typewriter down and leans over my left shoulder.

I pause and take a deep breath, waiting for inspiration. I write, *'Qui est blanche avec des taches?'*

It is not unusual in our family to fluctuate between speaking French and English in one conversation. Gilbert, who speaks English well, says, "Who is white with spots?"

He laughs, leans over me, and types the answer. *La vache.* "Of course, a cow. But seriously. What do you think?"

"My old typewriter sounded like tac tac tac. The new one says tic tic tic. It's not quite noiseless, but it appears to work very well." I type a few words and admire how the carriage and letters move smoothly, unlike my old one. "Thank you so much. *C'est merveilleux*. The letters are big and clear. I will use this to help organize and write my memoirs."

"We knew you would like it," Paule says, kissing me on the cheek. "Now, enjoy getting to know your typewriter and write more wonderful tales! I will come and get you when it is time for dinner."

"You're leaving me all alone with this machine?" I ask them, my eyes sparkling.

"Yes, *Grand-père*. I told *Grand-mère* I would help her put her silver tea set back on the tall oak cabinet," Gilbert says as he grabs his sweater and leaves the room, Paule following close behind him.

The room is quiet again. I idly touch the keys on the top row of my new typewriter and muse about what story to write next.

*The Mayor on the Mountain*
**Yokohama, Japan, 1904**

Henriette draws small circles with her finger on the tall entryway windows as she gazes at the mist over the harbor. Champagne rain has followed us from Paris and may even turn into snow. I watch as she turns and looks at the automobile parked in our entryway.

"Louis, what are those two big boxes in the back of the automobile?"

"It is a small desk and typewriter combination that arrived at the customs office last week. Since I am going up the mountain, I offered to deliver it to Mayor Kobayashi. I was able to lift the desk by myself, but it took two of us to lift the weighty typewriter."

I come closer to see what Henriette has drawn, but the drops have all gathered at the bottom of the window. I take her cold wet hands to warm them between mine.

"Is the mountain trip dangerous?" she asks, drawing near as I give her a kiss on the forehead.

"No, and it is worth the trouble to be in good standing with the mayor."

My attention is drawn to our children playing with marbles on the floor and singing a Japanese song they learned from our new Japanese cook. Madeline returned to Paris to be with family, so we have hired a new woman named Sachiko. The children don't know the meaning of the words *Shita-Kiri Suzume,* a traditional fable. The cook told me it was about an old man, his greedy wife, and a hurt sparrow. The children, however, smile and giggle to the rhythm of the words.

I leave Henriette to go greet her mother in the salon. *Grand-mère* smiles, puts down her linen embroidery, removes her glasses, and asks, "Where will you go today in your new motor chariot? Sightseeing up in the mountains, or instead down to the sea?"

"Anywhere a motorcar can travel. Now that I have had a few months of practice driving, I am ready to go even farther. The plan for today is to visit an upland village. The mayor has invited me to his town to demonstrate my motorcar. There may even be snow in the mountains! I will tell you all about it when I get back."

"Papa. Bring us candy from the International Market. Please!" says Edith, our five-year old, as she rolls a marble and it crosses the oriental rug.

Henriette, cozy and warm by the fireplace in the salon, says, "It's so cold outside, and driving will be colder still. I hope you are carrying extra gas and oil, tools and heavy ropes, anything that might be needed for repair or an emergency?"

"Yes. Of course, I am always prepared."

"Please be watchful when crossing creeks or shallow rivers. There are many where you are going, and you must make sure the water level does not reach the carburetor."

"Henriette! I'm surprised by how much you have learned about cars! I appreciate your concern and I promise I'll be safe." Eager to get underway, I kiss my family goodbye. My petite handlebar moustache tickles my children's cheeks, and they rub their faces as I walk away.

Full of optimism, I go down the steps two at a time. Once at the automobile, I check the boxes in back to be sure they are secure on the padded back seat bench. Satisfied that all is well, I open the driver's door, climb in and settle into the front seat that extends to the other side, more like a sofa. I start the engine and I am ready to go.

I have planned well for this trip. I will drive through the mountains and up to the town, visit the mayor and offer him a ride to a neighboring settlement. Our drive itself will promote the future of the automobile and my business in Japan. Fortunately for me, the mayor speaks English very well. He told me he graduated from the Yokohama Commercial School where the boys had English lessons in the morning, and the girls had English classes in the afternoon.

I maneuver the narrow winding roads, waving at the locals. I marvel at how they use horse drawn carts to come into Yokohama from their remote homes. Some villages closer to the city have access to trains, but not this one.

I drive by old lodgings and rest houses at regular intervals along the way, a great help to slower travelers. Trees have been planted to give travelers shade at their rest stations. At one of these covered spots, a worn cart rests against a fence. The owner brings a bucket of water to his horse. His two young boys have come with him, happily involved in a game of hide and seek behind three old pine trees as their father rests on the back of the cart. They remind me of my children, always making up new games to play.

They stop their game when they hear my noisy vehicle. Charmed by children, I wave at them, smiling, and they respond by jumping up and down, arms greeting me and then waving goodbye.

The countryside roads in Japan are narrow and certainly not made for cars. Travel roads have always been important in Japan for postal, government, and military purposes, but horses and carts are smaller. It is a constant challenge to decide who moves off the road if I meet someone on a narrow lane. The terrain is often a deciding factor, and it is usually easier for my automobile to go backwards than to turn a horse and cart. I try to accommodate the other vehicles.

As I cautiously negotiate another sharp corner, my carefree outlook changes. Snowflakes begin to fall like powder on my windshield. As the motorcar begins to climb to higher elevations and switchbacks, my heart beats faster. Will the car slip? Will I get stuck? I have never driven in the snow before. After cresting one hill, the car starts to show signs of fatigue. Steam escapes the radiator, and I have had to stop more frequently to replace the lost water.

At one point I realize that I still have several miles and switchbacks to go before I reach the village. I put on the brakes, jump down, and lean against my automobile. I turn to the back seat and look under the cardboard boxes, hoping to find a jar of water, but all I find are ropes and an empty bucket. Frustrated, I lean against the car again and gaze at the ditch beside the road.

That's it! The ditches have accumulated several inches of snow. I grab the metal bucket out of the back seat and scoop up some white powder. I place the pail on the hot radiator and watch the snow slowly melt. After repeating the process several times, I am finally on my way again.

The trip has taken longer than expected, but I finally see the village ahead. As I slowly motor onto the main road of the village, I see shops lining the road. One shop has baskets of dried fish on long wooden tables under a canvas awning. I laugh when I see a market sign printed in English offering extract of chicken. Underneath the sign is a tray of brown eggs, of course! On the other side of the road, is a textile market. The shop has flowing silk yardage hung from bamboo poles. The bright colors would attract anyone to their store. Some children are peering out of the second story windows above the shops, waving to their siblings to come have a look at the horseless cart I drive. I smile and wave a greeting to them. I imagine what the children are saying when they see me.

Perhaps they see a giant, green, metal beetle with wheels instead of legs—as tall as a five-year-old. Ten shiny spokes radiate like sunbursts from the center of each wheel. The beetle has two long sofas on its back for passengers. There is a cover that attaches to a clear window at the front of the insect. On the right side, the driver holds a tall mushroom-shaped steering wheel. The best parts are the two dragon eyes in front with metal eyebrows that dance up and down as the beetle goes over bumps in the road. And when I rev the engine, the children hear the creature roar! A giant dragon-beetle!

I laugh to myself as my creature scuttles through town. After passing a dozen buildings, I see a sign, *Yakusho Government Office,* nailed to a wooden building.

I park my muddy motorcar, wishing there was a place to wash it. After taking time to brush pine needles and dust off my jacket, I enter the office.

I am greeted by Mayor Kobayashi. I wait to see if he will shake hands, and he does. I notice it has become more natural for me to bow, too, when meeting fellow businessmen. The mayor eagerly says, "Let's go outside and see the new motorcar. My staff is excited to see it, too. We all want to go for a ride."

"Of course. But first we need to get your heavy desk and typewriter out. We can carry more people if we have more room," I tell the mayor.

While two employees unload the boxes, I apologize for the mud on my automobile, and inform the group about the advantages of the new motorcars. "The ride is fast, stable, and best of all, it is enjoyable." I wait as the mayor translates in much longer sentences. I can understand parts of what he is saying. My fluent brother-in-law taught me the basics and is my tutor.

"It is good you have a canvas cover on your automobile. I think we can fit two people on the bench in the back. The tall fenders should keep most of the mud and snow from the road off the car. Now take us for a ride, we are ready! I will sit in front with Monsier Suzor! Staff! Join us on the step under the doors and hold onto the side of the car," he says, pointing to the wide step on the side of the automobile.

"Mayor Kobayashi. You mean the running boards? Perhaps six people on this little car is too many."

"This motorcar is made of steel! It cannot break. No problem for us and no problem for the motorcar. You worry too much, Monsier Suzor. We are ready!"

I acquiesce to the mayor's logic. To differ would show a lack of respect. I don't like, though, that he is telling me things about my own motor car without any experience. But this is a business agreement, and so I respond respectfully, "Alright. *Chotto* ride."

The Mayor laughs at my use of the Japanese word. "A little ride! Yes, a *chotto* ride."

"Welcome aboard, Mayor Kobayashi. Sit next to me in the front. Two can ride in the small seat in back. The other four of you need to keep your feet on the running boards and hold on to the outside of the motorcar."

The car holds out, groaning from the strain, and slowly moves forward. I am becoming concerned about the tires and our fuel supply. I know that most tires can last for 1500 miles under best conditions, but mountain roads, snow, mud, and water add stress to the rubber. What started out as a fun excursion has become a worry for me. It is almost impossible to get replacement parts if we break something, or parts can take months to arrive.

I try to focus on the beautiful scenery on the mountain. We look down from rocky ledges to the fertile valleys and patchwork rice paddies a few miles below us. The views are stunning. In a quiet moment, as I look around, I wonder if coming to Japan was the right thing for our family. Would I have done better in Paris if we had left Adrienne and Jules to their fates? I don't think so. Maybe I am just tired.

Keeping my thoughts to myself, I return Mr. Mayor and his jubilant but muddy staff to their office after a half hour ride. Beaming, Mayor Kobayashi removes his glasses to wipe a few muddy smudges off, thanks me, and promises to share his excitement with other government officials. He and his staff will enjoy sharing their motorcar adventure with the village, proud to be the first to ride in an automobile.

The mayor is part of a growing community in Yokohama that look to progress as a benefit for Japan and its people. The automobile is a giant step in that direction.

I look at the coach clock in the car and see it is almost three o'clock. I must make it down to the valley below before dark. Since I have had so many problems, I decide to make more regular engine checks, even if that means driving in the dark. Overheating shouldn't be a problem going downhill, but the air is getting chilly.

After a half hour, I stop for a routine check. As I do so, I look over the hood of my automobile and see the sky turning grey, a sure sign of more snow. Chilled, I wrap my scarf around my neck and put on a pair of gloves. Jumping down from the car, I look at the front tires. Both are fine. Checking the rear tires, I see and feel that one is completely flat. I squat and stare at the tire. There are no good options. I know driving with a flat will damage the axel, so I jack up the car and take off the tire. I look at the worn inner tube. I'm stuck. And I don't have a spare tire with me. The car, indeed, did carry too many people on my tour with the mayor. And I am cold and hungry. I brought some apples and cheese, but they are long gone. It is past dinner time, and I imagine Henriette waiting with a plate for me.

My gut plunges, and I try to keep my mind from distress. Instead, I try to think of options. I walk to the side of the road and distractedly pull damp old grass from a ditch as I ponder. Then, clump in hand, an idea takes shape.

I rip more grass from the ground. Shaking the snow off, I stuff the inner tube with the grass and the roots, making a solid tire. After an hour, I have a makeshift tire ready to reattach. I climb into my car, and warily drive down the mountain into the oncoming darkness without another problem from the tire or the axel.

When I finally return from my excursion, Henriette meets me at the door.

"Where have you been so late? Give me your scarf and your hands. They are frozen!" she says, taking and rubbing my hands in hers.

She looks at my suit pants and says, "What took place on the mountain? Your pants are covered with mud from the knees down and your shoes would best be left outside. Sit down and I'll help you with your shoes and tell me what happened."

After recounting todays misadventures, I say, "Henriette, in the morning I will order spare tires from France. And," I say winking at her, "I think I need to add Michelin Tire dealer to my list of business ventures."

# Chapter Eight

Vladivostok Port where the hired Siberian trappers were to begin
their risk laden trip to Hamburg, Germany

# Chapter Eight
Library
Manor de la Noeu, France, 1948

The drawing room at the chateau was much more ornate, with lovely plaster floral motifs on the ceilings. The walls in my new, small library are made of plain stucco, but we have collected pictures and other art pieces for years and will use them to decorate the rooms. Abundant light shines through the tall windows and helps my aging eyesight.

I hear a familiar scratching on the open grey shutters. I put down my newspaper, stand up, and cross to the other side of the room. Our Siamese cat, Fujiko, insists on coming in after her morning expeditions. She meows as she enters, and when I sit back on the sofa, she immediately curls up beside me waiting to be recognized and petted.

She is good company. Very quiet. I stroke her fur and return to the business of my newspaper. The economic impact of the war has caused endless problems. Some people think the economy will improve quickly with political and social reforms. Sadly, I am too old now to partake in the fun and challenge of new business endeavors.

When I was in Japan, I was so attuned to the business culture that I took numerous risks and did better than most. But not always.

Fujiko gets up, arches her back in a stretch, and crawls into my lap. As I caress her smooth silky fur, recollections of an ill-fated gamble get my attention. I gently pick up the cat, look into her blue eyes and say, "Fujiko. Your beautiful coat reminds me of Siberian furs. You are as soft as sable — but you smell much nicer."

I stand, place her on the sofa, and go to my desk to consider how to tell this prickly story.

*Siberian Roulette*
**Yokohama, Japan, 1905**

A man of imposing presence looms over the traders, not only because of his ample size, but also because he stands, arms crossed, on top of a sizeable wooden crate overflowing with Siberian soft gold.

His bushy, unkempt red beard and gruff voice demand attention from the international merchants on the Yokohama dock. He has rented a garage to house a fur trading fair. Fur merchants looking to buy pelts directly from hunters can do so when they disembark at the busy port. I am fascinated by the volume of pelts, and I have many questions for the merchants. I wave a hand over my head to get the burly man's attention.

Alexei Vasilievich sees me and beckons me over with a single arm swing. As I approach, the Russian jumps off his crate of furs, removes his soiled gloves, and we shake hands. He even smells rough.

"I am Louis Suzor," I say to him. "I am here to see your fur operations. I may be interested in doing business with a trader," I say, my eyes riveted on the hectic exchange of furs, reminiscent of ants on a hill organizing sugar granules. The piles of animal fur and skins reek.

He guides me around the raucous warehouse, taking time to gruffly shout out directions or call out a boisterous greeting to another hunter.

"Monsieur Suzor. Best furs come from Siberia. Look here," he says, holding out a pelt for me to touch. "Siberians know how to kill animals and keep the fur not ruined. Feel it. This is wild sable fur, the best. Farm fur is not so good," exclaims Alexei, enjoying being a fur guide and enthusiastic for a new customer.

Furs in Yokohama these days are imported as fast as silk is exported. I look around and see black and white fox furs. Workers move a bundle of wolf furs packed in sawdust onto a cart and to the dock. I jump out of the way as another worker guides several bundles of what look like squirrel pelts out of the warehouse and towards the train station.

"Mr. Suzor, Japanese like squirrel coats very much. Two or three hundred squirrels in one coat. Very warm and attractive. You and I know ladies like to look rich," grins Alexei, nodding at me.

I am distracted again as I see a dozen containers overflowing with beaver and rabbit pelts. Alexei thunders at the crew, "Don't be reckless people. Pay attention and crates will not fall over."

I notice two crates labeled in Russian, but I don't recognize the fur. "What are these?"

"In English, walrus, seal, and sea otter. Hunters like these skins very much. Good to keep people warm in Siberia!"

We return to the front doors of the garage and stand beside several bundles of sable furs. I absent mindedly stroke the almost weightless fur, silky and satin-like. If I close my eyes, I feel like I am petting a kitten. No wonder the fashion houses in New York and Paris have a demand for these pelts, famous for being warm, beautiful, and durable.

Alexei shouts out more directions, pointing right and left, and returns to me. "The fur is for hats, gloves, shawls, boots, and coats. You are interested in buying pelts? I think you are French. You have nice suit. You work for fashion house? White polar bear fur we have over there," he says pointing towards pelts layered in sawdust and salt in the back.

Careful to avoid contact with a dirty crate, I stand aside, brushing salt off my shoes and answer, "No. I am not here to buy fur. I am interested in shipping furs, importing and exporting."

"You must buy fur to ship fur. You are very lucky man. I have 15 hunters leaving in two days. They go Vladivostok, Omsk, Moscow, Poland, and last in Hamburg, Germany. You pay money here and furs available in Hamburg. I will give you more information in the morning. You and I know this is good business opportunity. In Russia we say, 'Do not hurry to reply, but hurry to listen.' Tomorrow you come back. Now," he turns his head and shouts, "back to work!" to anyone who will listen.

I say goodbye and leave, thinking through this incredible opportunity. The fur trade is like the California Gold Rush fifty years ago. With the sale of the furs to my clients in Hamburg, I could make enough money to buy a freighter. My ship would travel between Marseilles and Yokohama—the debut of the Suzor Marine Transport Company! The more I think about it, the more excited I get.

I drive over to the consulate office and look up my brother-in-law, Jules. I explain the undertaking. He is more hesitant than usual to support this new business idea, but I convince him to walk back over to the fur market with me.

"Louis," he says as we walk. "You know the outcome of a successful expedition, but have you considered the chance of failure?"

I think it over and say, "I won't be going on the trip, so there is no personal risk. Since the Trans-Siberian Railway has expanded, the trappers have safer ways to transport and—"

"Hunters still have to deal with dangers like disease or accidents. Wolves and bears can inflict a lot of damage on a hunter. Then there is melting ice swallowing fur sleds. The weather could be a problem, too. And what about this Alexei? Do you trust him, Louis? You have experienced rewards from speculation before, and if Alexei can be trusted, financing a big venture like this could produce a remarkable success."

"My insurance business and import-export company are doing well, but I am of a mind to expand the businesses. I will need a freighter to develop new markets in the future," I add, trying to get him to share this risky decision.

"You are the only one who knows if you can afford this gamble. Assess the risk to you and your family. Talk it over with Henriette. Sometimes getting some sleep before a big decision is a good idea," suggests Jules.

The next day, I return to the market to meet with the Russian trapper. I hear his thunderous voice over the other traders and walk towards him. He sees me and jumps off a crate of pelts. We meet in the middle of an aisle of furs. "Alexei Vasilievich, I have decided to finance an expedition. Tell me. How long will the trip from here to Hamburg take? I will make arrangements to have a business associate meet the lead trapper there."

"Mr. Suzor, you and I know this is a good arrangement. Trip takes three maybe six weeks. Who knows, with bad weather, maybe it will take longer. Ivan Nikolavich is a good trapper and leader. Very experienced trapper," assures Alexei, brushing his hands together and resting them on his hips.

At the end of the day, arrangements are complete, money has changed hands, hunters have been hired, and the troupe of trackers leave to hunt soft gold — the wild Siberian sable furs. I watch from the dock as the trackers row smaller boats out to the larger ship in the outer harbor. Next stop for them will be Vladivstok, a major port city in Russia overlooking Golden Horn Bay, near the borders with China and Korea. The Trans-Siberian Railway will be their base until they arrive at Hamburg.

Several weeks pass and I start to second guess my decision. Six weeks go by, and I have not heard anything from Alexei Vasilievich or my associates in Hamburg. I anxiously meet with Jules again in his office.

"Jules, I have a bad feeling about this. I am fearful I made the wrong decision. My business associates in Hamburg have not seen or heard from the trappers. They tell me it is late in the trapping season and there are not many fur traders in the harbor. What am I going to do? I trusted and financed Alexei and now I am ashamed for possibly making a mistake that cost a great deal of money."

"Louis, I had a bad feeling about the Russian trader. You were eager and Alexei gave you every reason to believe in his fur hunters and traders."

"How am I going to tell Henriette? The family has been adjusting well to our new life in Yokohama, and I was sure this would fulfill my business intentions."

"*Bien sûr.* Surely, it will be difficult. So, you didn't talk it over with Henriette? The best you can do now is accept it, and focus your attention on your other businesses," says Jules, level-headed as usual. Of course, he doesn't have to be the one to tell Henriette about my costly gamble.

"You are right. My decision was too hasty. I wanted to expand my company too fast, and I took an unnecessary risk. Henriette is right. I must slow down and control my impulsivity. Oh, I'm sure I'll hear about this."

Trying to bring a little levity to the situation, Jules puts his hands on his hips and loudly imitates the Russian fur trader, "You and me both know all things are difficult before they are easy."

# Chapter Nine

Louis and son Georges (born 1906) in whimsical photograph.
Yokohama, Japan ca. 1909

# Chapter Nine
Manor Library
Manor de la Noeu, France, 1948

I lean forward in my faded green velvet armchair, pick up a small stack of photos, and look at the one on top. I am holding two strings supporting my son Georges as if he were a marionette. Suitably, he is wearing a pastel blue and gold court jester's costume. I turn the hand-tinted photo over — Yokohama, 1911. Georges was only five years old.

My heart aches. We lost Georges to a glider accident when he was 24 years old. I miss spending time, especially fishing, with him. He would catch fish, and I would place them on the river rocks and carefully sketch their contours on rice paper. If he had not died, would he be going fishing with me and Gilbert today?

"*Grand-père*. Lunch is on the table in the dining room. Here is your cane," Gilbert says, picking it up off the floor and handing it to me. I stand up and steady myself with my cane. I've been sitting all morning and my hips are complaining. "I'm looking forward to our adventure this afternoon! And the maid has agreed to make trout caviar if I catch a female in the family-way — we already have the champagne. I'll get your charcoal pencils and drawing tablet after lunch."

Caviar. Russian caviar. Japanese caviar. I used to like the roe, but it no longer appeals to me. The scent reminds me of the Russian fur trader and my losses. I will politely eat a bite tonight if we get some. And I wonder what Gilbert and my other grandchildren will think when they read my *memoire*.

*Pulling Strings*
**Yokohama, Japan, Circa 1907**

"Where are you going, Papa?" my son, Louis, asks.

Holding the front door open, ready to leave, I answer, "Off to Tokyo for a business meeting with a banker. It is not far, only 16 miles. But first I must stop by the waterfront to check on a shipment. I'll be back tonight, not too late. *Au revoir*, my darlings."

"*Au revoir*, Papa!"

I never tire of going to the harbor. The merchants are from many countries, so the traders usually have new and interesting products to see and possibly buy. I drive along the commercial quarters and head north to the customs offices. The port is alive with expectant activity, as a ship from Vladivostok, Russia, has arrived in the outer harbor carrying *ikura*, red caviar. From the automobile's window I can see, in the distance, Russian sailors hoisting the barrels on sturdy ropes and chains, transferring them to the waiting smaller ship, which will be able to navigate the shallow harbor.

Within a half hour, the smaller boat arrives at the wharf. Russian sailors jump from the boat and hurry up the wooden dock for carts to transport the crates of roe to an open warehouse on another pier. Russian fisherman and sailors unpack the roe swiftly as buyers jostle into line to assess the wares and bargain for their companies. I have heard the price and quality of the red roe goes down every two hours because more salt must be added. The best roe is purchased quickly.

I park my automobile at the end of the docks and walk on wooden planks over to the canvas-covered outdoor fish market. Merchants and buyers pack closely, like sardines. Wooden crates of the salted roe sit on low platforms. The smell of discarded fish is so strong, I take short breaths until I get used to it. The stench reminds me of the rank outdoor fur markets.

Japanese men in kimonos and sandals walk around the crates, while some sit on the floor at low tables on tatami mats. Several Chinese workers weigh the caviar on huge balance beam scales. One lifts a full drum onto a steel balance tray while another loads weights onto the opposite tray. After the amount and price are determined, money changes hands.

Albert Moreau, my friend with an export business and an expert at roe, is here early to buy Russian caviar to can and export into Asia. He finds me looking at the contents of four oak casks of shiny caviar. He is familiar with the caviar trade, but this is my first time watching the exchange *en plein air*.

"The medium color and size are the sweetest," he says. "Not as good as the caviar in France, but the Japanese love it." He then draws my attention to a Japanese seller and buyer. Pointing them out, he says, "Watch those two men. See? The two men in blue and white kimonos by the warehouse door? They are bartering for a good price."

I don't understand what is happening. They are not speaking; instead they are putting their hands in each other's Kimono sleeves. *"Très intéressant!* It is a bit bizarre, no?" I am perplexed by the peculiar behavior.

"This is how it works. Look at the tall man. He is the seller. He reveals the price for the caviar using his fingers concealed in his kimono sleeve. Now look! The buyer is reaching his hand in the seller's sleeve, counting fingers. Here is where it gets interesting. The sale is complete if the buyer takes his hand out. However, if a buyer wants to barter, he rejects the offer and offers a price with his own fingers. Keep watching. They may go back and forth for a while. And it is all in the name of confidentiality. No one else here in the market knows the final price, which means the next buyer might buy at a higher or lower price than this man."

Buying and selling caviar in this quantity would never be done this way in France. Once again, I am fascinated by the cultural difference in business transactions. In Paris, there would be a set price or perhaps an open auction at the dock. Prices would be displayed for all buyers, just as bread, fruit, and vegetables are sold in the public markets.

As I look around, the scene before me becomes even more animated as groups of men negotiate according to this foreign way of conducting business.

"Fascinating, isn't it?" Albert asks. "Look around for a bit. I need to go to the front desk." But before he can leave, we hear a loud voice with a Russian accent.

"You and I both know this is a good price."

I can't believe it! I turn, and sure enough, there he is. *"Mon Dieu,* Albert!" I say to my friend. "It is Alexei Vasilievich. I would recognize that voice and red hair anywhere. You remember the Russian fur trader I told you about? It's him!"

*"Ah, oui.* I remember your terrible loss at his hands."

"Should I say something?"

"Absolutely approach him. It has been several years—you deserve your answers." I feel angry and compose myself for the upcoming interaction. "See me before you leave," Albert says, "and tell me what you find out."

I work my way through the busy market towards the Russian fur trader, bumping into people along the way, not knowing what to expect. I feel my heartbeat quicken and I start to sweat. I hope my anger and frustration don't show.

"Mister Alexei Vasilievich. I would like to talk to you," I call to the massive Russian, who stands with his hands on his hips beside a mass of caviar casks. He turns around and we make eye contact. He smiles with surprise, walks over to me and gives me a robust handshake. I step back and brush off my suit.

"*Bonjour*, the Frenchman. Nice to see you. You are here to buy black gold, our Russian *ikura*? You know *ikura* is Russian word?" he asks, sounding like an overly friendly salesman.

Before I can speak, Alexei says, "Da. Da. I am sorry about the trappers. I don't know what happened to your hunter and trader, Ivan Nikolavich. I never saw him again. The other hunters never saw him, either. You know, there are many problems for hunters. It is very risky work—wild animals are dangerous. And wolverines are always angry! Nasty animal but beautiful fur. Worse than bear or wild boar. Or maybe something small like tick or mosquito made Ivan Nikolavich sick, maybe killed him. I am sorry we lost him. He was a good and brave hunter," he says, head down, looking at the floor, attempting to look remorseful.

Clearly, I will not get any money back.

This is a waste of time. Two years ago, I resigned myself to the idea that I had made a hasty investment with bad consequences, but I didn't expect or want to see Alexei again. "I don't want your black gold. Do you really think I would do business with you again?" My forwardness surprises me, and catches him off guard, too. "No. I will tell my fellow businessmen to avoid you and your caviar or anything you sell. Good day." I turn to leave and feel my cheeks flush.

Alexei Vasilievich waves and bellows after me, "You and I both know this is true for now. Maybe other time."

I hear the paper market signs overhead ripple as breezes pick up. The winds from the mainland are welcome as they blow the smoke from ships away from the city. I take a deep breath and the fresher air takes some of my stress with it. I walk to the front desk and meet up with Albert. Looking back at the crowded market, I tell him about my short and futile meeting with the Russian.

"Louis, I don't think you will ever have cause to do business with him again. Our company has cut back on buying caviar, whether it is fresh or canned. Some businesses found the caviar sold as Russian was really from the United States! There is a shortage of sturgeons in Russia and other countries from overfishing, so the prices fluctuate, and when you don't know where it is from, it is best to leave it alone," says Albert. "At least you were able to confront the Russian and perhaps put the debacle behind you?" He puts on his hat and straightens his jacket.

"Yes. Now is a good time to let that story end. Thank you for coming with me and showing me the business side of caviar," I say as we shake hands and I leave the foul-smelling warehouse.

I walk to the end of the wooden dock, step up into my motorcar and settle in my seat for the ride to Tokyo, trying not to think of how much I lost to Alexei Vasilievich. I start the car, and the noise of the motorcar alerts pedestrians to stay to the side of the road. I also notice how, since the roads have been dry without rain for a week, my automobile leaves a cloud of dust behind me. I make a mental note to slow down when meeting another vehicle on the road.

After a bumpy ride on gravel roads, I arrive on the outskirts of busy Tokyo. Electric trains wander through the streets, shifting rails when necessary. Rickshaw drivers adjust their course of travel, careful to avoid pedestrians, farm carts, and other rickshaws. And me. Some drivers wear straw hats, while passengers carry delicate umbrellas and fans to avoid the sun. There are so many umbrellas it looks like multicolored mushrooms dancing to and from the center of town.

As I near downtown Tokyo, the streets get busier. Large business signs loom over the shops. The tops are tilted towards the road so people can read them. Chinese paper lanterns bring color to the storefronts and encourage customers to enter. I drive slowly, always watching for children, families, and horse-drawn carts. I smell the salty pungent air of the outdoor fish market on one street as I drive past. As I approach the bank, I look up the street and see wooden poles with paper awnings shading the grateful merchants and customers at the popular Shijo-Dori market. Tall narrow silk banners display the names of the various shops in artistic calligraphy.

I park on the side of the street and descend from my Clement Bayard motorcar, just barely avoiding being struck by a horse-drawn carriage owned by the Tokyo postal service. Interesting that my next project relates to those carriages. I step back against the bank wall to let a group of school children walk by on their way to the city park. Some of them slow down to return my smiles, then they speed up to catch up with their classmates.

I dust off my jacket and slacks, run my fingers as a comb through my hair, then lift my chin and approach the front doors of the new Mitsui Bank. I adjust my tie, and finally twist my mustache. Appearances are important. I feel confident in this new venture.

The doorman greets me with a bow and asks, "You have a meeting with Mr. Hiroaka?" I nod. "I can take you to his office. Follow me down this hallway."

Mr. Hiraoka is tall and slim, dressed in the latest European style suit, custom made by the best tailor in town. I spoke with him at my tailor's shop when I was picking up a new suit last month. The dark blue suit and azure tie compliment his professional appearance. He bows and greets me, and we exchange pleasantries about our families. He draws a chair near his desk and motions for me to sit. He returns to sit across from me at his long teakwood desk.

First things first. A young clerk comes into the office, bows, and pours two cups of hot aromatic tea from a white and blue teapot. I notice three blue herons painted on the pot, as if they are waiting to catch a fish in an indigo pond. The clerk places two cups of tea on a silver tray and sets the tray on the desk.

"Please have some tea. How can I help you today, Mr. Suzor? It is always a pleasure to work with you and your innovative business ideas," Mr. Hiraoka says in perfect English. I wish I could speak Japanese that well. I'm lucky English is the Lingua Franca of international business in Japan.

I lean forward from my chair and place one hand over another on his desk. "Innovative and productive concepts, as I see it, are essential for such a large city. Have you noticed how long it takes for your bank and businesses to get mail? Look outside. Horse drawn carriages are impractical and too slow for such a large city." He looks outside the window, and nods slowly. "The city limits keep expanding as Yokohama and Tokyo annex new villages. There are 450 thousand residents in Yokohama, and about 2,000 of them are foreign residents. This is the perfect time to organize and publicize the automobile for public service and transportation. The Emperor supports progress. I would like to order mail trucks for your city, and I hope we can work together on this venture," I add with aplomb, leaning back in my chair.

The clerk comes in with fresh hot tea and refills our cups. "You do have some very good points," Mr. Hiraoka says. "Progress is a priority for us. But I have an important question for you. Did you contact your banker in Paris?"

I put my teacup on the desk. I feel my right leg begin bouncing with nerves. I immediately sit up straighter to stop the movement. A British diplomat friend told me that a trembling leg, called *bimbo-yusuri* or poor person's shake, shows nervousness and bad manners in Japan and China. The nervous bouncing signals that you are bad with money — unfortunate behavior in a bank.

My leg under control, I reply, "The French banker doesn't understand your country. He refused my request. I have accepted it now, but I was disappointed when I was in Paris last month. My banker thought it was a ridiculous idea because there are no wide roads here in Japan and children play outside, so it would be impossible to drive safely. He advised me to forget the idea of importing cars to Japan, saying the venture was doomed to be a financial disaster."

Mr. Hiraoka pauses and takes a sip of tea, looking at the blue bamboo branches on his teacup. While he is weighing my request, I add, "The

French banker has never been to Japan and hasn't seen the progress and opportunities in your city."

Mr. Hiroaka hesitates and excuses himself. "I need to consult with a colleague." I take this as a good sign—he is interested, if cautious. But I understand caution, especially in the wake of Alexi Vasilievich. In his absence, my leg tries to dispel my tension, so I stand up for a moment and shake it out before sitting again—just in time.

Mr. Hiroaka returns and takes a seat behind his desk. "We have an idea that is good for you and this bank. We propose a temporary business venture, sharing responsibility three ways. The bank advances one third, you invest one-third, and one-third is made of shares sold to the public."

This is a good deal, I know. "Wonderful," I say, before the deal can change. "Thank you, Mr. Hiroaka!"

"I still need to check with our bank director to give you a final decision. Assuming it goes through, the papers and authorizations will take a few weeks to complete. Mr. Suzor, this is a very helpful progressive business idea for Tokyo and Yokohama."

Mr. Hiroaka stands up, and I follow suit. We bow, and then shake hands. Mr. Hiroaka is a businessman and a friend. It is a shame we don't socialize more, but I live on the Bluff where foreign residents live, and he lives on a hill on the other side of town where the Japanese businessmen live.

As I drive home, I feel wonderful. I am convinced that my idea is fundamentally safe and sound, and that my efforts will eventually pay off. When I arrive home and settle in, I talk my day over with Henriette. She agrees that it is a safe risk, not like some others, and confident that financing some of the project out of my pocket will not put our family in danger.

A short week later, I hear back from Mr. Hiroaka—the bank director approved the deal. I take another trip through the colorful crowded streets of Tokyo to see Mr. Hiroaka, passing villagers pulling carts. The mail trucks will make their life easier, I'm sure.

I disembark from my auto, and I turn right and enter the bank. Mr. Hiroaka has all the documents ready and, after a ceremonial cup of tea, we finalize the transaction.

As I leave the bank, Mr. Hiroaka says to me, "Let me know when you get your next shipment of automobiles. My wife and I would like to buy one."

"I will have one sent over with the mail trucks. You are first in line for the next automobile," I say, enjoying our growing friendship. We bow and shake hands, the best of both worlds.

Back in Yokohama, I go to my office and work hard at arranging shipping and purchasing documentation. When I was in France last month,

I contacted several different automobile manufacturers and toured their factories. I didn't have the funds then to place an order, but the agents were very friendly and helpful, and I was able to identify which company would be the best option for me. Now that I have the funds, I send a telegram ordering 25 trucks, adding one car for my private use and one more for Mr. Hiraoka, a total of 27 automobiles from the Gobron & Brillie factory. Feeling confident, I also ordered a few Delaunay-Belleville automobiles for my dealership in Yokohama. I order replacement parts and extras for repairs, since none are available overseas. I will wire the money when the shipment arrives. I also send a telegram to the Michelin tire manufacturer and place an order for tires.


A week later, the Michelin representative replies: *'will send rep stop are there cars in japan stop'*

I send another telegram, keeping my message below ten words, as each word is expensive: *'want michelin franchise contract for all japan stop.'*

I will work exclusively with Michelin for every automobile. *"Finalement!"* I think to myself sitting back in my desk chair, right leg bouncing easily now. The Siberian experience was a difficult lesson. Alexei had me on a line then, but this time I hold the strings.

# Chapter Ten

Clement Bayard automobile with factory in the background. France

# Chapter Ten
Library
Manor de la Noeu, France, 1949

Another year passes and I have not even finished half of my stories. The photos alone are not enough; I want my descendants to have a sense of my experiences in Algeria, Japan, and France. Every moment has a story. I want my tales to inspire them to think about their lives, too. I hope they will see a little bit of me in themselves through the experiences I share. I exhale and look around my library. How will I know when I have finished?

I look at the white wall to the right of the doorway. My son, Louis, framed-in part of the wall and we built an aquarium into it. A yellow and black striped butterfly fish is on the left. Following him is a Moorish idol, black and white striped with a magnificently thin dorsal fin. Other Hawaiian tropical fish hover, ever ready to whirl and spin.

But they never will. I carved them out of wood and painted each one, Julius Bien lithographs guiding my paint strokes. I have never seen these fish in person, but I have felt them in my hands.

Henriette comes into the room and sits by me on the sofa, carefully adjusting her dress over her knees. I glance at her and see silver streaks in her hair, just on the sides. Always elegant, she wears a string of pearls everywhere, even when she dallies in the garden. Is she getting even more petite?

"Louis, are you taking a break from writing? You were staring at those fish, even though they weren't moving." She puts her hand on my arm and draws herself nearer.

"*Cherie*, the fish are like my stories. Each one is different and going a different direction. It's a bit frustrating, I must admit."

"Yes, Louis, and right now they aren't going anywhere—like your stories."

"And I have so many pictures to sort. I'm making time to spend with you and our friends, but in doing so, I'm afraid my project is lacking some attention," I say giving her a kiss on her cheek.

"Well, that is very sweet of you," she says. "And, for now, I will sit here with you and admire these motionless fish and enable you to not do your work—for today. But, darling, do not give up on your stories."

I smile. What a wonderful wife, steady at my side for so long. I gaze at the fish I transformed from blocks of wood into an aquatic museum, and I remember the first tropical fish I met under glass on a steamship.

*Ocean in a Box*
**The South China Sea, 1911**

I stand at the railing of the ship, returning to Yokohama. The ship sailed for ten days from Saigon to Shanghai, and we are just now leaving Shanghai harbor. I can barely see the International Settlement from where I stand on the promenade deck. The buildings fade into the ocean mist as our ship chugs slowly towards Japan.

I have been in Paris, visiting our daughter, Andree. She is asthmatic and her lungs cannot tolerate the thick smoky Yokohama harbor air, so she lives the life of a little Parisienne with her grandmother. Andree was born in 1901 in Japan, but she was always sick and in the hospital. After a few years, we had to make the difficult choice to send her back to France to be with Henriette's mother. Henriette's sister, Adrienne, is there as well now, and lives a little less dramatically since the shock of Jules's death in a motorcar accident in Zurich five years ago. He had been the French Officer of Public Instruction, and they were on government business at the time of the traffic accident. Now, at just 29 years old, Adrienne is a widow.

I worry about not being in Paris with Andree if something terrible happens. Last year there was a great flood in the city. The Seine River rose eight and a half meters, causing damage to most of the buildings, and I wasn't there to help my mother or daughter. That was a natural disaster, but I also have concerns about crime and safety. This past August, someone stole the Mona Lisa from the Louvre Museum! Who would do such a thing? The possibility of something happening to my family in Paris leaves me uneasy. So, I carry the burden of worry, but I keep it to myself.

Our family members miss their little dark-haired Andree and her bright smile, but there is no other remedy. Fortunately, she loves her grandmother, and enjoys her friends and family in Paris. But my heart aches whenever I think of her and feel the distance. We only see her every few years, as it sometimes takes three months to get to Paris via steamship, and another three to return. But it is better than the boarding school I went to, I'm sure— I hope— where my brothers and I were at the mercy of unforgiving nuns.

These thoughts whip through my mind as quickly as the wind on my cheeks. The ship travels at 17 miles per hour. Weather and currents can change the speed of the journey. But travelling in first class offers many opportunities to a businessman. I am fortunate that I learned to speak English when I was a child, since most European businessmen have the English language in common.

I look forward to seeing familiar old friends on the ship, but I also see this trip as an opportunity to meet new people. I will often go it alone and ask to join a table and exchange business trade cards as I leave. Mine includes my name and address and a list of my business services from insurance to automobile sales. I am starting to use more newspaper ads, too, and am finding them quite effective for bringing in new clients.

In addition to businessmen, missionaries and government officials are also in first class, along with some adventurous characters out to leisurely see the world. I visit with them, too. You never know. A government official or a wealthy traveler could be your next customer!

Second and third class, as well as steerage, are below us and we rarely see them. They are mostly workers looking for jobs.

I leave the outer deck rails to go back to my cabin, my intention to read the newspaper. I must be up to date on world news to partake in conversations. We can't talk business all the time.

I pass a mirror at the end of the hallway and see my hair covering the top of my ears, and notice that my moustache is a bit unkempt, too. I decide the newspaper can wait. I go down the hall and up a short flight of stairs to make an appointment with the coiffeur. The barber suite is decorated with ornate mirrors and the finest oriental rugs. To my surprise, the barber seats me right away.

"Monsieur Suzor, it is so nice to see you again. I believe I gave you a haircut several months ago on your trip to Marseilles. More motorcars? How is the business in Yokohama?" Max, the portly German barber, asks in English.

"*Tres bien*! Thank you. I am eager to get home before a shipment of auto bodies and frames arrive. They need to be assembled by hand and I want to be there to supervise the work," I say running my hands over the velvet arms on my chair. "I'm looking forward to having the 25 trucks assembled, buffed, and shining! And, of course, sold to new motorists."

"Please lean your head forward, Monsieur, while I trim the nape of your neck." I go quiet while he trims, then, when he is done, continue my story.

"Max, the copper glistening grills and crimson red and black bodies will look like an army polished and ready for a parade! I already have a large hangar built specially for them."

"Monsieur, you are so excited you cannot stop speaking! Please wait for a moment while I trim your moustache," he says with a laugh. I chuckle to myself, too, and continue my daydreaming about my new undertakings as the barber uses his scissors close to my mouth. "Well, there you go, Monsieur Motorcar. You look quite refined again."

I look at my reflection and turn to see both sides. "Thank you, Max. I am pleased," I say as he removes the white cotton bib from around my neck.

I step out of the barber chair and brush off my slacks, before paying the bill. As always, I leave a good tip.

"It is always a pleasure to see you. What will it be next? Airplanes? I heard there was an air race from Paris to Madrid last May," Max asks with a smile.

"There were too many injuries and a few deaths. The race has now been suspended, Max. I will wait until planes are a bit safer before I buy one!" I reply as I turn to leave the barber shop.

I return to my cabin. A quick change of clothes before supper is in order, as I will be dining with my friends and business colleagues. The ship's staff has made up my bed with clean sheets and an embroidered silk bedspread and two pillows. A large armoire with two full length mirrors holds itself securely against the wall with the help of metal straps in case of rolling seas. I cross the room, open the armoire, and choose a fresh white shirt and grey jacket. As I change, I hear the supper gong. I look at my reflection one last time, adjust my cravat, cross the room, and close the door behind me.

As I walk down the hallway, I hear piano music coming from the bar. I go up three stairs and turn into what looks like a Parisian ballroom. The decoration is almost theatrical with heavy drapes, oriental rugs, darkly polished wood walls, and beamed ceilings. Orange chairs with gold ornate arm rests wait for guests to claim them. A haze of smoke rests in the air, as some passengers have come in early for a before-supper cigarette or cigar.

I see a Dutch business associate, Mr. Kerr, standing by a doorway where the air is fresh. He has a fashionable white handlebar moustache, an ample paunch, blue eyes, and greying curly hair. I join him at his tall table to have a drink and enjoy the lavish plates of cheese, though I will pass on the Russian caviar. The bar is generous with their caviar, hoping the salty brine will make patrons thirsty and want more drinks.

"Well, here you are—Father of the motorcar in Japan! I hope you and your family are doing well," says Mr. Kerr after spooning himself a generous serving of roe onto a too-small toast round. He is the owner of a renowned silk export company with offices in New York, Amsterdam, and Paris.

"You flatter me, Mr. Kerr! And how goes your business?"

"More of the usual silk trade dealings. Some people prefer French silk, and some prefer Japanese silk. Fashion houses have their favorites, too. Our silkworms seem to be content and very busy. As you know, Japanese raw silk is of excellent quality. We have some mills in France that have been thriving with worms imported from Japan. Some earlier worms died out from a pandemic, but that is in the past. The new ones are expected to stay healthy and grow well," adds Mr. Kerr, pausing while the server delivers two whiskeys. "While you have human children, I keep myself busy with silkworms!" he chuckles, taking a sip.

"Your silkworm family appears to be thriving. I'm happy to hear your investments are doing well. We continue to have unforeseen occurrences as well with the motorcars."

Another man comes towards our table and introduces himself. I greet him and ask him to join us. Perhaps he has similar interests and we can all benefit from meeting each other. After shaking hands with Mr. Wilson, I tell him briefly about my automobile business and Mr. Kerr tells him about his silk business. Tall and slim with a ready smile, Mr. Wilson is a young American on a pleasure trip to Japan. He says he is an adventurer, and he is going to visit an American friend who lives in Yokohama for several months. They plan on traveling by train or boat, perhaps even making time for fishing.

"Mr. Suzor. I'm sure you have some stories to tell from your motorcar adventures in Yokohama," says Mr. Wilson.

"Well, a few months ago, I encountered a horse and cart loaded with salt on the way to our summer home in the mountains."

Mr. Wilson says, "Please tell us what happened. Everyone likes a good story!"

"I have an interesting one. So, I am driving on a very narrow dirt road on the way up Usui Pass to our mountain summer home. I go around a bend and am suddenly face to face with a horse and cart. I put the car in neutral and wait. I see a villager in a blue and white cotton kimono shirt and baggy tan linen pants. He anxiously holds his horse's harness, looking right and left, clearly not knowing what to do next. The road is too narrow for either of us to pass. The horse, with large terrified eyes, starts to cautiously retreat to get away from the strange machine in front of him. The tall load on the cart wobbles from side to side. The horse backs the overburdened cart into a pond, and a large number of packages wrapped in straw tumble off into the water."

Mr. Kerr asks, "What was in the packages that fell into the water?"

"This was the distressing part of the event. The packages were salt for the village. The salt fell into the pond and started to dissolve in the water where the villagers raise fish. The salt probably killed the fish."

"What happened next? Was there anything you could do to help?" asks Mr. Wilson.

"I tried to help the man, but he refused any assistance. The man bowed and apologized. He said he was sorry and asked forgiveness. Imagine that. This seems to be normal in my dealings with many Japanese people I encounter. The situation would not be so polite if we were in France!"

"And definitely different in America!" adds Mr. Wilson.

A waiter approaches our table just as I finish the story. "Would you like to order, gentlemen?" he asks. We turn our attention to the supper menu. "Last night I had mutton cutlets," Mr. Kerr says, "Tonight I will order the Petits Fillets Mignon. How about you?"

"The fillets will be perfect. I'll also have the giblet soup, please, as the aroma has been tempting me since I came in here. And plum pudding with brandy sauce should finish things off well," I respond.

Mr. Wilson places his order and tells the waiter his table number. He excuses himself to join his group for dinner.

"Let's go to the dining room," says Mr. Kerr as he finishes his drink and sets the glass on the table. "We will be at the Captain's table tonight. And I'm looking forward to more automobile stories!" He puts on his hat, hungry for another elegant meal on the ship.

After I direct the waiter to bring my dinner to the captain's table, I follow Mr. Kerr. The dining room is up a short flight of stairs at the bow of the ship. I use the railing, as I have been thrown off balance by a wave or a turn of the ship's wheel one too many times.

I walk across the room to the captain's table at the front of the elegant dining room. Behind the table and against the wall is a moving masterpiece, a vibrant ocean in a box. A glass window spans the front of the wooden box, giving viewers a glimpse of the undersea world. I have seen these on other ships and in a few homes in Paris. I find myself drawn to watching the inhabitants, remembering Jules Verne's book *20,000 Leagues Under the Sea*. I'm grateful the giant sea squid could never fit in this box!

Before I sit down, I walk closer to see how the box is made. I can feel the sides and back are wood. Inside I see the water-tight pitch coating. I put my hand on the glass and feel the warmth from the light inside. The tropical clown fish and others require a heated home.

"Incredible, isn't it?" asks someone in English. I turn to see Mr. Moller, an American friend. We shake hands. "I heard from a steward that the saltwater is replaced regularly to keep plants and fish healthy. What a job!"

I agree as we walk back to our predetermined places at the Captain's table. Each place setting has a card with our names carefully scribed, placed behind the gold trimmed plates.

A man at the head of the table stands up, Captain Klein. I know him from previous trips and enjoy his company and stories. He greets us and invites us to be seated. I am happy to find I am seated facing the colorful aquarium. I find the movement soothing. I think I will come back tomorrow and sketch one or two fish in the morning.

A waiter comes to our table and I order a fine French Bordeaux. As our meals are served, we share stories about our business adventures and our lives away from our home countries. As the evening goes on, we compete to follow each story with a better one.

Mr. Moller from America mentions something about a dead rat with the plague being found in Tokyo. He then goes on to a case of cholera on the ships, not suitable conversation for the Captain's table. Americans can be so crass sometimes. This is not a good way to encourage new business connections.

Thankfully, Mr. Kerr quickly changes the subject. "Mr. Moller. Ask the waiter to tell you what that ugly brown thing is resting on the gravel in the aquarium. Ask him to tell you in Chinese."

Mr. Moller asks, and the waiter, with a twinkle in his eye, says, *"Yu."* We all burst into laughter, except Mr. Moller, who looks confused. Mr. Kerr explains to the American that *yu* means fish in Chinese. Mr. Moller breaks into a hearty laugh, too.

I notice there are a few gentlemen admiring the fish in the aquarium next our table, and since we have all finished our meals, I invite them to join us for a brandy. After introductions and a new round of drinks are ordered, Mr. Kerr asks for another story.

Looking at the aquarium, I decide to tell a fish story. "Alright, gentlemen," I say, after a sip of warm brandy. "I will tell you about driving in a snowstorm, a near fatal accident, and a basket of fish." The men turn their attention to me, and I continue. "As I told you, it was snowing. A lot. There was a heavy layer on the ground, so much that the engine noise was muffled, and it was unusually quiet. Every few minutes I had to stop and scrape off the snow that had gathered and frozen on my windshield. I remember looking at my frozen hands, wishing I had brought gloves. I was just starting to feel more confident driving in the snow, when suddenly I heard a cry and the autocar shuddered, as if I had hit something. I brought the automobile to a full stop. As I stepped down from the vehicle, I prayed it was not a dog. Unsure of what I would find, I slowly looked under the car." Waiting several seconds, I reveal, "I saw a body." I pause again, watching Mr. Moller, Mr. Kerr, and the captain looking at each other in surprise.

*"Mon Dieu!"* the Captain exclaims. "Did you kill the person?"

"No, thank goodness. I hadn't seen her because of the snow on my windshield. She was a large woman with black hair, pulled into a bun. She was wearing a blue and white kimono and several sweaters. The lower part of her ample body was lodged awkwardly between the front wheels. I quickly got back in the car, shifted into reverse, and moved back a few feet to clear the woman, and then helped her back on her feet. She appeared frightened, but she miraculously didn't show signs of an injury."

"I told you he has good stories. True, too! Keep going, Louis," encourages Mr. Kerr.

I continue, "Snow usually has no odor, but I could smell fish." I halt briefly for effect. The men pause and look curiously at one another. "I said to the frightened lady, 'Are you all right? I am so sorry. *Sumimasen.*' Her half-frozen fish were scattered all over the snow. 'Let me help you put them back in your market basket.' We grabbed the cold trout and slipped them to her wicker carrier. My hands were already cold, and now they smelled terrible, too. Thankfully, the snow cushioned her fall. And lucky for both of us, she was plump and had a large behind which stopped the car and probably saved her life." I look around the table and can't help but laugh at the surprise in the men's faces.

"That was quite a fish story, Mr. Suzor," Mister Moller, the American, says. "Now I have one to share about my nephew in Malaysia." We look at him expectantly as we sip our brandy.

"He was quite a rascal. He and his friends put jellyfish into mud puddles where the nuns had to walk to get to church on Sunday mornings. The church wasn't far from the convent, but it was the only way through the jungle to get there. Since the children were hidden behind the giant leaves, they felt they wouldn't get caught. Unlucky for them, they made so much noise laughing that the nuns found them, grabbed them by their ears and brought them to Mother Superior! And you know how those Catholic nuns can punish small children!"

We get a good laugh out of that story, imagining the jellyfish surprising the nuns. After a few more stories are told, the captain rises. "Excuse me, gentlemen. But I must check in on the first mate before retiring for the night. I hope to see you all again, soon."

I decide to retire for the evening as well. I push my chair back and stand up. I walk around the table and shake hands with the remaining tablemates. "Good night, gentlemen. Here is my business trade card for each of you, and I would be pleased to have one from you as well. I hope we can be talking advertisements for each other in the future. Thank you for a very entertaining evening. I look forward to seeing you tomorrow." I turn away from the group and walk down the short flight of stairs, holding the railing.

I turn right and go down another flight of stairs and then the hallway, to my cabin. I open the door and instantly feel relaxed. I take off my jacket and hang it in the oak armoire. I look at a statue of a carved carp anchored to a corner of a desk. I walk over to it and feel the artistic curves. Could I carve a piece of wood to capture the grace of an angel fish, just as I hope I captured some business revenue prospects this evening?

# Chapter Eleven

Louis and friends attract curious onlookers in downtown Yokohama.
Clement Bayard automobile.  The company logo, a statue of
Pierre Terrail, Seigneur de Bayard is on the hood.
The license K denotes Kanagawa prefecture.

# Chapter Eleven
Library
Manor de la Noeu, France, 1949

I lean back and rub my hands together. They get cold when I type, probably a circulation problem. I stand up and walk over to the tall narrow window facing the morning sun. My coach clock is on the sill hanging from a small tree I carved from wood, the timepiece resting in a cradle of roots.

I pick up the sunbaked silver clock and immediately feel the warmth in my chilled hands. I gaze at the face of the timepiece in my palm. Across the middle are the words 'Automobile Club.' I return to my desk for my magnifying glass, hold it over the clock, and read the tiny letters below, 'Yokohama Automobile Garage.' I still feel the heat from the silver case and beveled glass. After I have adsorbed all its warmth, I place it and the magnifying glass on my desk. I sit back in my chair and consider writing a story about my automobile garage in Japan.

Henriette comes to the doorway. "It's almost time for lunch," she says, coming into the room. She sits on the sofa in front of the Japanese tea crate that holds my paper memories and looks through the pictures on top.

"The crate is still beautiful even though it has some scratches and the lacquer seems to be wearing off, even after all these years. The faded orange and pink chrysanthemums and green leaves still hold their color and charm. Sometimes I feel like the box, getting older and fading," says Henriette.

"Yes, we are getting older, but, like the flowers, you are beautiful and still hold your charm," I respond, happy to tease her. She laughs.

"Lunch is ready, Louis. It's your favorite, onion soup. And have you had your watch repaired yet?" she asks, eyeing the coach clock on my desk.

"No, not yet. It still says two o'clock all the time."

"Well, Louis, at least it shows the correct time twice a day," she says, smiling at her remark.

"*Toujours la Comedienne,*" I say, laughing at her quick reply. "I'll be right there."

I pick up the large coach clock, walk back to the window, and return it to the base of the tree, carefully hanging it by the metal bow that encircles the winding crown. Looking at the hands of on the clock, I wonder why time keeps going forward, but my memories wander in the opposite direction.

## Mechanical Marvels
### Yokohama, Japan, Circa 1912

I park my car in front of the garage, get out, button my coat and lift my collar against the harbor wind. Fall has blown in from the sea and I am ready to be inside, protected from the gusts that rush around the warehouses. A month has passed since the trucks arrived in Yokohama, and it is time for a periodic visit to the garage to check on operations.

I open the door to the garage, careful that the wind doesn't catch the door and wrench it out of my hands. The scent of raw grass mats on the dirt floor mixed with oil meets my nose.

I walk over to the manager and greet him with a bow and a handshake. "Mr. Tanaka. How are you? And how are the employees doing?" I look around the shop and see rows of heads bent down, intent on their work. Before he can answer, I ask, "Mr. Tanaka, why are so many people working on Saturday?"

The garage manager proudly announces, "I decided to clean all the engines this weekend. All your employees are working. Careful and thorough cleaning is important for new trucks."

Thirty employees sit at individual tables close to the floor. Several kneel, and others sit cross-legged. Some mechanics wear blue and white kimonos and indigo linen and cotton *momohikis*, Japanese traditional pants. The other half wear western slacks and wool coats, some with kimono tops underneath. I take a deep breath, and I look around the warehouse, stunned by what I see. The trucks are on one side, the cloth hoods on the other.

I walk up to the first *kacho*, a mechanic, pause, and silently observe him. He sits comfortably on a tatami mat polishing and sorting engine braces in orderly piles by size. They took every engine out of the trucks, and then dismantled each one. Completely.

The *kacho* avoids eye contact, a Japanese form of respect, and continues his project. I walk by several other tables set up with similar tasks. Another *kacho* cleans and sorts nuts, gears, and bolts, making clean shiny towers on his worktable. The towers look like a village of tall Buddhist temples.

Each table has a wooden box under it for oil-soaked cotton cloths. Behind the tables are stacks of clean clothes waiting their turn to be used. The hammering and the sound of employees talking distracts me, but not for long.

*Mon Dieu!* This could ruin me. The engines came completely assembled from France and were made to stay that way. I cover my mouth with my right hand and remain silent, not ready to speak. Mr. Tanaka does not appear to sense my fear; perhaps he thinks I am in awe.

Mr. Tanaka continues to walk beside me. "Workers use solvent to clean all the pistons, generators, and magnetos. All the old oil is gone, and the parts are getting clean and dry," he announces with pride. The parts glisten and sparkle from the light filtering through the upper garage windows.

The crew smile when I walk by. Some take a break from their work, step back, smile and bow. I make a small gestured bow in return, and look at my manager, "*Alors*. So, the parts from all twenty-five engines are mixed, no?"

Beaming, he replies, "Yes. They are so clean. There is no problem. We can put the engines back together."

There is nothing I can do in front of this *fait acompli*. It's done. There is no need to say anything now until I compose myself. I excuse myself and exit the building without saying a word, look up to the sky, and make the sign of the cross. Ever since I spent all that time with the Catholic nuns, I send prayers when needed. Today I need it. I pray the wind brings a message to Saint Christopher, the patron saint of drivers, for help. Any help.

I slowly climb into my automobile and drop onto the seat. I take off my hat and scarf and remove my jacket. I feel warm despite the cool breeze. I wipe my sweating forehead with a cotton handkerchief. Still too warm, I take the metal clock off the dashboard and rest my forehead on it, feeling the cold metal absorb some of my fears.

I have no idea how to put an engine together and lack the mechanical ability to do so. I have always put my trust in my employees when it comes to fixing engines, but they have never taken an engine completely apart. Or assembled a new one. Now all the parts are mixed together. How will they know which bolt goes on which engine? I remind myself that they can look at an engine and intuitively know what to do quickly and effortlessly. But that is when the engines have all their pieces together, assembled, in context.

I return the clock to the dashboard. I decide to go for a drive to settle my rattled nerves.

I start the engine and drive away from the harbor garage. I compose myself by thinking about the inauguration day for our twenty-five new postal trucks. The new drivers, mechanics, and their families paraded through Yokohama, the first people to ride in the latest modern trucks.

The cherry trees had just started to drop their thin red and green leaves in preparation for winter, and excitement was in the air. I rode with Mr. Hiraoka, my friend from the bank, in his new car. The seat bench spanned the front, leaving ample room for both of us. The car had jolted forward, and we were on our way, followed by the new trucks.

96

The noise was deafening at first. I turned around to wave at my two daughters and two sons who rode with Henriette and a driver from the garage in the mail truck behind our car. They were so happy, and I saw young Louis calling out to me, but there was so much noise I couldn't understand what they are saying. Henriette waved to me, and I smiled back.

Mr. Hiraoka shouted to be heard above the noise, "Your postal trucks are a true success. And I am very satisfied with this new car I bought from you! My family is so proud when they ride with me. Thank you, Mr. Suzor!" He maneuvered his auto to lead the parade through each dusty street. Spectators cleared out of the way just like Parisians scatter when they see or hear a fire truck. As we cruised along the streets, people on the sides of the roads looked on in awe. Some merchants stood on the side of the street with bamboo poles balanced across their heads, stacks of baskets filled with trinkets hanging from either end. A precarious portable market!

"You are welcome, of course," I called back to him. "My business successes are yours as well. Companies are sprouting up like young rice shoots in newly flooded fields. Your bank is helping many others grow and become managers of import companies and garages."

Mr. Hiraoka shouted over the noise, "There is Japanese proverb, perhaps written for you. 'The day you decide to do it is your lucky day.' We share your good fortune."

Starting this business was not easy. I hired fifty employees chosen from the best mechanics available. All of them had to learn how to drive. Undertaking a project this big required some luck.

Each succeeding truck bounced up and down, and finally the parade rounded the corner into an open space under the cherry trees. We jockeyed the trucks around, trying to fit them into the park. My mechanics and I had successfully introduced The Imperial Company of Postal Trucks to Yokohama!

When the engines turned off, my children ran across the grass and led me to our lunch site. Yokohama Park was still warm enough for a picnic. After a lunch of cheese and ham on French bread, Georges asked, "Papa, can we go and play with other children under those trees?"

"Of course, you can, but don't be gone too long. We will be leaving in about an hour." The children made some new friends and played hide and seek behind the elm and cherry trees. A perfect afternoon behind the wheel of my new company.

Today is different. I find myself on a familiar road near Tokyo. Focusing on the road helps with the stress, and I start to cool down. But my bad luck is not over for the day. The automobile coughs a few times, then lurches forward, and stops. I have heard that cough before, and I know the remedy is gasoline. I let out a sigh and sit back on the leather seat, considering my options. I had been too preoccupied with my worries to check the tank before heading out on such a long drive.

I hear the rumble of another motorcar coming from behind. I look in my rear-view mirror. The driver slows down and stops behind me, jumps from his automobile, and walks up to the side of my car. He is dressed in modern slacks and a tan jacket. He takes his hat off and I see his black hair is thinning. He has a ready smile and approaches my car with confidence.

To my surprise, one my former garage managers greets me. "Ah! Monsieur Suzor! Are you just taking a rest, or do you need help?"

"Kaito, is that you? I haven't seen you for a long time. I heard you bought a new garage in Tokyo. Are you on your way home?" I ask, leaning over my car door, trying to look unworried.

"Yes, Monsieur Suzor. I have a new garage and a new family in Tokyo." He furrows his forehead. "It looks like you have a problem with your automobile?"

"Well, Kaito, I am embarrassed to say that I used more fuel than I expected, and I need to get back to Yokohama."

"I have extra fuel. Let me help you. I can put it in your tank," he says, returning to his automobile without hesitation. He reaches over his back seat and takes hold of a large red metal gas can. He hoists it out of the car and brings it to my thirsty automobile. Thank goodness it carries five gallons. He unscrews the metal spout, lifts the can, and pours the fuel into the tank.

I open the door and step down from my automobile, fumbling in the pocket of my jacket. I withdraw some money and try to pay Kaito.

"No, Monsieur Suzor. Please don't pay me. It is an honor to help my former boss."

I am touched by his kindness. I thank him, and I promise to return the favor someday. We part ways and continue to our homes. I feel fortunate and distracted from some of today's stress.

I force myself to give the workers a chance to put their mechanical skills to the test. After three days of anxiety, I go back to check on their progress. I am relieved to see that the skilled crew, through tremendous perseverance, has put the engines back together.

"Mr. Tanaka, it looks like the trucks have survived their surgery," I say with only a little uncertainty. I try not to think of the means the unexperienced crew must have used—hammering?—to reassemble the engines.

"Yes, Monsieur Suzor. After trial and error, the mechanics are experts now. They can fix any car." He starts one truck to show me that it works.

"But Mr. Tanaka," I say above the noise, in partial jest, "The trucks seem much noisier than before. Is this a problem?"

"*Okina oto*. Loud noises sound more powerful. Our noisy trucks will get more respect from people if there is a big sound." Just then, as if to demonstrate, a young mechanic drives out of the garage yard in a truck. The roar startles the children playing in the street beyond, who scatter and squeal with delight.

# Chapter Twelve

From left: Andree, baby Georges sitting in Edith's lap, Louis (in a dress and a hair ribbon popular at the end of the Victorian era for very young boys), and sister Paule.

# Chapter Twelve
## Manor de la Noeu, 1950

The Christmas holidays are over, and I finally have the time to get back to writing. As I walk through the dining room towards my office, I pass my lovely wife packing boxes of extra holiday dishes to put in storage downstairs.

"Louis, look what I found under the stairs. It must have been put there when we moved from the chateau," she says, pausing her packing and gently handing me a long wooden box with dovetail joints tied with linen string. "Do you remember this?"

I lean my cane on a chair and take the box with both hands, recognizing it immediately. "Of course, Henriette!" One side of the box is gray from smoke damage. I put it on the table and carefully untie the brittle string.

"Open it and we can hang it up in the hallway if it hasn't been damaged. It shouldn't be in direct sunlight. The silk is too fragile."

I lift the rolled-up silk and paper scroll out of its box. The top outer layer of paper has some grey smoke damage, but as I unroll it, the rest is in perfect condition.

"Henriette, I hope I look this good when I'm over a hundred years old!" Laying it on the table, I see the two russet and tan painted carp, and imagine they are happy to be out of the box and swimming, again, in a pond of silk after all these years. The ribbon edges still shine when the light touches them. I gently hold the end of the roll to keep it from falling off the table. "It's a wonder we still have it. Yes, the hallway, that's a good idea. But let's hang it up higher since we don't want the cat to play with the little iron figures at the bottom." The figurines hanging from the bottom are two small cast iron men, and their weight keeps the scroll hanging without curling. In Yokohama, the Japanese would have hung the scroll lower towards the ground, for viewing from a sitting position on floor pillows. But we Westerners hang scrolls higher.

"I'll ask Bernard, our neighbor's son, if he can help hang it in the hallway later today. I don't want either of us standing on chairs," Henriette says, raising her right eyebrow to make sure I don't try it myself.

I nod my promise. "Thank you, Henriette." I roll it back up and hand the scroll to her. I take my cane from the back of the chair and continue to my office. On the way, I rub my fingers against each other and notice some ash residue from the box remains on my skin. At my desk, I sit in my chair and take my handkerchief out of my breast pocket to clean my hands. I remember that day when something was given, and something was taken away.

*Something Given, Something Taken Away*
**Yokohama, Japan, 1912**

I see a man standing on the porch outside my settlement office. He shifts his weight from one foot to the other, clearly waiting for someone. He carries a long, narrow wooden box, with an envelope tied to the top. I rise and cross the room to open the door.

"Hello. May I help you?" I ask as we bow. "Wait...I recognize you. Daisuke Yamada-san? Is that right?" My former employee is well dressed in Western slacks and a tailored jacket and shirt.

"Yes, Monsieur Suzor-*sama*, that is right."

"What a pleasure to see you, Daisuke Yamada-san!" After several more bows and handshakes, I invite him into my office.

"The same to you, Monsieur Suzor-*sama*. I've been gone three years." He pauses, then continues. "As you remember, I resigned from your business. *Ah*, my job was to collect money from customers, but, if you remember, one customer did not pay. I was so ashamed, and I still regret I couldn't get the money for you. That was my job. I am so sorry that I was a disappointment to you," he says, bending his head forward.

I sit on a chair and motion for Daisuke to sit across from me. He sits on the edge of the chair, wooden box in hand.

I look him in the eyes and assure him, "Daisuke. *Bah, no.* It was not your fault. You were a good employee, one of my best. I was not angry then, and I am not angry now. I wanted you to stay but you insisted you must leave. I am pleased to see you. You are doing well? You look happy and successful, too." We converse about our families, old times, and our respective current business ventures. Soon we run out of things to say, and he hands me a thick envelope.

"I would like to give you this, Monsieur Suzor-*sama*."

"Should I open it now?"

He nods his head, giving me permission. I carefully open the rice paper envelope. *Mon Dieu!* It is full of money. I look at Daisuke, then back at the bills. I close the envelope and hand it back to him.

"Daisuke, please take the money back. You did nothing wrong, and you do not owe me a thing."

"No, Monsieur Suzor-*sama*, please keep it. I will lose face if you return it to me."

I stand and walk to my desk, and then back, stopping in front of him. "*Bah, oui.* I understand. But I will lose face, too, if I take it all. So, take half the money back. Let us split our respect for each other." I sit again. At first, he refuses, but after some convincing, he agrees to take half.

I am touched by his integrity. His sense of honor for himself and others is admirable, and he is so decent. He is a perfect example of the Japanese tradition of respect. I feel honored to know him.

After our financial decision is made, he puts his hands together and bows his head, and then offers me the wooden box.

I open it and see a roll of silk and paper. I gingerly lift it from the box, unrolling it to reveal two carps painted in stunning shades of rich brown, captured on silk by a master. Two little cast iron figures are looped on the bottom of the scroll.

I take in a deep breath and pause, not knowing what to say. I smile and marvel once again at the kindness and artistic integrity of the Japanese people. "Daisuke, I am so honored. This is an antique and very valuable kakejiku. *Duomo arigato*. Thank you so much."

"*Doitashimashite*. You are welcome. The kakejiku is for the interest due on the debt, which is now finally settled." We laugh and stand to bow to each other. Our business is complete, and I open the door for Daisuke and follow him outside. From there we go down three stairs and stop to wish each other well, bowing once again for good measure.

As I walk to my automobile, I pass five metal buckets filled by the fire brigade and placed by my office. The city has grown so much, so quickly, that Yokohama leaders are working hard to keep the citizens protected. The roads between homes in Honmoku have been widened to decrease the chance of fires spreading to older wood and bamboo houses.

As I drive home from my office, I admire the crooked pine trees shaped by years of salty sea winds. On the southwest coast of Tokyo Bay, Honmoku sits on cliffs carved by years of pounding waves.

When I arrive home, I step down from my automobile and walk over to greet my energetic sons, Louis and Georges, who are playing outside the guesthouse. They are pulling a cart, pretending they are a rickshaw driver and passenger. They drop the wagon and come running to meet me.

"Papa! What are you carrying in that box? Is it for us?" they ask as they walk with me to the porch. From our porch windows we can see ships come and go; a source of relaxation and inspiration. We often watch fishermen and their wives mending nets among mounds of seashells.

"No. It is something from work. I will tell you about it later," I say as I place it on a tile shelf in the large stone back porch. "I want to show your mother and the girls, too."

I sit on a cement step to visit with the boys. "Papa! The fire brigade came by today and we watched them fill the water wells with long hoses! They were dressed in red and yellow coats, the same as the firemen in the watchtower wear," Georges, already six, tells me, waving a stick pretending it is a fire hose.

"The firemen came by my office today, too."

"And they sprayed us with water!" Louis, three years older, says. "It was so cold we had to change our clothes afterwards. But it felt great!" I can't help but laugh at their enthusiasm. They run back to playing rickshaw outside, and I walk up the stairs to see if my daughters are home, too. They have been living in Tokyo at a boarding school for Western and other children. They come home on the weekends unless Henriette and I are out of town. To my delight, Paule and Edith open the door and greet me.

"Hello, Papa. We missed you!" Paule says. "Would you like a lemonade before dinner?"

I stand up and go up the stairs and in the front door. "Yes, Paule, that would be wonderful. Where is your mother? I have a gift for the family tonight."

"Mama is in the kitchen with the cook. I'll let her know you are home."

Paule returns from the kitchen, lemonade in hand. I sit down on the sofa and take a refreshing long drink. I attempt to put it down, but there is no room on the coffee table. Sections of newspapers are spread all over the tabletop.

Edith comes over to the coffee table and moves a stack of pages before sitting next to me. "Papa! We were reading the new issue of the Japan Weekly Mail. Did you hear about the French gentleman riding on his way to the bank in a rickshaw? He collided with a horse and cart and was thrown to the ground, injuring his face and hand."

"Do you know him?" asks Paule.

"Yes, it was Monsieur Mauger. He is okay and says he is not pressing any charges. Of more concern to me today was the news that a mine washed ashore and exploded on the beach," I add. I enjoy that my daughters are grown up enough now that we can discuss politics and the news. I know that not many fathers approve of their daughters speaking about politics, but I believe we live in a rich International community. There are many points of view from different countries. A German and an American can bring a new point of view to a discussion. Our girls' classmates come from Japan, China, Britain, America, and France. They may not appreciate it now, but they will as they get older.

"Did you read about the mutiny of Awaji Maru?" Paule continues. "The ship arrived at Nagasaki. The paper said that 300 mutineers were secretly killed on an island! It was only seven miles from a Siberian port."

"Yes, I heard the report. But you never know if information has been changed by the newspapers. Perhaps it is a made-up story to warn laborers to work hard and stay with their ships," I tell my girls.

"What do you think? Do you think it is real?" Edith asks. But before I can answer, Henriette walks in from the kitchen.

She kisses me on both cheeks and sits across from me. "What a wonderful treat to have all of us together for dinner tonight." She looks down at the paper spread across the table. "Are you girls reading this?"

"Yes, *Maman*," Edith answers.

"I am impressed. Louis, have you read the report on rats found with the plague? The paper says there have been seven cases reported in Osaka! Five new cases of cholera were reported and three were proven fatal. And the Hakone district is dealing with a rabies outbreak. *All* of the dogs without owners will be killed."

"Maman, do you think those stories are true?" Paula asks, applying my question to her mother. "Papa just said that some of the reports may be false. How do we know for sure?"

"I don't know, darling. That is a good question. Maybe," she says, looking at me, "it is time to go back to Paris," says Henriette. She begins to gather up the newspapers from the table, in preparation for dinner.

"Henriette! I didn't know you were wanting to go back to Paris," I say.

"Oh, I don't know. I think about it from time to time. Are we going to be here forever? I think this city is becoming unsafe."

"Oh Henriette. We must always be careful, no matter where we are. Paris has its own problems with rats. There are robberies in all cities. And anywhere there are poor people while the price of food and housing increases, there will be friction. Even if we go back to Paris, we will still be dealing with the same problems."

"Louis, *mon chéri*," she says, pausing to look at me. "Remember when little Louis was born, and we were robbed? It was even in the *Japan Weekly News*."

"Yes, Henriette. I kept the newspaper article and put it in the tea crate with my pictures. That was a frightening day."

"What happened?" asks Edith.

"In the middle of the night, Louis was a tiny baby, and the robbers threatened your father with a sword."

"What?!" exclaims Paule. "Why have we never heard this story? What happened?"

"Well, we woke to a man standing over our bed, threatening us," I tell my daughters. "We didn't tell you the next day because you were too young, and we didn't want you to feel unsafe. He wanted money, but not the 40 yen and eight shillings I had in my coin purse. Instead, he stole my two swords hanging on the wall."

"It was so frightening," Henriette said.

"Well, it is over now. Danger is everywhere, Henriette. But so is safety. And tonight, we are here, together. Besides, it's not every day you get to be in the paper!" I say, trying to raise her spirits with some humor. "That day was newsworthy. But best to look forward."

The girls clear the newspapers off the coffee table, and the cook comes in to tell us that dinner is ready. I call Georges and Louis in from playing and tell them to get washed up. Once we have all sat down at the table and our *coq au vin* has been served, I relay to everyone what happened in the office this afternoon.

"Is that what was in the box, Papa?" Georges asks.

"Yes, and after dinner I will show you the beautiful scroll." We eat, and it feels wonderful to have the whole family together, minus, of course, our dear Andree, who is in Paris with her Grandmother and Tante Adrienne. Henriette seems to be in a better mood, but I am surprised she raised the idea to return to Paris. Is she missing Andree?

After dinner, I bring in the scroll and show it to the family. Henriette is as delighted as I am, but the boys seem uninterested, and the girls are not as impressed as I thought they would be.

"It's—Well," Edith says.

"Old-fashioned," Paule finishes for her.

"Oh girls. It's a 50-year old scroll painted by a Japanese master. It's not a Parisian piece of décor. This is a priceless gift. Louis," Henriette says, lightly touching the edge of the silk, "Your former employee is a wonderful man. Put it some place safe. I'm concerned the painters might damage it if we put it up right away."

"Always practical, *ma chérie*," I say to her. "I'll bring it over to the guest house to store with the rest of our things."

"Oh, that reminds me. I had the gardeners move some furniture and the tea crate with all our pictures to the guest house. The crate really isn't a beautiful piece of furniture, but I know it is important to you. And it has kept our photos and postcards clean and safe since we came here," says Henriette.

"You're right. I remember the day my first order of coach clocks came in that tea crate. I'm glad you had it moved. Paule and Edith, would you please help me move most of our art pieces this weekend, in preparation?"

"Papa, we already did it after lunch. Mama told us which ones to take."

"Perfect! You have become very grown up and helpful in your 12 and 13 years. Thank you!"

After dinner, I bring the scroll back to the porch, intending to walk it over to the guesthouse. But the sun is setting behind the land, and dark is approaching from the harbor—the night sky is growing deep navy. Our garden glows in the remaining evening light. Shades of gold and orange drift through the trees rustling in the gentle evening breeze.

I set the scroll on the window ledge, promising myself to bring it next door tomorrow. Instead, I stand and watch the evening arrive, a masterpiece of muted sunset colors. It has been a long week, and a bit of time to myself is a precious commodity.

When I turn to go back into the house, everything is quiet. The children are in bed and Henriette and I are ready to follow. I think of Andree, so far away in Paris. She will be going to bed in about seven hours. I pray she will sleep well.

Henriette and I go to our room and get into bed. I can feel the ocean winds have picked up a little, wandering up the rocky cliffs to our home, drifting in from the open window. Dreams will come easily as the sound of waves lull us to sleep.

But not for long. My dreams are interrupted by a whiff of smoke. I wake, confused. Was the smoke in my dream? No! I roll over and grab Henriette by the arm, shake her awake, and tell her to get the children. I jump out of bed and look down the hall to see black smoke coming up the stairwell. How can we escape? We can't go downstairs.

"Henriette, out the window over the kitchen. *Now!*" I yell. I pull on my trousers and shirt from beside the bed, right over my pajamas. I rush to follow Henriette, still in her pajamas and silk bathrobe, down the hallway. We yell and pound the walls, trying to wake the children. Paule and Edith appear at their door, wide-eyed.

"It's a fire!" I yell. "Get the boys!"

The girls run to wake their frightened brothers. The floor is starting to feel warm beneath my feet. The girls emerge from their room, each clutching a brother by the arm, and follow Henriette to the window at the other end of the hallway. The young boys are screaming. I hear the cracking of burning wood, and my lungs are stinging. I grip the corner of my pajama shirt and I put it over my mouth and nose. I turn my head to see just the tips of flames ascending the staircase at the other end of the hall. Henriette has the window open, and I help lift the children through and onto the fire escape platform I made, never expecting to have to use it. Henriette and the children quickly descend the ladder as I climb out of the window. The last thing I see of the inside of my home is flames climbing into the hallway.

I descend the ladder and join my family, standing across the large yard by the guesthouse. The wind from the harbor, so appreciated a few hours before, is now fanning the flames as clouds of sparks light the sky like fireworks, billowing smoke rising like dragon's breath. The sound of the house cracking shakes the ground, and Henriette and I hold the children close.

"Papa, where is the fire brigade?" cries my son, Louis. "The firemen told me today they help put out fires. Where are they?"

"I don't know, Louis. They haven't had a chance to get here yet. I really don't know the answer," I say picking up Louis, trying to instill calm while I am tormented inside. The flames are eating everything left in the house. Thank goodness many of our possessions were moved to the guest house for the painting project. But not everything. Some valuable paintings remained in the house. The painting by my mother's cousin, Sir John Everett Millais, is gone forever. Our clothes, furniture, dishes. Up in flames. We stand in shock, barefoot and in our pajamas in the cold night, but warm enough from the heat of the fire.

"Papa, here they come! I see the wagon! Hear the bells?" asks little Louis, wiping tears off his red cheeks.

The wagon appears with the fire brigade fighters. Five men in heavy jackets jump off their wagon and put a hose in the water wells. For safety, their trousers of heavy cotton have been wetted down, along with their hats and gloves, but the weight makes it difficult for them to move quickly. One man holds a cumbersome hose, but there is not enough pressure to reach the house with water.

"Henriette. Paule, Edith. Take the boys to the guest house. Stay there." I hand Louis to Henriette, and I run to the head of the fire brigade. I recognize him from business meetings with city workers.

"Is there anything you can do?" I ask the man.

"I am sorry Monsieur Suzor. *Sumimasen.* We saw the fire from the watchtower, but the wind is too strong tonight and the fire grew too fast. And the fact that there is no water pressure makes it impossible to save anything." He shakes his head. "I'm sorry, we are too late. All we can do now is work to make sure the fire does not spread. I'm so sorry. Stay at your other house and do not come near," he says, bowing and excusing himself.

I don't know what to say. I have no words. I turn and walk back towards the guest house, stunned. Henriette meets me half-way.

"Where are the children?"

"At the guest house, Louis. They are safe." She grabs my arm. "We are all together, Louis. *Mon Dieu.* We could have been burned up in the fire." I can barely hear her comforting words. All my work, my effort, gone. Thank god my business work is in my office now, and no longer in the house.

"Look, Louis! The chimney and the back porch are the only things not on fire." I look, and remember standing to watch the night arrive, just hours before. I had no idea what tonight would bring.

I put my arm around her shoulders. "We will build a new house. For now, we will find a house to rent on the Bluff."

"Let's figure that out tomorrow, Louis. Come, let's get back to the children," she says, leading me back to the guest house. The older girls are trying to distract the boys and calm them. When we arrive, the girls look up, and I can see that our presence calms them, too. I am so grateful we are all alive.

"Edith?" little Louis asks. "Please, can I sleep in your bed with you tonight?"

"Of course, you can. And Georges can sleep with Paule."

Henriette and I make sure the children are in bed, and then we sit together in the dark, holding hands in silence, watching the flickering embers through the window. I cannot comprehend the reality of what just happened. Only once the night is dark again do we, too, climb into bed. Anxious thoughts blend with threads of lingering smoke as we await daylight.

The next morning, a dream of glowing embers wakens me. I quietly get up before anyone else. I put on the pants and shirt I wore yesterday—the only clothes I now own. I leave Henriette sleeping in the guest bedroom, and cross from our room through the sitting room and silently open the guesthouse door. I walk next door to the remnants of our home. Smoking timbers lay on the ground like a burnt forest. A few neighbors walk quietly along the road to see what happened. I walk up the steps to the stone porch off the kitchen, one of a few places left standing. The tile shelves have somehow been left, untouched by the fire.

Resting on the ledge where I placed it last night, the kakejiku scroll rests in its box. I pick it up with both hands and blow a layer of ashes off the top. I can't believe it. I look up and out onto the bay, where cargo ships move in and out. I am fortunate my business is still intact, so I can rebuild my life, yet again.

I carry the scroll to the guesthouse and carefully open the door. I go in and put the scroll on my Japanese tea crate. Careful not to make any noise, I walk over to an armchair and remove the white cotton sheet that covers it. I sit down, and exhale. The only things I hear are my children breathing and an occasional cough. My family is safe. And so is the scroll resting on the tea crate that keeps our family memories out of harm's way.

# Chapter Thirteen

The Grand Hotel opened in 1873. With a beautiful view overlooking Yokohama harbor, it was considered the height of Western culture and elegance in Japan.

# Chapter Thirteen
## Manor de la Noeu, 1951

I hear scratching at my library window. I go to open it to see our cat rubbing against the windowsill. There is a chill in the air this morning, reminding me that summer is leaving. Fujiko jumps in and leads me back to my typewriter. I sit down and she climbs into my lap and settles there, purring like a little motor.

I have lost sleep over the last story about the fire. The house burned 40 years ago, but writing brought the nightmare back, and I felt as if it had just recently happened. I pet Fujiko and take a few moments to collect my thoughts. I pick up a sheet of thin typing paper and feed it through the large roller. I move the carriage to the right, think for a moment, and begin to type. The keys move, but the page remains blank. Nothing except a few ink smudges; the ribbon has faded beyond what I can eek out. I exhale, annoyed that I must leave my library and go to town. I pick up my cat, arrange her on a chair cushion, and leave the room.

I walk down the hallway to the drawing room calling for Henriette. I see her outside, watering her plants on the patio. Standing at the doorway I ask, "Henriette, will you come to town with me? I need ribbon for my typewriter, and I could use more onionskin paper. We can stop at the bakery on the way home."

"Louis, the maid said the car keys are lost. I've looked everywhere for days," she says avoiding eye contact as she walks across the patio and into the house, passing me. I turn and look at the hallway table where they are usually kept. How can they be misplaced so often?

But then Henriette sighs. "Louis, please come sit next to me," she says, putting her basket down on the table and sitting on the couch. "I can't lie to you." I cross and sit next to her, wondering what she is talking about. "The doctor says your eyesight is getting worse and driving may be dangerous. I know you are careful but driving too slow is not safe. It is just as bad as driving too fast. I am concerned about people on the road, but I worry most about you. Our maid has been hiding your keys to keep you safe. I told her to because I know you want to continue driving. The doctor suggested I do it."

"What?" This is a surprise to me. "If the doctor says I can't drive, then I will find another doctor! I have my French driver's license, and it's for life. I'm not dead yet!" I can feel my irritation and anger grow. I rise and walk outside onto the patio quickly, before I say something I might regret later.

I go for a short walk around the manor, down a lane lined with maple trees in full fall colors. I used to be able to walk several miles, but a short walk to the end of our lane is all I can muster even with my cane. Some of our close friends have passed away and, as I stand in the cool morning breeze, I realize I am slowing down, too.

I really need more time to think this over. I don't want to surrender my car and my freedom, but my eyes and legs are giving in to aging.

By the time I get back, Henriette has arranged for our neighbor, Albert, to drive us to town. He is in a cheery mood and expresses interest in buying our car. I am not ready for this conversation, so instead, I silently sit and look out the window. I can't help but notice that trees are a bit blurry, and some cars in the shade are hard to see. I hate to admit it to myself, but Henriette is right. The time has come to give up my license. As we drive through the dappled maple-lined lane to town in and out of tree shadows, I remember being the first to get a driver's license in Yokohama.

## Rules of the Road
**Yokohama, Japan, 1912**

Several months have passed since we lost our home to a fire. The police determined that the fire was caused by arson. There are Japanese who have become poorer since Western foreigners, mostly British and Americans, arrived. They are not wrong to be angry. Food is expensive and it is hard to afford a home in the city with progress and prices rising. The police believe that these people — technically criminals, but also people resentful with how things are changing — were at fault for the fire.

In any case, our friends and neighbors helped us with our immediate needs, like clothing for Henriette and the children, and some furniture. We moved into the apartment over my office in Yokohama, and all the children were in boarding school during the week, so it did not feel crowded at first. But eventually, on the weekends, it felt too small, so I decided to rent a European style home with ample room for our family and guests. We live again on the Bluff, or *Yamate-cho*, 150 feet above the sea at the south side of Yokohama Settlement.

Since we are rebuilding our lives, I decided that now is as good a time as any to build a new summer home by the sea, where, when school is out, the whole family can live together with plenty of space. I am quite pleased with the Japanese style construction, which is a surprise to many of our Western friends. When a typhoon raged through the Kanto valley, leaving a path of destruction, the construction workers were able to pick up the pieces and put the house back together, because it was built with notched beams instead of nails. After the shock of losing so much of our lives, I wanted to make our summer home was typhoon resistant as possible. You can replace windows, but not children.

As I drive from our rented home to the commercial district, a cool, grey haze descends on the busy Yokohama port. I hear fog horns as I follow the *Yato Zaka,* or what we call the Camp Hill Road, and eventually pass behind the Grand Hotel to the French Consulate. When I finally arrive, I park my car and jump down, but instead of going inside I walk around a row of parked rikshaws and towards the port office a few blocks away. I stay on the dusty walkway at a prudent distance from the swift rikshaws.

I have arranged a meeting with the local official in charge of the transportation committee and a representative from the police department in order to discuss drafting a new set of rules to help drivers and keep the public safe. The number of cars and drivers in Japan is growing rapidly. Wooden carts share the road with horses, rickshaws, an electric train, and new motorcars.

The old port building is clean, but the wood outside shows the greying effect of salty marine air. I go up the steps and open the heavy solid pine door. Inside, I look around and see a large oak rolltop desk with dividers neatly arranged for writing quills, ink, and rubber stamps. On shelves behind, stacks of paper and documents sit on tidily arranged wooden boards. The desk doubles as the front office counter. I notice four teakwood chairs neatly tucked under a tea table in a corner, blue and white china cups awaiting tea.

Two gentlemen walk into the room from a rear office. I see a familiar face, Mr. Sasaki, a regional authority and representative of the transportation board. Following him is another acquaintance, Officer Ozeki of the Tokyo district police. They are both wearing European-style suits. After exchanging short bows, I shake hands with the gentlemen. Mr. Sasaki motions the two of us to follow him to his office down the hall. On entering the office, I see, as is the custom, a teapot awaiting us, a welcome guest at any meeting.

While we settle in brown leather chairs, Mr. Sasaki calls down the hallway for a clerk to serve us. After tea and the required small talk, I start the discussion.

"Look at the many new changes in Yokohama and Tokyo these days, gentlemen. With the arrival of automobiles, I see some new challenges. The rickshaws and other transportation are all competing for one road, causing mounting confusion. I am here to share solutions for this area and your citizens," I say, placing my hand on my right knee, making sure my leg doesn't start bouncing.

Mr. Sasaki responds, "The Emperor has expressed a desire for a modern country. I am honored to serve the policy of the Emperor. We welcome progressive ideas, Monsieur Suzor."

I take a sip of tea and put my cup down, admiring the blue and white geometric designs. "Well, most importantly, I see a need for laws for all drivers. We had similar chaos in Paris: dogs being run over, children getting into cars and accidentally driving into fields, cars blocking the roads, and hospitals admitting numerous inexperienced drivers."

"I think you have very good point," Officer Ozeki says. "My wife says it is not safe to walk on roads in Yokohama and Tokyo. We need more sidewalks, too. Conversations about these needs have already started in our local government, and I am happy to help coordinate this project. Tell me your ideas, and I will share them with our authorities."

I nod. "Perfect sense. Well, we need street signs posted in the roads like the system used in France. And we need a booklet printed explaining the meaning of the road signs, and how to obey them. In addition, another book could be printed with regulations, codes of the road, and helpful suggestions." The gentlemen seem genuinely interested. "I took the liberty to create some proposals," I add, as I hand them both several pages of neatly typed documents.

"Thank you, Monsieur Suzor," Mr. Sasaki says. "As I said, some of us have discussed a few of these ideas already," he says, leafing through my proposals. "One suggestion was to use pictures with words because we have many languages in Yokohama, and some local people never learned to read."

Officer Ozeki says, "We can print rules in English, French, and Japanese. It makes good sense to duplicate the rules of roads of France. You are the French foreign automobile expert. If we get approval from the board, I will give you full assistance with our local authorities."

I look at Officer Ozeki and make my closing request. "I would like your permission, if you agree, to teach a group of your police officers the procedures for administering written exams and automobile maneuvering tests for driving licenses," I say, feeling a tremble in my right kneecap. The thought of a Frenchman teaching a group of Japanese policemen in English is a bit daunting. I hope I am ready for the challenge.

Officer Ozeki pauses for a few minutes as he mulls over the idea, "This strategy will serve the Emperor by keeping cities and citizens safe. I believe licenses provide protection for Japanese people and our foreign guests." He hesitates. "However, some will not agree with your ideas right away—it takes time for some people. I will bring your ideas to the committee when I speak with them. As I see it, you can start training officers as soon as we have an agreement and written authorization. Of course," he adds, laughing, "Monsieur Suzor, you need a license, I will personally administer the driver's test for you. If you pass the written and driving tests, you will receive the first driving permit in Japan."

Gratified, I laugh as well. "We should do it soon, because with all of the new traffic on the roads, we don't know how many tomorrows we have, yes?" Our conversation turns to deciding which day I will take my test, and we close the meeting with a sense of progress in the air.


A few weeks later I take the test. Of course, I pass. And a month after our initial meeting, I walk from my office to the police department to receive my new driver's license.

Inside, Officer Ozeki meets me at the rolltop desk. After our greetings, I sign my license, verifying that I will follow the preliminary rules, licenses, and codes of the road. The paperwork has recently been determined by the committee and approved by the Emperor and the local officials.

I rub my hand over the beautifully embossed cover for my license. The brown leather is embossed with a mountain scene, and on the bottom right hand corner is scribed, *With compliment, Suzor, Ronvaux, and Co. Ltd. Yokohama*. I had the covers made as an advertisement for my business, and as a gift to the police department. I carefully put the license and its cover in my coat pocket and turn to step aside, looking at the three men behind me who have lined up to take the test.

With the new excitement surrounding motorcars and touring this beautiful country, these motoring friends and I are starting an automobile club. "Hello gentlemen," I say. "I hope you are well prepared for this test. The test is quite rigorous. Lots of new rules and regulations. Any of you who pass, let's meet at the Grand Hotel at five o'clock to celebrate our new driver's licenses and begin our gentleman's club!"

"We will see you then," says my friend and colleague in the export business, Albert Moreau. He shakes my hand confidently, as do the other men, Robert Martin from the Asian Silk House and Philip Durand, a diplomat from the United States Consulate. I leave to go back to my office for the remainder of the afternoon.

A few hours later I walk into the lobby of the Yokohama Grand Hotel, a center for social life in this busy port city. I marvel at how remarkably similar it feels to European hotels.

Inside the expansive lobby is a large, curved wooden counter separating the reception area from the waiting room. Behind the desk teakwood mailboxes with room numbers assigned to the current guests line the wall. The hands on the Victorian clock indicate that my friends will arrive soon. The lobby is peaceful and quiet for now, as most businessmen are still at work or out for the afternoon.

I sit in an upholstered wooden rocker to wait for my friends. I look out the wall of windows onto the panoramic view of this evening's maritime activity, from huge ocean liners to small fishing boats. A waiter comes to me, and other guests, with a tray of cocktails—a blend of gin, brandy, and champagne. I gladly accept one, taking several sips. The ceiling fans hum as they create a welcome breeze, and I can feel myself begin to unwind from the long day.

Over the whirring sound I hear a familiar voice. I turn to see Albert Moreau walking towards me. He takes off his hat, revealing his balding pate. "*Bonjour*, Louis. *Bravo*! Congratulations on your license! Isn't it a beautiful day for driving and for fragrant cherry blossoms?"

"Yes, it is. *Très bien!* You passed!" I say, standing to shake his hand.

"Of course, I passed. I didn't want to miss the fragrance of flowers in the wind as I drive. But in all seriousness, I am looking forward to teaching some of my employees to drive. They are like little children fighting over a toy, always badgering me to let them have a turn at the wheel."

"Look. Here comes Mr. Martin. Did he get his license as well?'

"I believe so. It would be an embarrassment if he didn't since he owns three motorcars! Oh, and Philip Durand said he would be a little late and to start without him."

The three of us stand up and move to the lounge to start our very first meeting of our automobile club. We sit in white linen covered armchairs in a half circle facing the evening view. Some junks bob on the sea, their sides reflecting the evening light on the lazy waves. Other ships are just tiny specks in the distance, a longer voyage still ahead of them before they arrive here in the harbor.

Albert hails a waiter and grabs a champagne cocktail for himself. Robert Martin orders a red wine from Bordeaux and a fragrant tray of imported French cheese and ham. "Let's get started," he says, "I have a lot of ideas for this driving club. The future of automobiles is ours to share with the local and international community in Yokohama. I hope you brought notes. I did."

"Many drivers are unfamiliar with the remote parts of this breathtaking but rough country," I say. "They are often afraid of getting stranded or running out of fuel. We can organize safe adventures to different areas and with a group of motorcars, like Nikko and Mount Kindo Myogi. No one would get left behind."

"And this is just the beginning," Albert says. But before he can continue, Mr. Durand, the tall American, enters the room. He reaches for a cocktail from the tray held by a Chinese waiter, lifts the crystal glass off the tray and takes a few gulps emptying the glass in true American fashion. He sets it back on the tray before helping himself to another drink, which he carries over to our group. "Sorry to be late. I hope I haven't missed anything."

"Philip, did you pass the test?" asks Albert.

"Well, no. I didn't take the test because the office was closed. I don't know why they close two hours for lunch. But I'm sure I'll be fine without a license for now. I have an American license and that should be enough. Maybe next month." I catch him up on my ideas of hosting group excursions. "I wholeheartedly agree, Louis. Each month we can organize outings to different places, depending on the weather. The outings could be open to anyone," adds Philip as he settles into his chair, shading his eyes from the setting sun.

Robert sits up straight in his chair and raises his index finger to get our attention. Already a member of several International clubs in Japan, he states, "I believe we need a president, vice president, treasurer, and a general secretary. What do you think?"

I respond optimistically, "Robert, how about you be president, Albert can be vice-president, Philip, treasurer, and I will be general secretary." The men nod, and we toast the completion of the board.

Robert adds, "An important consideration, as we have done in other clubs, is to invite the Imperial Prince of Japan to accept the Honorary Presidency of the Automobile Club of Japan. In fact, out of respect, we should call it the Nippon Automobile Club."

"*Mon Dieu*, that is an excellent idea! And it will make our club more attractive to Japanese motorcar owners!" I say, thinking to myself that more club members mean more connections with people who may become my future clients for automobiles or insurance.

"There are a few jobs that all three of us must share. We need to make road maps, so people will know which motorways are safe, and which have missing bridges," Robert says.

"We could also create a pamphlet of suggestions for emergencies. A list of supplies would be helpful. Members can share their experiences and advice at meetings, and we can add them to the pamphlet," adds Philip. "We have all had to improvise at one time or another."

"I couldn't agree more," I say. "Two weeks ago, my family and I returned home quite late in the dark from a hiking trip to Mount Asama. It isn't always easy to get children back in the automobile in a timely manner. On top of being late, the automobile lights wouldn't turn on. The carbide lights were out of acetylene, and we were driving on a narrow winding road, overlooking a rocky drop to the valley below." I pause, then continue. "My first thought was to turn back, but the road was too narrow." I pause to take a sip of wine and place the glass on the table. "I had to improvise. So, I made a lantern. I dipped paper in car oil from the can behind the back seat, and then wrapped the dripping mess around a candle. Then I pulled a bamboo pole from the back of the car—we use it to support the car canvas top when it rains—and tied it all together. I then secured it to the hood of the car. We creeped down the winding road, narrowly missing falling off the cliff onto the rocks below. But, eventually, made it home safely."

"Louis, how did you happen to have a candle?" asks Robert.

"I always carry candles. We must be prepared for anything. I will put that on our list of emergency supplies."

"It is amazing how we have had to invent ways to solve new problems every day," Philip agrees. And if you had been in a group, someone else would surely have had a portable headlight. Louis, add that to your list!"

"These new vehicles in a foreign land have been quite a challenge. I agree that traveling in a small caravan is a fabulous idea," Albert says. "This makes me think. What if we develop a guide with a written review of different villages and attractions? We could include travel information on hiking as well." We all nod in agreement with this brilliant idea.

President Robert Martin adds, "Our family went to the Tea House at Nikko. We didn't know there was such a beautiful Temple, the Iyeyasu, with curving blue and yellow tile roofs. We went inside and saw sacred texts on the walls and a famous carved ornate gate in front of the temple was painted in orange and gold. It was quite remarkable, breathtaking. We could include information about places like this in our guides."

"Our family motored up to Nikko several weeks ago, too," I add. "It would have been nice to have had some information before we got there, since there was so much to see. We spent the night at the elegant Nikko Hotel. The next day we hiked to Urami Waterfalls, one of three in the area, as well as visited multiple temples, and learned about the spring and autumn festivals from locals. We were grateful to find a shop selling popular postcards, because there was too much to remember."

We discussed many more ideas for another hour, agreeing to meet again in two weeks.

"Thank you so much for bringing us together, Louis," Albert said.

"Oh, *Merci* to you, too, all of you gentlemen," I reply. "We now have the first driver's licenses and the first automobile club in Japan, The Nippon Automobile Club! Cheers to us all!"

# Chapter Fourteen

This photo was Louis' idea promoting the Michelin tire company.
This photo was made into a poster and decorated the walls of
Michelin dealerships in France.
The last one seen by the family was in 1984.
The photo was taken in their garden in Honmoku
where they built a new home after the fire.

## Chapter Fourteen
## Manor de la Noeu, 1952

Henriette is in the drawing room getting ready for guests. It seems our preferred pastime lately is to have dinner parties. My wife is better at planning, but I excel at dinner conversation and interesting stories.

I bring in the stories that I have rediscovered from my research and writing. I have somewhat reorganized the pictures in ten-year increments. As I get older, it is increasingly difficult to remember which child is in what photo, and where we were at the time the photo was taken. Writing stories is sometimes difficult, but I find telling them to friends is easier.

Our guests will be here soon, so I get up to go to our bedroom to get changed. Before I go, however, I choose a few pictures from Japan that might add some interest to the evening and lay them on top of a stack of postcards.

Later, as I emerge from the bedroom changed for dinner, I hear the buzzer announcing our guests, Mr. Archambault and his wife, Margot. I shuffle to the door.

"*Bonjour!* Welcome *mes amis*," I extend my arm for Margot, cane on one side and guest on the other. "Come into the drawing room for an *aperitif*. Henriette is in the kitchen with the cook and will be here shortly."

Mr. Archambault is a close friend and Michelin tire dealer. He settles into the sofa as the petite antique chair is too small. He used to have an athletic build, but French pastries have won him over. He leans forward, resting his elbows on his knees.

"Louis. It is so good to see you. I have wanted to tell you that we finally got our poster from the head office. Other dealers have received theirs, too. Some clients make a special trip just to see the geishas in the antique car with your boy dressed up like Bibendum, the mascot of the Michelin Tire Company. Ingenious idea."

"Oh! That was forty years ago now. Automobiles look a bit different now," I add.

"Achilles. Tell Louis about the new tire. They call it a *Cage* à *Mouche*," says Margot, indulging my interest in cars. She sits comfortably in the small Louis XV chair facing Achilles.

"Yes, it's called a fly trap, like the plant. It has loops of wire from the hub to the tread. And steel cords around the tire mean longer life and less heat," answers Achilles.

"That is indeed remarkable. Margot, did you know I once had to stuff a tire with grass to make it down a mountain in Japan? How times and tires have changed."

Henriette comes into the room to join us. "Welcome, welcome," she says kissing our guests' cheeks. "I heard you from the kitchen. Louis, tell Margot and Achilles the full story about the day the geishas came for photos."

"Excuse me for a minute," I say as I take hold of my cane, stand up, and go to my library to retrieve the photo. As I return with the picture, I see my mother's red tortoise shell clock on the mantel of the sitting room. I look down at the picture.

"Well, let me tell you a story," I say to our guests, as the clock choruses, "Tic toc, tic toc."

*Three Geishas and the Michelin Man*
**Honmoku, Japan, 1912**

Clip, clop, clip clop. I hear rhythmic horse foot falls come to a halt behind our new Japanese style summer home, followed by a neigh. I go to the back porch, open the door, and go outside to greet the travelers in the carriage. I watch as the driver carefully helps three geishas down to the road below. Their platform shoes can be a challenge on the steps.

"*Kon'nichiwa*. Hello, and welcome to our home," I say as introductions pass around with the required proper bowing and little eye contact. The driver returns to his carriage to wait.

A few months ago, I thought it would be a good business advertising decision to show geishas with the car in order to appeal to our growing number of Japanese customers, since many Japanese citizens are looking to buy an automobile. I met with the director of the geisha house and discussed the possibility of a photography session. After a conversation about what I was looking for, she agreed and informed me of the rules of their dress and conduct. An older geisha would need to be present to chaperone the younger apprentices.

The director told me that the word geisha is made of two parts. *Gei* means "art." *Sha* means "the person who does it," referring to dancing and singing. I have always admired Japanese art, and I thought the geishas wearing kimonos and *oshiroi* white makeup sitting in my car would make a great photograph.

I invite the entourage into our home. The older geisha comes in first, followed closely by her two apprentices. They keep their heads bowed, as is their tradition. One has a ready smile, but the other is more serious.

"*Kon'nichiwa*. Hello, and welcome to our home," I say again as introductions pass around with the required proper bowing. The geishas remove their *okobos*, or platform sandals, and walk into the room in *tabis*, traditional button-down socks with a split for their toes. My son, Georges, finds this an appropriate place to practice speaking Japanese.

"*No namae* Georges," he says as his introduction. The shortest apprentice geisha smiles and says, "*No namae* Hamako. Seashore child."

The older geisha bends down and takes my son's hand, "My name is Azuma, meaning Spring. And this is Emicho, beautiful butterfly," introducing the second apprentice geisha.

Henriette smiles and motions for the geishas to follow her into the living room, inviting them to sit and share tea. They choose to sit on pillows on the floor, very close to each other. They look like newly planted flowers clustered and blooming together in a spring garden.

Azuma, the oldest, wears a pale lavender kimono with red silk around her neck and a brighter gold obi around her waist. A lace shawl covers her shoulders in case of an unexpected breeze.

Hamako, like the others, wears a black wig. Her blue kimono with yellow chrysanthemums has a spring green obi tied with a golden cord belt. Emicho is dressed in a gold and red print kimono and red obi. A *kanzachi*, an ornate hair adornment, falls gently down the left side of her face.

The geishas nervously attend to their kimonos making sure the fine silk is not crinkled. They politely decline our invitation for tea and Azuma asks for a room to prepare and adjust their makeup. Before the pictures, they will apply more white powder and add red lipstick.

Henriette says, "Please come to my daughters' room. Take your time and come out when you are ready."

The Japanese blossoms follow my wife, and she gets them settled. I see her coming down the hall to the drawing room and I ask, "Henriette, has the tailor arrived with little Louis' costume? Louis must try it on in case there are last minute alterations."

"The tailor should be here soon. The gardeners have cleared the lawn and tidied up the flower beds. The azaleas have been groomed and the carts have all been put away. And some tables have been moved to the tennis courts in case we need more room," she answers, and I notice a sharpness in her voice as she is getting a bit tense. Too many people to organize.

I hear a knock at the door. The maid answers and welcomes the tailor. I go to see if I can help him with anything.

"Where should I put the costume, Mr. Suzor? How about the drawing room?" The tailor is carrying an awkward large cotton sack, which holds the suit.

"No, no. There is a guest room down the hall. I will show you," I say, as I guide him down the hall, making sure not to disturb the geishas. Little Louis and Georges follow us into another room.

"Papa, can I try it on?" asks my oldest son. He tries to get it out of the bag but needs help. Georges, his little brother, takes hold of the white stuffed fabric tires as they wrestle Bibendum, the Michelin mascot costume, out of the bag and onto the carpet. The tailor patiently helps my son into the outfit and pulls his arms through the cotton rings before stepping back to admire his work. The fit is perfect.

"Look, Papa. The head looks like whipped cream with spectacles," says Georges. "Can I wear it, too?"

"Yes, but you will have to wait until afterwards. You are too short to wear the costume for the photos. Oh, Georges! Did you wash the tires and the headlights like I asked you to?" I forgot to check about this earlier, and it would surely add a wrinkle to the plans for our photo shoot if he forgot

"*Bien sûr*, Papa. I washed the car and the tables, too," he answers. I can only hope the cushions are dry at this point.

When we return to the living room, my daughters are sitting on the settee admiring fashion plates in a magazine. "Papa, I don't know why you won't let Paule and me be the models in the pictures. We have new beautiful dresses that would look more modern than the geishas' kimonos. Their robes are traditional and old fashioned," adds Edith, looking to her sister for support.

Paule nods in agreement and holds up a magazine, "Look at these latest fashion drawings from Paris, Papa. They use Japanese silk but design modern French drop waist dresses and skirts. Don't you think we would look nice on a postcard or a calendar? We could carry umbrellas and look very *chic* and *à la mode*."

"Yes, you would look lovely, but are you Japanese? No. You are French." The girls scowl at each other. "I want the local people to see a geisha in the car, to realize that there is an option to quit using rickshaws and to buy motorcars," I tell them. "The Japanese like to hold onto traditions, so the geishas will represent their customs and the car will show they are forward thinking," I tell them. "Edith," I say to my eldest. "The Geishas are our guests, and we need to treat them with respect. After the photographer takes my business photos, I will have him take a picture of the two of you in your new dresses from Paris. We should get a family photo as well."

"When will the photographer be here. Papa?" Georges asks, coming into the room.

Looking for a distraction, I take George's hand and say, "Let's go outside and wait for him."

The photographer has already arrived when we get to the garden. I ask about the weather and if the conditions will work.

"The lighting is good and there is not much wind. The sky is blue, and the sunlight is not too bright. Perfect conditions for taking photos." says Mr. Farsari. "I see that you have a pagoda over there in the garden. Park the motorcar in front of it, and the stones in back will look like a waterfall." He starts setting up his camera. "I think we are almost ready for the geishas and the children."

"Georges, run inside and tell your mother to have everyone meet us outside by the cement pagoda in the garden," I say, giving him a task. He runs into the house to tell Henriette, and I can tell by his speed that he feels important.

As we wait, Mr. Farsari and I discuss photography. "The camera has become a great source of income for photographers like me. You know tourists love postcards, and businessmen like you, Monsieur Suzor, benefit in advertising, posters, and calendars. The great thing about photographs is that a hundred years from now, the pictures we take today will tell a wonderful story to your descendants." I appreciate his long-view perspective, beyond our current advertising efforts.

Soon, everyone meets in the garden, except my daughters. They are miffed and are choosing to miss the event. Louis has been wearing his costume all this time, and although he is getting hot, he has not complained. He is ready.

Georges, in blue shorts, a middy top, and a white straw hat offers to go in front and crank the engine. He is not strong enough to start it, so the photographer says, "Stay there, Georges, you will look great in the photo."

The geishas, wearing platform sandals, need help stepping up into the motorcar, so I offer my arm to steady them one at a time. I don't know if they have been in a motorcar before, and the expressions on their faces are serious. However, I am not concerned, as Japanese automobile customers don't expect smiles, just the traditional serious visage. The geishas stand, umbrellas ready.

"Papa. Is it time for me to stand by the car?" asks little Louis. "I have the cup full of nails and broken glass ready," he says, showing it to me.

At this, Henriette turns quickly and asks, "Why does he have those?" The geishas look at each other not knowing what to think about the nails and glass either.

"Henriette, it's alright. It is part of the Michelin advertising campaign. *Nunc est Bibendum*. It's Latin for 'It's time to drink.' The advertisers are showing that Michelin tires drink up obstacles on the road."

Henriette raises her left eyebrow. "This Bibendum also smokes a cigar in the posters. Do you think our son should have a cigar, too?"

"No, of course not. He's too young," I say, smiling at her quick wit.

Mr. Farsari is ready. Tripods and cameras are placed, geishas are settled, Georges is at the front crank, and Mr. Bibendum raises his glass of nails for all to admire. Mr. Farsi takes the shots.

"I have five pictures of the geishas and your boys. Do you want any more pictures taken?" Mr. Farsari asks.

"Yes, my daughters would like a few photos taken. And we should get a family photo. But first I must get the geishas on their way."

I walk over to the automobile and help them down from the car. *"Arigatou,"* I say in thanks to each of the ladies and we exchange appropriate bows. My youngest son, Georges, comes over and joins in, practicing his limited Japanese with Hamako. The driver has been watching from the side garden and I hear him make a noise clearing his throat indicating it is time for the geishas to leave. Perhaps they have another engagement after our photo session. The geishas go into the house to collect their basket of belongings and go out the back door to their carriage. I paid the geisha house when I reserved them for this afternoon, so this task is complete.

Paule and Edith come out to the garden after they hear the carriage leave. Mr. Farsari takes several pictures of the young ladies in French fashions by the pagoda, by the automobile, and one with Paule standing in front of the passenger door, and Edith at the wheel.

"When I get a driver's license, I will take you and our brothers for rides all through the countryside," says Edith, holding onto the steering wheel, to anyone who is listening.

"We aren't in a hurry for that," I tell my daughter.

I turn my attention to Mr. Farsari. "I have been thinking about what you were saying, about photographs holding stories for my decedents, and I believe you are right. Thank you for capturing this day for us, for all of us. I look forward to seeing the final photographs."

"My pleasure, Monsieur Suzor. My pleasure," he says, shaking my hand. "And I will bring the photos to you when they are ready." He nods, and I watch him walk towards his automobile. Indeed, I feel that a piece of my legacy has been documented for future generations, and future stories.

# Chapter Fifteen

Louis in the driver's seat and Henriette in the back seat, sharing an
afternoon ride with friends along a coastal road in
Japan's Kanto region.

## Chapter Fifteen
Library
Manor de la Noue, 1953

I sit at my desk idly petting Fujiko. She stretches before settling down for her mid-morning nap on my cashmere lap blanket. I have started keeping it on top of my tea chest beside my desk and it is now her favorite spot.

Henriette walks through the doorway with a bundle of mail in her hand. "Louis, look at that cat on your blanket again. Should she share your blanket when she eats mice for breakfast?'

"Henriette, we eat pigs and cows and share a blanket at night. I'm sure it's okay. Ah! I see you have the mail."

"Yes, there is a postcard for you from Gilbert," she says, sitting on the sofa.

"I'll come join you," I say, standing slowly. I look forward to hearing from my grandson. He has finished school and is taking some time off in Asia before he joins the military. He hopes to be a Zouave as well. He reminds me of myself, when I was young in Algiers. He must be having incredible adventures, and I'm sure our friends are delighted to have him visit for the summer.

I settle in next to Henriette. "Look! Three postcards, not just one! One from Hong Kong and two from Japan. Here. You can read the one from Hong Kong first," she says and places it in my outstretched hand.

The picture is a harbor view at night from Victoria Peak, the highest point in the city. I turn it over. Gilbert writes that one tram brings visitors up to see the view, and one to bring them back to the busy city. He loves the people and the food, and he hopes we are doing well. Not much information, but that is why postcards are so popular — just a note to say hello.

"Louis," Henriette says. "Gilbert sent two postcards from Yokohama. One is the picture of the rebuilt Grand Hotel, and the other is the Queen's Tower Customs House. Look at the streets. They are wide enough for four cars to pass comfortably. Remember when we lived there, how narrow the roads were?"

"Such changes. I have seen that Customs House. It looks more like a mosque with its white tower. What does he say on the card?"

"'Dear Manyette and Daddy. I tried to find where your house and office were, but with so much reconstruction over the years after the devastation, it was impossible to find. Nonetheless, I am enjoying my travels. I hope you are both doing well. I will write a letter with more information soon. Love, Gilbert.' Funny, he still calls me Manyette."

"The shortened form of Ma Henriette, the name I call you sometimes. No one calls you grandmother."

"I prefer Manyette, really. Grandmother just sounds like an old lady!"

"Let me see the Grand Hotel," I say, taking the other postcard. "Oh, progress can be a wonderful thing!" I say. "Inspiring, isn't it? Don't you wish we could go back, Henriette, even just for a visit?"

"No, Louis. My traveling days are over," Henriette says. "I am happy to live vicariously through the younger generation. Here, I'll leave this postcard with you, and you can read it again and look at the picture if you'd like. I'm going to the drawing room and write a few postcards of my own, and a letter to our children," she says. She kisses me on the cheek and rises to go to her sitting room.

I get up and cross to the tea crate. I move Fujiko to the floor before removing the top of the crate. I turn the lid upside down, put her blanket in it, and place it on the sofa. She comes back to her comfortable bed and settles in. I go back to the crate and lift out a cardboard box of postcards from Japan—there must be a hundred. I shake my head, as I look through them. The first has two monkeys eating noodles with the English words, 'Happy New Year 1905' across the front. The next postcard has the year 1906 depicted on an abacus. There is even an Art Nouveau geisha hiding behind a *wagasa*, her *washi* paper and bamboo umbrella.

I smile when I run across postcards from one of our trips to the magnificent waterfalls and temples of Nikko. Postcards were just beginning to be popular then, and my daughters collected as many as they could. We would send them through the postal service to our friends and family in Europe, and it was always an exciting day when we got one back through the mail. Sometimes when on a trip, like to Nikko, we would send ourselves a postcard without a message—just for the fun of receiving something in the mail, and the additional opportunity to receive a souvenir with a postal date. It is nice now to have the date, but it is a bit of a challenge to discern the year. The dates are written from right to left according to the year of the Emperor's reign. They did not use our European dating system. Very confusing. Turning the image of the waterfall over, I see Edith mailed this one to her sister. I look at the pastel painted photos and remember my many trips to the mountain temples.

*The High Road to Nikko*
**Japan, 1913**

"Motoring to Nikko is like travelling in a beautiful postcard, but we can see the true colors," I tell my friends as we meet and get ready for an expedition to the mountains. We are waiting outside my automobile for the other four motorists and their guests to arrive at the city park.

Today the high road is the best road. And the only road. We will climb Usui Pass. The pass from Nagano to Gunma is only about seven miles long, but there are 32 switchbacks along the way, and some are very steep, so the trip to the top can take several hours. Spring is a perfect season for motorcar outings to the magnificent mountain vistas of Nikko. Albert, Hans, and I are leading a small automobile club motor-tour to this natural wonder of Japan, just as we imagined the day we earned our licenses. We are riding in my new burgundy Delaunay-Belleville, a beauty with pearl-gray leather upholstery. The artfully crafted woodwork is honey-colored birds-eye maple. The car is roomier than my last one and can carry six passengers. Henriette likes it because it is much more elegant than our first motorcar, and the passengers in the back seat are higher than in the front, so the children can easily see where we are going. All the accessories are in bronze and copper, and there are even silver bud vases on each side of the passenger seats for flowers!

I hear the rumble of other motorists coming into the park. After they stop, I walk over to greet each one. We decide who will follow whom. Lucky for me I am the leader, so I won't get the dust and gravel that automobiles kick up.

"Alright my friends. Let's get going," I shout so all can hear. I climb into my vehicle and sit behind the steering wheel. Hans shares the front bench with me while Albert sits in back. I start my engine, and around me other motors grumble at first, then roar, then settle into a low growl. As the line of dragon beetles leaves the park, I turn to Albert and Hans and remind them, "This is a business trip as well as a pleasure outing. We must be sure to document any new information on this trip for the growth of our club! And don't forget postcards."

We leave the city and ride through increasingly rural areas. The cars are too noisy, so we can't talk much. I'm happy just looking at the valley and vistas. I see tea plantations with women and men bent over filling their wood-strip baskets with precious tea leaves. Some women are dressed in blue cotton kimonos with a red fabric belt wrapped around their middle. They wear skirts under their kimonos, and they all have on white cotton scarves tied at the back of their heads. After picking leaves at one plant, they pick up their large baskets and move to collect more—arduous work for a cup of tea.

Several carts pulled by men pass our group going in the opposite direction. The carts are filled to overflowing, but nothing falls out. Another man pulls a cart transporting four people up the road to a train stop. Buying a horse may be too expensive and feeding it could be an additional difficulty. Some families on the sides of the road are walking on foot to the station carrying baskets of perhaps some personal belongings, maybe food for the train ride. A small child sleeps on top of colorful cloths in another large straw hamper. A man carrying that basket takes out a kerchief and wipes his forehead as he keeps moving ahead. I wonder how far he has walked. And here I sit in my French automobile.

I stay on the main road and pass the train station, one of several on the pass. As we drive, I marvel at the beauty of the different trees and flowers at the higher elevations. Pines and azaleas add to the mountain vistas, and purple and yellow wildflowers blanket the hills.

As we meander up the switchbacks, rocks on the dusty road ahead start to slow us down. I look behind us. All four vehicles advance at a snail's pace up the hairpin turns. Men are taking off their jackets in the heat, despite the dust. Women put up their colorful paper umbrellas and wave fans to cool off. I'm struck that we look like a flutter of butterflies on our way to the temples.

We maneuver the next switchback on the road, and I abruptly stop my vehicle, letting the engine idle. Albert stands up in the automobile, turns to face the other motorists and waves for them to stop as well.

"Albert, what is going on here?" someone calls from another car.

An unbelievable spectacle meets our eyes. "Hans, have you ever seen anything like this before?" I ask my friends.

We watch a parade of houses moving up the road, laboriously assisted by the local villagers, who sing as they work. The houses roll over long logs. As the house advances, the last log is picked up and brought to the front to allow the house to move forward again. The children in our caravan squeal with excitement. They have never seen a house move up or down a mountain path.

Turning off our engines, drivers and passengers alike jump down from their motorcars and approach the few villagers, who look equally surprised to see us on the road. Using our limited yet functional Japanese and many gestures, we try to find out what is happening.

I bow and ask, "What is happening? Why are you moving houses?"

A villager, familiar from a previous encounter during my last visit at the hotel, steps forward and returns my bow in greeting. We look at our dusty hands and, with a chuckle, decide not to shake hands. He smiles as he

140

wipes the sweat off his face with a dusty cotton kerchief, seeming happy to take a break, as do the people working behind him. He appears to be interested in our group of foreigners, and he speaks English quite well.

"Hello. My name is Koji. I remember you, Mr. Suzor, and your automobile. I work at Nikko Hotel, but today we move our village because of avalanche. Eight years ago, there was very big avalanche—so many big rocks went into Lake Chuzenji! The water level got too high and flooded the village. We moved our village up the mountain, but last week, rock avalanche fell on the village. So today we move what is left of our village, again."

We marvel in disbelief. Houses balance on six wood logs laid across the path, as the villagers push crowbars with difficulty, strong arms stretched to their limits, moving a few feet at a time in the afternoon heat of the higher elevations. We hear the local workers start to sing again in unison, using the song to keep in time with their work.

I feel a bit of a breeze, but not enough. I see Albert has walked ahead to look at the moving spectacle, and he turns back to us, waving his arms and points ahead. "*Mon Dieu!* Look! There is a railroad track well ahead of the villagers. It appears the villagers are trying to push their heavy wooden homes to the track to make it easier to move them forward on the rails.

An unsympathetic British man—who is more interested in his experience coming up than in the shared experience of the moment—calls out, expressing concern that we will be late getting to the hotel and miss dinner. I wish I could stay and watch the villagers, but I need to respond to my business and guests. And, in truth, the man who called out is right, as we still have two rugged miles to cover.

"Best of luck to you and your workers. Perhaps we will see you, Koji, at the hotel," I say, as I motion for our group to return to our cars. I step up and into the driver's seat and start the engine. Our caravan rumbles to life, and I cautiously lead our group around the villagers and their unstable homes.

My thoughts return to the family walking to the train station lower down in the valley. And now this mountain community. I can't help them move their houses, and I know that these villagers can't afford a car. Could I import buses from France? It would allow families to go from their homes by bus to trains and then to many other destinations. Yokohama has trains and electric trollies, but people outside of the city could benefit as well. It would change their lives for the better. I will talk it over with my friends after dinner.

The clamor brings my attention back to the task at hand. The villagers were noisy, but our automobiles are downright deafening. Ahead, I see a railroad station captain with a red flag frantically waving his arms running towards us from the train station house.

I stop my motorcar, jump down, and run to meet the frightened railroad captain.

"Danger! Danger!" he yells. "I hear a train. Not the scheduled train!! Tell the villagers!"

Through many gestures, broken English and Japanese, I calm the captain down and communicate to him that the villagers are not close to the tracks yet. When he realizes they are safe, he breathes a sigh of relief. The unscheduled train passes us, and chugs away wandering down the hill.

We get back into our automobiles and continue our journey. After many more switchbacks, the Nikko Hotel finally comes into view. As we drive up the road, we feel a gentle wind sailing across the lake bringing relief in temperature. We turn off our engines, and as I get out, I overhear a British woman exclaiming over the beauty of the azaleas in bloom, their discomfort already forgotten. "The whites, reds, and purples make me homesick for England," she says to her husband, as he holds the door open for her. "Look, there is even wisteria climbing the front trellis by the entry. I was told it was beautiful here, but it is so much more."

"Mother," asks the woman's son, "Will we be able to go out in the little sail boats tonight? I can see some on the lake. William and I want to go fishing, too. We brought our fishing poles, remember?"

His father answers, "There is a light breeze on the lake. Yes, you may go sailing with your brother after supper. And tomorrow will be good for trout fishing."

I can't help but join their conversation. "Did you know, children," I ask, "that this mountain is considered a special holy place? It's a good thing we weren't here 50 years ago." I pause. "I was told that the mountain was closed to women, horses, and cows! A Buddhist priest claimed it as a holy place. Only men could be on the mountain. But that was then. Anyone can now go up the mountain, and many European embassies have built vacation houses around the lake. You children are very lucky to be here. Tomorrow we will see waterfalls. And some temples. You will even be able to go inside some of them. You can buy color postcards for souvenirs or to send to your friends back home."

But the boys aren't listening. They are much more interested in preparing their fishing poles for tomorrow. As they run off, I say to the adults, "There is a Japanese proverb that says, 'Do not use the word magnificent until you have seen Nikko.'"

"I understand completely," says the gentleman. "We look forward to our time here. Will you be at dinner, Mr. Suzor?"

"Yes, absolutely. I will see you there. Until then, enjoy your afternoon!" The couple smile and follow their children down the trail towards the lake.

I smile, satisfied that the people for whom we have created the tour are satisfied. When everything has been unloaded and my friends have gone their separate ways—likely to the bar, or to go fishing themselves—I turn towards the hotel and walk into the lobby. The sitting room overlooks the lake, and I sit down in a large bamboo and white cotton armchair to take in the scene. Lake Chuzenji has been stocked with trout for about 20 years, and I watch the fishermen on the shore pulling in their catch. I wonder if they are catching *iwana,* a different kind of fish that the locals use nets to catch.

After dinner, I retire to the lounge armchairs overlooking the lake and mountains for a brandy with Albert and Hans.

"Louis, I can see you have something on your mind. You look energized and you should be tired from the long trip. Even your bouncing knee looks eager to say something!" says Albert.

"Just a nervous twitch. You are right. I am troubled by what I saw today. The families walking long distances to the train and the one person carrying four passengers in his cart looked exhausted. Outside of Yokohama and Tokyo I see old people walking great distances and families with small children. And here I am, a European out for a pleasure drive in their roads. It leaves me feeling uncomfortable."

Albert says, "Yes, I thought you were awfully quiet on the trip. Not your usual jovial self."

I have a sip of brandy, and add, "I am encouraged, though. Buses. We have them in Paris. What do you think?" I say, starting to feel a little excitement for a new project that would be so helpful.

Hans adds, "There are many towns far away from trains in the Kanto region. I think you may have a great idea. Can you get buses from the Clement-Bayard firm in France?"

"I'm sure I can," I say, swirling a warm brandy snifter in my hand. "I think I could order some and sell them to smaller local transport companies, creating new jobs. But first I will have to check with Mr. Hiraoka at the bank and the local transportation board," I add.

Albert finishes his brandy and puts it on the table. "Louis," he says, standing, "I think your idea for buses could benefit our automobile club, too. Members could join if they didin't own an automobile. We could include a bus in our excursions! Superb idea. We'll talk about it more tomorrow. I can see you are not tired, but I can feel myself slowing down. I think it is time for me to retire for the night. Goodnight gentlemen!"

Hans stands up as well and says, "Louis. You have a knack for turning obstacles into opportunities. I look forward to talking about it more tomorrow, but for now I am going to retire, too. Goodnight Louis. Albert."

I bid them both a good night, order another brandy, and take in the postcard perfect view of magnificent Nikko.

# Chapter Sixteen

The train to the family summer home in the mountains. Trains were
built in 1893 to go along the steep mountain slopes, and bridges
carried passengers to Karuizawa, a popular mountain retreat
for the international community.

# Chapter Sixteen
## The Market
## Nice, France, 1953

After five years in La Noeu, we have moved to Nice in southern France. My Japanese tea crate has been put to good use once again, as the memorabilia were packed away and moved carefully. We came for year-round sunshine and to be closer to my son, Louis, who works in the flower wholesale business. He brought me along to the Cours Saleya flower market this morning. While he speaks with exhibitors, I slowly amble down the rows of blossoms and people, secure with my cane for balance. The fragrances of the geraniums and fuchsias linger with me as I lightly touch tender sunbursts of dhalias and chrysanthemums. I duck my head to avoid a group of small birds, colorful *chardonneret*s, as they swoop in and out of the outdoor market.

My son catches up to me, takes my free arm, and says, "Papa? Are you ready to get a coffee? Paule said she would meet us at Café D'Azur. We are just three shops away."

"*Bien sûr*. I could use some energy," I say, and we leave the market and head to the café. When we arrive, we choose an outdoor table and sit under a green and white striped awning. As we wait for Paule, we watch the busy market.

"*Et voilà!* So, I finally find you two," Paule says as she arrives, and we greet each other with the customary French kisses, high on the cheeks, sometimes two, sometimes four times, depending on what part of France we are in. I pull a chair out for Paule to sit next to me. She looks like her mother with her wavy hair starting to grey.

"Papa. Look at these postcards," she says, as the waiter brings three cups and a carafe of fresh coffee. Paule smiles a thanks and continues to show me the pictures of the interiors of trains. "I got them on the *Mistral* yesterday. The train, pulled by a steam locomotive, goes from Paris to Lyon, and then Nice. And at 80 miles an hour!" She places them on the table so I can see them.

"You still love postcards, Paule, but how they've changed since you and your sister collected them in Japan. Look at the colors! The red and black engine looks a lot different from the tiny grey train we rode into the mountains in Japan." She nods. "And these passenger compartments look quite deluxe, unlike the benches and open windows in that little train. At home, I was looking at the postcards I saved of the train station near our summer home."

The waiter returns to refill our cups, and brings a tray of pastries, from which we choose our bakery treat. I choose a *mille-feuille*. As the waiter leaves, I notice a small bird—a parrot—land on the back of a vacant chair. I recognize it as an inseparable, or—as some call them—a 'love bird' because it snuggles its head with others when sleeping.

"Look, Louis and Paule. I have seen a few of these small parrots in Nice, visitors from Africa, I believe. That one looks just like the bird in Japan that caused so much trouble on the train. Do you remember that day?" I ask my daughter and son.

"Papa, how could we forget?" says Paule, crumbling a part of her pastry, discreetly dropping it on the floor to watch the little green bird eat and hop about.

## Midori Bird Gets a Ticket to Ride
## Japan, 1914

Washed out roads and heavy grey clouds convinced me this time to take the little grey train to and from our mountain summer home. The children must start school soon, and until the roads have been repaired, the train is the only way to return home to Yokohama. The trip can take hours, as we are 80 miles north west of Tokyo, and at 5,000 feet in elevation. Today is our last day of vacation in our summer cottage.

Our summer home in Karuizawa is a retreat from the city's summer heat. The two-story house has enough rooms for our family and several guests. Numerous windows invite the welcome mountain breezes to enter and swirl out an open door. Bamboo shades keep the rooms comfortable, and I especially like to hear the rain on the cedar-bark roof. We can have gentle drizzles or terrific downpours. Open wood-slatted balconies on the top and the bottom floors are a perfect place to sit and watch visitors walk down the tree covered lanes.

Henriette comes out of the house and meets me on the front porch. "The bus will be here at the house to take us to the train station in thirty minutes," she says. "Please have Paule and Edith help get the furniture covered in the house. I asked the boys to get the outdoor furniture and bring it inside. And please have everyone bring their bags to the porch."

"Yes, Henriette," I say, feeling unsettled because there is so much to check and double check before we go.

Normally I would have things packed in our automobile, but this time our autocar was left in the city for the summer. This means that we are taking the bus to the train station. There are about 200 cottages in the *gaigin-mura*, the foreigner's village where our house was built. We are one of 400 local homes, so buses are helpful to many people. Each bus can hold about 10 passengers at a time. These vehicles are smaller than the 20-seat Clement-Bayard buses — 30 in all — that I imported to Yokohama and promptly sold to small local transport companies.

"Papa," says Louis, coming onto the porch. "I have checked the downspouts, and Georges and I brought in the furniture from the decks upstairs and downstairs. We decided to leave our hiking boots and poles here. We want to climb Mt. Asama again next year if the volcano agrees!"

"That sounds good, Louis. If you are ready, bring your suitcases to the porch. And get grandmother's bags as well. Please," I add. He nods and goes inside to help my mother. Henriette's mother and my mother have both spent a lot of time with us in Japan. Our children are lucky to know and love them. And I am proud all our children are growing up to be kind and responsible.

I hear Edith from inside the house, "Paule, I can't close my suitcase! Is there room in yours?"

I open the screen door and call to everyone, "I want everyone on the porch right away.

The bus will be here in 25 minutes. Trains don't wait for girls to pack their dresses. And Paule and Edith, you still need to cover the living room furniture with the sheets."

"Yes, Papa, we know! Just a minute," calls Edith.

After bringing their suitcases onto the steps, the girls race back into the house to cover the furniture. I organize everyone's luggage, making sure we have everything. Henriette's mother limps to the front and settles herself into a porch chair and, Shingo, our *geboku,* who has been our household helper since we came to Japan, brings a forgotten bag to the porch.

Finally, my children, mother, and wife are ready. The cook, who lives in Karuizawa, will close the rest up after we leave. I can relax now.

I lean against a pine post on the porch and look at my family crowded on the porch. "The only one missing is Andree," I say. "We just aren't complete without her. She must be getting ready for school in a few weeks, just like all of you."

"Papa, when will she be back? Why can't she come to the mountains with us?" asks Louis. He was born two years after Andree—they have all grown so fast.

"Andree has asthma, remember? She was always sick and coughing for hours? The air in Yokohama has too much smoke from the ships coming in and out of the port, and because of that she couldn't stay."

"Oh. Yes," says my son, Louis. "She would try to race us but would get out of breath. Her cheeks were always red, and she would wheeze."

"Yes, Louis, you do remember." I tell the same story to them every time they ask. But the explanation leaves me sad for Andree. On top of that, I feel frustrated because I cannot fix her medical condition.

"But Papa. You say the mountains are healthy for us," says Georges.

"This is true for most people. But do you remember last month when the volcano on Mt. Asama sent out a plume of smoke? And the ashes? If Andree breathed in the ashes, her chest would hurt, and we'd send her to the doctor again. No, the air in France is much better for her."

"I just got a post card from her. She seems to be very happy at school," Paule says. "Tante Adrienne takes her to the theatre in Paris and they have fun going shopping. I wish I could go shopping for fabric and shoes in Paris!"

"Me, too," adds Edith, turning towards her sister and responding to her prompts. "I saw her last pictures and she looks *so* fashionable. Her hair is so pretty tied with that big organdy ribbon. And she was wearing a white linen skirt and button up middy blouse with those shell buttons. The military styling looks so chic, don't you think?"

"Did you see the other picture with the matching double-breasted coat with the gold buttons on the sleeves?" Paule asks.

But her answer is interrupted by the sound of a *mejiro* bird chirping. I turn my ear to the sound, then look back at Edith and raise an eyebrow. She slowly pulls a towel off a small brass bird cage revealing the feathered *chanteuse*.

"The girls couldn't resist buying it at a market in the village, Louis," says Henriette. "Isn't that pale green pretty? And such a lovely song."

"We have a *bird*?" I asked. What more do we need after five children?

"Oh Papa," says Edith. "It's so cute. It's always on the move in her cage, and she hangs upside down, sometimes. Look!"

"The girls have named it *Midori*, Japanese for green," says Henriette with finality. She seems to like the little bird.

Just then the bus arrives and there is nothing to do but take the bird with us. I take my mother's arm and walk her to the bus, while Shingo and the boys shuttle our suitcases. We all climb on board. Shingo makes a final check to make sure we haven't forgotten anything on the porch, and then climbs on behind us.

"A bird, Henriette?" I ask, sitting down next to her.

"Louis, the cage is tiny. It will be just fine. The girls can take turns carrying it on their laps. Oh, Louis," she sighs. "The songbird reminds me of Adrienne and her singing at our parties." I think to myself that, honestly, I prefer the bird, but I say nothing.

The ride to the station takes ten minutes, and when we arrive Shingo and the boys help move our packages from the bus to the train. Henriette and I help her mother up, and then I hold the birdcage as Paule steps into the train.

Out of the corner of my eye, I see the ticket master coming my way, his short legs and arms pumping to get to me before I board. He steps in front of me. "Do you have a ticket for the bird?"

"A ticket, sir?"

"The train rule says animals must have full-fare ticket," he says in a gruff voice.

So much trouble over a bird! "Ah, no, sir. Surely the rules do not apply to a bird so petite in such a tiny cage. It doesn't need a seat. My daughter will hold it on her lap," I say, trying to step around him and onto the train. But the stout official will not move away. I realize he isn't going to back down, so I pay the extra fare for the bird and he walks back to the station. Letting out a big breath of irritation, I get onto the train. It has been stressful getting here, and I don't want to leave the bird behind, on principal, let alone the fact that the girls would be very disappointed.

Just as I climb on board, I pause and think. I feel like I have a point to prove—this is a ridiculous situation.

"Shingo, may I please have your salamander?"

"Excuse me, Mr. Suzor?"

"I need your salamander, please, Shingo. And quickly." I hold out my hand, and he takes a jar with a salamander inside of it from his handbag, and hands it to me.

I step down towards the platform and, with a wave, call out after the conductor, "Excuse me!" The conductor turns. "My servant has a salamander the size of a finger in a mustard jar. He is bringing it home for a cure for some sickness. Does this animal also require a ticket?"

"Louis!" pleads Henriette from inside.

"Is it alive, the salamander?" asks the conductor, returning to the doorway.

"It is difficult to tell," I reply, slowly turning the container towards the conductor.

He shifts his weight on his feet and sweat develops on the official's brow, and he wipes it with a cotton handkerchief. He doesn't seem to like amphibians. He scratches his head and leaves to consult with his supervisor.

As he returns, Shingo rises from his seat and crosses to stand with me at the door.

"Your *geboku* will have to pay for a ticket for the salamander," says the conductor, handing Shingo a passenger ticket for the salamander.

I take the ticket from Shingo and shake my head. "My *geboku* travels at my expense," I reply. Sometimes the cultural differences are infuriating— bending the rules is apparently impossible. No exceptions. And there is no room for comment.

The conductor takes my money and leaves. I hand Shingo his salamander and its ridiculous ticket, and he returns to his seat, cowering a bit, likely from discomfort at my blatant challenge of the rules.

I sit and join my family; Henriette shakes her head and looks out the window, over the terrain. She wouldn't say anything more on the train, but I'll likely hear about her discomfort tonight. The train finally begins to roll down the mountain, and we are headed home. The young boys are quite interested in the salamander now, as it is, indeed, alive and moving slowly up the side of the jar. Shingo lets Georges hold the jar.

"How do you eat a salamander?" asks Georges.

"The Japanese medicine shop dries it and makes into powder. For stomach-ache and worms. It makes the sickness go away," Shingo replies.

Edith looks at her sister and raises an eyebrow, obviously feeling a bit sickened by the conversation. Smiling, Paule asks me, "Do you remember our coachman? He used to get extra money selling the urine from our horse. Since the mare was white, the medicine was guaranteed to work."

"For specific illnesses, one cup every morning certainly works," adds our servant, nodding his head.

With a shake of her head, Edith settles in for the ride down the mountain. The engine chugs slowly down the tracks. I relax in my seat next to Henriette and feel comforted by the sounds of wheels turning on the tracks towards home.

# Chapter Seventeen

Mariko and her dog playing in the Suzor garden. Yokohama

## Chapter Seventeen
## Nice, France, 1954
## — Henriette Speaks —

A friend is driving Louis to Tours for a car show, so I have time to clean up after my husband. He does get a bit forgetful. He's seven years older than me, and I can see his health and strength are starting to fade.

I try to help him as much as I can. I bought a large basket at the flower market last month into which I can collect the pictures and notes he casually leaves on tables and windowsills throughout our home. Everywhere. He was once so organized with his paperwork, but his mind has changed with age, and with the eight years of this project of his. Louis is certainly reviewing his life under a microscope.

Basket cradled in my left arm, I go out to the patio. The day is sweet and sunny, and my red geraniums and impatiens are overflowing their ceramic pots. I breathe in the fragrant scent of lilacs and marvel at how flowers on the Riviera flourish and flaunt their colors. I pick up a group of photos strewn on a glass coffee table, then go inside to the drawing room. More papers and photos. Even a few yellowed newspaper articles.

I pick up a copy of the Japan Weekly News. I remember that it was a favorite of ours while we lived there since it was printed in English. We all knew English as well as French, and we were able to converse in Japanese. I add the newspaper to my bouquet of paper memories and continue down the hallway, past the hanging scroll with the two Japanese carp, and walk into the library.

I place the basket on the tea crate. This box holds our memories of Japan — those formative years that shaped our future lives. We were blessed to live such an adventure. Two photos drop from the carrier to the floor. I pick them up, look at them and pause, taking time to remember that day. I sit down at Louis' desk to study the old black and white photos. I feel a cloud of sadness, and I wonder what happened to the little one who once could have fit perfectly in my wicker basket.

*Mariko*
**Yokohama, Japan, 1917**

Desperate cries from outside interrupt the piano and violin duet. Edith and Paule pause their playing and look toward the door. "Mama, those boys really must stop playing tricks on us," says Edith. As the oldest, she often takes charge of her siblings.

"Go tell them to stop," I say, adjusting a picture on the dining room wall, as small earthquakes rearrange our paintings on a regular basis.

She gets up from her piano bench, and Paule sets her violin down on the sofa. The two go to the door and open it. But her brothers are nowhere to be found. Instead they hear a wiggling, noisy bundle wrapped in a ragged towel laying in a basket. We all look at each other, speechless, hearing the screams of a distraught child.

Edith bends over and with both hands underneath the worn-out wicker carrier, she brings the child inside. Paule clears off the sofa, and her sister puts the new arrival down. Hearing the cries, Amah, our Japanese help, comes into the living room to see what is going on. The girls step aside, and I place my hand on top of a worn grey towel. I unfold more fabric and see a round, pink angry face looking at me. Tucked into the towels are two empty baby bottles. I remove more layers and can see she is a little girl, hungry and quite thin, dressed in a colorful, but worn, baby kimono. She begins to calm down when she sees us hovering over her, but then she starts up again.

Amah comes close to the basket, looks at me and extends her arm. "May I hold the baby?" she asks. I nod, and she picks her up.

"Madame Suzor, the baby is so thin. She needs food right away. She is not strong—look, she needs help holding up her head. And see the back of her head, here?" Amah shows us a flat instead of rounded head. "This little girl has been laying on her back most of her short life. She needs food. I will wash these bottles and fill one right away with warm milk," she says as she gently passes the little one to Edith.

"She looks like the Japanese Meigi baby dolls we played with when we were little," Edith says, enraptured. "But this one needs a bath and some clean clothes." She sits down, and we all stare at the baby and each other, shocked. Amah returns a few minute later and gives Edith a bottle of lukewarm milk for the baby.

I sit down on the sofa next to Edith and look at this child, discarded like a dog, and left on a stranger's doorstep. The baby is clearly comforted by the warm milk. "*Mon Dieu*, who would do this? I wonder if she could even be a year old. We will need to contact the authorities soon."

"Mama, please don't tell anyone. Not yet. Please!"

"Why not, Edith?"

"I don't like the idea of calling the local police," Edith says. "What could they do that we couldn't? Please, Mama, we can keep her."

*Grâce à Dieu*, I think to myself. Just then, I hear the rumble of Louis' automobile at the front entrance, and I've never been so relieved to hear that machine. I stand up and go to meet him at the door.

Louis opens the door and the boys, Georges and Louis, walk into the room in front of their father. Nobody is saying anything, only looking at the three of them. Even Amah stands quietly behind the sofa.

"Paule, why is your violin on the floor? I thought this is the time you usually practice?" Louis asks. "Don't you and Edith have a recital next week?"

"Edith, what are you holding?" asks Georges.

"It is a package that was left on the steps," offers Paule.

The bundle starts to cry. Louis looks at me in disbelief. I cross my arms in front of me, shrug my shoulders, and look back, feeling numbness. I need to talk to Louis in private about the child. I am not going to raise another child, but I do want her to be in a safe place.

The boys join their sisters over by the couch, looking down at the tiny girl, trying to make her smile. The sweet baby doesn't know it has been renounced. Edith hands the empty bottle to Paule, and she heads for the kitchen for more fresh milk.

"Papa, can we please keep her? She won't be any trouble, I promise. I will take care of her," begs Edith.

"And I will help, too. Maman won't have to do anything," adds Paule.

"I hardly think so. I need to talk it over with your mother, and we will tell you as soon as we arrive at a responsible decision. You two girls watch the little one while we talk. Amah, will you join us with tea?"

"Yes, of course."

"We will be in the other room if you need something," I tell the children. We cross to the dining room and close the glass-paned doors behind us for privacy. Louis pulls out a chair for me, then joins me at the table.

As we wait for Amah to bring tea, I say quietly to Louis, "I wonder what the circumstances would have to be in order to provoke making such an agonizing decision. I can only imagine that the parents were very poor. The towels around her are old and she is so very thin. Perhaps they felt a European family without financial difficulties and with a Japanese maid, cook, and children would be a better able to raise and feed her?"

Amah arrives with a tray, which she places on the table. She sets the table with a blue and white teapot and cups for tea. I can smell the fragrant dried jasmine blossoms and imagine them floating on top. She sits at the table with us and pours the tea.

"Amah," Louis starts as Amah pours. "You have lived in Japan all your life. You understand the local culture and we try to do what is right, but we need your help. What do we do?"

Amah is quiet, thinking, as she hands us the cups.

"Could the baby be a love child from a European and Japanese romance?" asks Louis.

"It's too soon to tell just by looking at her," I say, realizing that he didn't take a close look at her when he arrived. "This is not the first time this has happened here, in the international community. The baby and mother would be shunned in this community if a Japanese mother kept her, right Amah?" She nods slowly. "If the pregnant mother was European, though, she'd travel back to her home-country until the baby was born. No matter where, the child will often be left in an orphanage, and this is unfair for the children."

"In a way, I understand the need for a family's sacrifice to keep a child safe and give her a chance at a better life," adds Louis. I can tell by the look on his face that he is thinking about our daughter, Andree.

"Amah, what do you think?" I ask her.

"*Ano*," she pauses, always using this expression to give herself time to think. Holding the cup of jasmine scented tea between her warmed hands, she responds, "If you take the baby, I can take care of her when you are gone for business or other reasons."

Louis sits back in his chair and takes a deep breath. "Amah, remember, we will be returning to France within the next few years. Our boys will be going into the military or getting jobs, and the girls will have completed school and may be getting married. Bringing a baby to France would not be possible for many reasons. Why shouldn't we give the baby to the authorities now?"

"She would be put in an orphanage, and many of those are too crowded already," Amah says.

"Do you know someone who would be agreeable to adopt the baby?" I ask.

Amah takes a sip of tea. "I'll think about people I know and tell you in the morning when we are rested." But the way she holds her head to the side, I know she is still thinking. Louis and I share a look as Amah continues. "To be honest, I always wanted a baby, but I never got married. But I must think and pray about that idea." She shifts her gaze towards the teapot. "I will take care of feeding her tonight. She can stay in my room. I'm very tired and I'm sure you are tired, too."

"Thank you, Amah, for thinking through options, and for taking care of her tonight," I say.

She nods. "Leave the teapot and cups, please. I will come back and pick them up."

We follow her into the drawing room and watch as she gently takes the now sleeping baby from Edith. Amah rocks her in her arms and a smile starts to tug at the corners of her mouth.

"Please, Monsieur and Madame Suzor. Do not call authorities yet," she asks, and Louis and I agree.


Morning comes, and I wake early in the pre-dawn dark. I did not sleep well, with thoughts about the baby interrupting my dreams. I go down to the kitchen. I stop in front of the door and hear a cooing, and Amah speaking. I open the door silently to see Amah holding the child, gently supporting the baby's head.

"Your skin is smooth and white as petals in tea," she whispers. "I think I will name you Mariko. It means Jasmine Child." Amah looks up and sees me in the doorway. "So," she says. "Life gives me a gift of Mariko. Mariko is not an unwanted child. She was just looking for me and my family."

Tears come to my eyes, and I nod. It feels so right to have Amah take care of the baby. Already she seems different. I remember when my first child was born, and all I could do was stare at her.

"All right," I say. "We will not call the authorities." I turn, and go back to bed, at peace.

# Chapter Eighteen

The Suzor family's entry in the Yokohama Armistice Day Parade.

# Chapter Eighteen
## Nice, France 1954

"Louis, I hear thunder!" Henriette calls to me. "Look how quickly the dark clouds are moving this way. We'd better bring in everything we need to keep dry." She is already out the back door, while I am still in the hallway behind. As she comes back in with her first armful, I hold the door open for her. "I'll pick up your box of postcards and photos. Hurry. Hurry."

"Henriette, you know I can't hurry. I'm older than you and my legs are slow," I say. I totter out to the cobblestones, but she is already coming back towards me with the last of my memorabilia. We make it inside just as the first fat drops fall from the sky.

"I'm glad we're on a hill," I say, as we enter back into the drawing room. "I don't know if there will be flooding or unexpected huge waves from the sea." It is our first storm living in Nice. "Come sit by me on the sofa, and we can watch the lightening over the water."

We sit down together. I lean my cane on a chair while Henriette puts my box of photos between us on the sofa. After putting on her glasses, she takes a few pictures out of the box.

I look out the window and see flashes of light brighten the sky and the Mediterranean waters. Close behind, a jagged streak lights up the billowing clouds. Thunder follows and I am glad we are home together.

"Look at the palm trees bend in the wind, Henriette." She looks up from the card and looks out the window. "They are so different than other trees we had in France," I continue. "Have you noticed one of our palm trees doesn't have a top? No fronds! Just a giant trunk in the ground."

"I hope we don't lose another one tonight," says Henriette, watching a distant flicker. I hear a gentle roll of thunder.

"Do you remember the oak trees at the chateau after the storm? Please say you remember. Nobody believes me when I tell them the rest of the story!"

"Yes, Louis. Nobody except your great-grand-children who go to bed with nightmares when you tell them the scary, and perhaps some made up, details," she says, knowingly raising one eyebrow.

"But it was true. There were four trees when we went to bed, and only one remained standing in the morning. Imagine the strength of that wind! After breakfast, Gilbert and I went to see what damage had occurred. We walked around the huge old fallen trees. The oak roots had many years to grow massive underground webs looking for water. Massive. But the relentless storm blew the trees over, dragging three huge root-balls out of the ground. And, remember? The roots unearthed three skeletons!" I smile at Henriette, waving my hands in front of me. "They were hanging and swaying in the country morning breeze!"

"*Mon Dieu*, Louis, I think I'll have nightmares, too," Henriette says. "Yes, I know the story. *Fini*."

"The bones were several hundred years old, and we contacted the former owners of the chateau to see who would come to take them away. The family was able to figure out through old family records who had been buried under the trees and were happy to give them a proper burial." She doesn't say anything more, rather she covers her ears, signaling this conversation is over.

I laugh and we both take a few photos out of the leather picture box resting on a cushion between us.

I take two off the top and show one to her. "Look, Henriette. The picture of our family in costumes for the parade in Yokohama."

"Oh yes, Louis! We did like to dress up in costumes, didn't we? And," she says, leaning towards me, showing me another photo from that same day, "everyone who was there will always remember this, too." Our family poses to the right while, to the left, overhanging the back of our automobile, is a rope noose, the criminal dangling as he should.

## The Yokohama Armistice Day Parade
**Yokohama, Japan, November 1918**

There are two things to celebrate today. The most important is a letter from my mother saying she, Andree, and Adrienne are safe and well in the Channel Islands with friends and relatives. Henriette's mother is with them as well. The letter was written four months ago. We haven't seen Andree for several years. She is 17 now, the same age Henriette was when we got married. My heart is heavy because I have missed so much of her life being so far away.

Since the beginning of the war four years ago in 1914, passenger boats were used to transport military troops, so travelling by sea to visit her was not possible. Postal ships were refitted and used in the war, so letters came infrequently. We lived in Japan with little communication from our mothers and prayed every day that they were safe. My mother in one rare letter said that they had left Paris and were staying with friends away from the French eastern war zone. We were all greatly relieved. I am anxious to hear more from them when communication lines open again.

The second reason to celebrate is the announcement that the war is over. Yokohama is especially jubilant, as Japan played a very important role in the war. Their navy worked closely with England and France making sea lanes safe in the West Pacific and Indian Oceans. The Germans held several South Pacific Island Colonies, and England asked Japan to help get the Germans off the islands and out of ports in China. The Japanese were successful and continued helping to escort British troop transport ships safely through Asian and Pacific waters. The Japanese also assisted the British in anti-sub operations against the Germans. Today we celebrate that four years of fighting and devastation on land and sea came to an end last week, November 11, 1918. Combat and hostilities have finally ceased. The British, Japanese and Americans, allies in the war, are celebrating the end of the tragic four-year war with a parade through downtown Yokohama. This year our family and others in the French community will honor our French countrymen and women, showing our love of France and our disdain for the WWI German soldiers, officers, and their last Emperor and King of Prussia, Kaiser Wilhelm II.

I hear the grumble of overworked engines. I look behind me and see automobiles overloaded with reveling parade enthusiasts — some people sitting inside, while others crowd together on the running boards. Everyone is excited to get in line for the parade. A man directs them to a narrow street waving a yellow flag trying to keep order. Other automobiles decorated for the parade drive by. We only have an hour until the parade starts, and I must continue on my way so my family can be prepared on time.

My first stop is the tailor shop, to pick up my sons. I left them with the tailor who is helping with finishing touches on the Kaiser. As I enter, Louis looks up.

"Papa. How does he look?" Louis steps back and admires a full-sized replica of the Kaiser, whose clothes are still on the table. Our tailor is a magician, turning cloth into a criminal. I wonder to myself what it will look like to have the stuffed Kaiser riding in my motorcar!

Leaning on a cluttered cutting table, twelve-year-old Georges is captivated by the process of making this figure look so real. "Papa! Tera-san made the face out of cotton and stuffed the inside with rice straw. He made the head and filled in the nose and chin with silk and cotton scraps. And he let us help, look! We got to sew on the eyebrows with black silk yarn, and there was even enough for a moustache." He places a black yarn remnant over his own lips. His brother grabs it and does the same. "The eyes and mouth look so real. I think we will fool everyone in the parade!"

My son, Louis, sits down on an ottoman, and makes last minute adjustments to the Kaiser on the tailor's table. He adds, "Tera-san sewed the head over one of his old mannequins. Then he gave us the special uniform to dress him in."

"Papa! Listen to this," George adds. "First, I told Louis to hold onto the body, but it was too heavy." He is holding back laughter. "The Kaiser's head fell off right in front of us." The three of us laugh. The tailor looks at the clock and doesn't smile. Today is a busy day for him with others waiting to pick up their costumes — we are running out of time. The tailor gives us some twine and rope, helping with suggestions, knots, and needles. The four of us finally get the cotton emperor's head and body back together. Now it is time to dress him.

Louis puts pants on the Kaiser, and I get his jacket and boots. The boys and I manage to finish dressing the former King of Prussia. He looks quite natural in his field grey jacket with brass buttons and a matching belt buckle. The feet are tight, but we manage to squeeze his stuffed legs into his boots.

"Have you seen the royal helmet?" asks Georges.

I reply to my son, lifting it off a shelf. "Yes. It's called a *Pickelhaube* helmet. Look at that," I say, pointing to the Coat of Arms on the helmet. The finishing touch is the officer's cape.

"*Voila!* There he is. *Le Diable Prussien.*"

Tera-san tells us, "I sewed rope around his neck and made sure it is strong. He's finished. *Arigatou gozaimasu.* Thank you, Monsieur Suzor. I am happy to see Kaiser Wilhem leave my shop."

"*Duomo Arigatou.* Thank you for your exceptional work, Tera-san. I hope we will see you at the parade this afternoon," I say with a bow. My sons follow suit.

The boys carry the Kaiser out to the car, barely able to stop laughing. I hope the police don't see us and think we have committed a crime.

With the Kaiser settled in the back seat, I get in the driver's seat. The boys squeeze into the front seat with me as no one wants to sit next to the criminal. I drive to Isezaki Street, careful on the turns not to let the Kaiser fall over. His helmet is quite heavy and pointed. I don't want him to put a hole in the pearl grey upholstery. Luckily, Louis tied him with a rope to the door handle.

Finally, we arrive at a side street at the beginning of the parade route where we have agreed to meet the rest of the family. I park my car and the boys jump down, open the back door, and they drag the Kaiser out and lean him against a truck I borrowed from my shop, careful so his head doesn't roll to the side with the weight of the helmet. Paule and Edith have met us here and are ready with flower chains to drape on the truck. My workers help them attach strings of white and yellow chrysanthemums from the roof to the floorboards. Even the tires are decorated with crepe paper. I put the French flag in the front of the car because, of course, we are French.

Henriette comes around the front of the automobile and asks, "Where did you get the sign on top of the car?"

"I made it myself. It says, 'Never Forget and Never Forgive!' We lost part of our country, Alsace and Lorraine, for forty-seven years to the Germans after the Franco-Prussian War. In this war, three years ago, the Germans used chlorine gas on allied soldiers and two French divisions in Ypres, Belgium. We got the land back, but not all the townspeople or soldiers. Thousands died throughout France. All in the name of competition for empires and another country's resources."

"Louis, yes, I understand how you feel. But today is a parade. Try to have fun! Take off that sign. Oh, here comes Edith, carrying your costume for the parade," Henriette says, trying to calm me down.

"I'm sorry, but the sign should stay on the truck. Look around. We are not the only ones who will never forget. Did you see the British truck with what looks like a Zeppelin in a trailer behind them surrounded by white crosses to honor those killed by bombs dropped by that aircraft?" I ask. But looking down the street I see many people who are just carrying flags and seem to be having fun. Well, maybe we are both right.

I see Edith coming around the truck with a cotton sack from the tailor.

"Here you are, Papa! You are now Sultan Suzor, our Ottoman Khan and ruler. As you can see, Mama, Paule, and I are wearing costumes from Alsace and Lorraine to celebrate getting the region back from the Germans." She pulls robes for me out of the sack and helps me button them on. I put on the belt with my saber attached, and with Edith's help, position my sultan's turban and fez cap. I am ready!

I turn to a young family friend who is approaching. Monsieur Aubree will join us in the parade. "Monsieur! You look like I did when I was a Zouave in Africa!"

"Monsieur Suzor. If there is another war I will enlist and become a Zouave like you," he answers.

"And Georges, Tera-san made your matching costume. He did a perfect job. And I see you are wearing the medals I earned in Algeria, too. I am quite proud of those, you know. Don't lose them!"

"I *won't,* Papa," Georges says with a slight look of exasperation.

I turn to Louis, who is sixteen and has changed into a French military uniform. He looks handsome in his *shako,* a heavy yet attractive hat used for parades. He looks so tall and reminds me of myself at that age.

I look at my grown children with amazement and my thoughts turn to next year. I know in my heart that it is time to return home to France. The war is over, and we were so lucky to be in Japan and not suffer like so many others did at home during the war. And it is time to see Andree again, too.

The children are growing up and getting ready to experience the world in their own way. Henriette and the children have let me follow my ambitions as I did my best to make a good life for all of us, far from our homeland.

My reflections are interrupted as my son, Louis, calls for help with the Kaiser. Before I can get there, though, he has handed the rope to Georges who stands on the top of the motorcar. He threads the rope through the metal hook on the wooden pole erected on the back of the truck. Louis grabs the rope and attaches it to the cotton Kaiser.

"It looks like you didn't need any help," I say. "You are all grown up and work well together." The boys grin at each other.

"You are just too slow, Papa," George gests.

"*Allez-y.* Let's get going," I say, dodging the taunt.

Georges says, "We must wait for the boy scouts from Saint Joseph's. My school is leading the parade with an honor guard through Yokohama." And just as he says this, his boy scout troupe turns the corner, marching. "Look! There they are! Start the car, Papa."

We wait for the scouts to pass us and prepare to follow them. As the engine idles, I find myself once again thinking about my family and our lives in Japan. I have learned in Japan that there are beginnings and endings sometimes at the same time.

# Chapter Nineteen

RMS Empress of Japan. The figurehead on the bow has been restored
and is in Vancouver's Maritime Museum.
A colorful fiberglass replica of the figurehead is in Stanley Park
in Vancouver, BC. Canada.

# Chapter Nineteen
## The Patio
## Nice, France, 1955

Morning sun and azure blue skies are a good reason to have toast and café outside on the patio. Fujiko finds a sun baked cushion next to my chair and curls up for a morning nap. Henriette has gone out front to get the mail as I find that even shorter walks are difficult, even with my cane.

I take the lid off the ceramic jam jar and scoop a spoonful of black currant preserves onto my buttered baguette slices. Accompanied with strong coffee and rich cream, this is the perfect way to start a day.

Henriette returns with a bundle of letters, places them on the table and sits down beside me. I pass her the jam and butter before I sort through the mail and pull out a letter from my daughter, Paule. I have been waiting to hear from her.

A silver letter opener helps me get to the paper, and I scan the letter, looking to see if she has agreed to help me with my writing.

"Louis, what does she say?" Henriette knows it has become more difficult for me to write my stories.

I sigh. "She says that talking or writing about those memories is like reopening a healed wound. Oh Henriette," I say putting the letter down. "Paule needs to write about the disaster and the following devastation. I know a lot about it, but I wasn't there. And I can't remember specific details from when I returned to Yokohama because I was in such shock. I want her to recreate that day before she gets older, like me, and starts to forget things."

"Well, you are right. She is the one with the story. But if she doesn't talk about it—"

"I understand that, but I know some day her children will be grateful to see it in writing.

It was a part of Japan's history and her own family's story."

Henriette nods, sympathizing. "Oh, look, Louis! Here is a letter from Nickie. I wish she hadn't moved to America. That's too far away for a grandmother's heart. Now I know how our family felt when we moved overseas."

"I'll read her letter next, after I look over the newspaper," I say, sipping my coffee. I pick up the paper and turn to the first page. "Look, Henriette, at this sailing ship in the news. Two men have started a shipping company, and this is their first ship, an Icelandic fishing schooner with three masts. It's called *La Douce France*. It sails cargo between Marseille, Algeria, and Tunisia! And they just bought their second boat, the *Côte des Légendes*."

"Louis, I know that tone in your voice," Henriette says with a smile. "Why don't you call them and see if they need a new business partner? You could finally have a shipping company," she says, laughing and putting down her section of the paper.

"You know I wanted that more than anything when I was younger, but that Siberian fur trader put an end to my shipping company before it got started. I think I still have the interest but not the strength. No, the business world has changed so much. I'd be too far behind now. And my mind is getting tired. No, *Cherie*. I won't be calling them."

We hear a familiar rumbling sound overhead and both look up at a silver metal eagle carrying its human cargo swiftly to the east.

"When we were in Japan, if someone told me a plane could carry 100 passengers from Paris to Delhi in 24 hours, with a stop in Saigon and Hong Kong, I would think the person was crazy. Remember when we came by ship to France in 1919? The world has gone from rickshaws to horse carts, to automobiles, trains, and now planes," I say to my lovely wife, as we hear another plane from a different direction thunder to the west.

## Homeward Bound
## On the *HMS Empress of Japan*, North Pacific Ocean, 1919

The ship tells us with a reverberating roar that she is getting ready to leave the inner harbor. My mother stands at the safety rail waving down at the dock to the members of the Union Church who have come to see us off. We are returning to France by way of the United States. My mother's friends from the Factory Girls Aid Society fight back tears as they wave, knowing they will probably not meet again. Mother is 76 years old and travel is becoming more difficult for her.

Friends look up from the dock and families look down from the ship, caught up in the excitement of adventures to come and the sadness of departure. We are riding a smaller ship to get out of the shallow Yokohama harbor to the *Empress of Japan*. She is patiently awaiting our arrival and will take us to Vancouver, Canada. From there the SS Princess Adelaide will take over, bringing us to San Francisco.

As we approach the white *Empress* ship, I can hear her rhythmic heartbeat and feel the strong vibration of her metal body. Holding onto the white steel rails, I am filled with exhilaration. And a little uneasiness. I am responsible for my grown children, my wife, and mother on this trip, so I must appear confident and optimistic in order to keep their nerves calmed. Fortunately, Henriette's mother is already in Paris. It is a long trip and we are at the mercy of the winds and waves. I take a moment before we reach the outer harbor to silently ask both God and Poseidon—the god of the ocean—for calm seas and a safe crossing. I've found it's best to have a good understanding established with both.

Aboard the *Empress of Japan*, I remain by myself, resting my arms on the metal rails. The smell of smoke and fishing boats lingers behind us in the harbor. For a moment I worry about work. My biggest upcoming challenge will be to continue running my businesses in Japan while living primarily in France. Hopefully the ships will travel faster, and I am confident I can find someone trustworthy to take care of my affairs in Japan while I am in France. I have several people in mind.

But the fresh air and blue water clear my thoughts, and I am looking forward to the time to sit with my family without business interruptions. My children are older now and will soon be leaving home to start their own families—this time is precious to me. Edith is already 21.

Henriette has taken my mother and the girls to get settled in our floating hotel. The boys have gone off to find their room, and then to explore the ship.

A familiar ship's steward, Mr. Holmes, approaches me on the upper deck. "Monsieur Suzor! What a pleasure to see you riding with us again. Is this a business trip?"

"Hello, Mr. Holmes, good to see you too. No, my family is ready to return to France. We are taking a vacation across the United States, most of it on the Santa Fe Railroad. We will go by train to New York, then by ship from there back to France."

"Mr. Suzor, you are always one for an adventure," he says with a chuckle.

"Indeed, Mr. Holmes. We are eager to see the States. My children all want to have a real Coca-Cola drink in California, not just the syrup like we have in Japan. We shall see how it goes," I tell him, leaning against the ship rail.

"What can I do to make your trip more enjoyable?" Mr. Holmes asks, lifting his cap and tucking his hair under the brim.

"Everything is fine. However, I am curious about the soldiers. How many people are on the boat?"

Mr. Holmes opens a notebook, turns several pages, and answers, "Yes, here they are. There are 110 adults, 28 children under fourteen, and an additional 445 soldiers. All total, 583 souls on board." He closes the portfolio. "Some exciting additional information, I don't know if you heard, Mr. Suzor, but the *Empress* has set a new speed record! She can glide through the waters at seventeen knots. We will be sailing for about three weeks, maybe a few days less, assuming winds, waves, and currents remain in our favor."

"Yes, I heard that. A shorter sail is always welcome. Thank you so much for your time, Mr. Holmes. I know you have a lot to do, and I must look after the family."

We finish our pleasantries, and I walk up the stairs on the starboard side of the ship, turn left, into a narrow hallway and take a shortcut through the smokers' lounge. Warm colors from the stained-glass windows cast orange sunbeams on the dark furniture. White and gold paneling with oak trim add to the Victorian décor. Leather seats and plush draperies enhance the feeling of luxury on the liner. Men gather around tables, socializing and drinking, and some even begin games of cards.

I leave the lounge, descend a short flight of stairs on the port side, and find our cabins in the wood lined hallways. As I approach, I hear chatter coming from one of our rooms. The door is open and Henriette, my mother, and our children are discussing possible room assignments. When I come in, Henriette hands me the room reservation cards. I look at the choices and decide for all of us.

"Henriette and I will take the room with the deck seats next door. Paule and Edith will share this room with *Grand-mère*, and the boys can have the next room. I believe it's just like this one," I add when Louis starts to protest.

"I like this cabin," says Edith, sitting on the three different mattresses, checking which is the most comfortable. "The brass beds and the oriental carpet are pretty. And look at the red and yellow cashmere bed throws! *Grand-mère*, you can have the bed closest to the doorway and away from the window. I know you don't like looking at the waves."

"That will be perfect," says my mother. She walks over to the plush velvet green armchair and sits down in it. "This chair will be mine for the trip. I take several naps a day, so this set up will be perfect."

As she speaks, Paule crosses to the portside window and stands on her tiptoes. "I like that we overlook the promenade deck," she says with a grin. "It's much easier to collect shipside gossip from an open porthole! We can guess which couples are married and which are not. Some may very well be married — but not to each other!"

"Paule!" exclaims *Grand-mère*.

"I'm only joking, *Grand-mère*," she says, though I suspect she's actually not.

"Mama, can we share your sun veranda?" asks Edith.

"What is this bar for, Papa?" asks Georges, overlapping.

"That is a safety bar. In case we hit an iceberg," I say, grateful to steer away from the girls' conversations. When Georges' eyes widen, I can't help but laugh. "But that's not going to happen."

"Louis," my mother says from her chair. "Please help me remember to get an extra package of souvenir postcards for Andrée. And don't forget to get a copy of the bath schedule for all of us."

"I will do my best, certainly," I say.

Henriette walks over to adjusts a large floral oil painting on the wall, reattaching it to a hook that is meant to steady it when the ocean waves have other ideas. "I should have had these hooks in Japan all these years. Straightening the pictures in our home was a nonstop nuisance," she said.

"Remember how the china plates fell off the wall, Mama, during the last earthquakes?" asked Edith.

"Yes," Henriette says with a sigh. "I will look forward to hanging the rest in our new home in France. I've missed them since I decided to take the rest down."

I look around the room and see that my mother is almost asleep. Preparing for this trip has been be tiring for her. "Why don't you girls let *Grand-mère* rest, and you two go out on the deck and see if you have any friends travelling on the ship. If not, I'm sure you will have plenty of time to

179

make some new ones. Boys, let your mother settle you in to your room next door." The boys nod; they have been waiting patiently. "I will go get each of you a blank ship's chart from the purser for recording our progress on the voyage."

"Mama, could we please have the ship's print shop make us some introduction cards to share on the boat?" asks Edith before Henriette can leave.

"No, Edith," Henriette says in a hushed voice. "You can use a pen and make your own. You are very artistic, and people would love to see your drawings. It'll give you something to do when you are bored." She turns to shepherd the boys to their room.

"Paule will probably be getting married to Maurice soon, anyways," says *Grand-mère* through closed eyes, "so she doesn't need any introducing." The girls shake their heads at each other and roll their eyes before leaving to roam the decks.

I go to my room for a moment of quiet, and I take off my suit jacket while I wait, hanging it in the armoire before sitting in one of the velvet chairs. When Henriette arrives, she removes her feather hat and sits down in the other chair beside me.

"They are all settled in," she says with an exhale. "I think we've made it on board in one piece, Louis. A minor miracle." Henriette and I rarely have a moment to talk in private. I reach out and take her hand.

"Henriette. I feel strange leaving my business behind. I'm glad the managers are running the business for now until I return, and they have always done a good job when I have been back in France on shorter trips. But I don't know who to put in charge of my affairs when we are living in France. It is different now. When I return, I'm thinking of perhaps leaving it in the hands of the Jesuit priest, Pere Machar."

"The priest, Louis?"

"Well, why not? He is a priest, no? He will have to answer to someone higher than me if he does something dishonest or deceitful."

"I don't know, Louis. Something feels off about that. Why do you have to decide so soon? Can't you figure this out when you return in several months?"

"I'd like to have a choice made by the time we get off the boat in San Francisco, so I can send a letter back with my decision."

"Louis, when you make hurried decisions, you are like a dragon that acts on impulse and leaves a trail of damage behind. And the costs. We are getting older and can't afford to lose your business in Japan. I think we need to know more about the priest. Can you send a letter for more information instead?"

Our conversation is interrupted by the dinner bell. "Well," Henriette continues. "We have several weeks to discuss this. You said you had some other people in mind. Let's take our time with this," she suggests.

I nod and pat her hand before rising to put on a fresh shirt and suit for dinner. Dressed, I leave our room and go next door to fetch my mother. When I get there, she is ready, dressed in a pastel pink cotton dress and a white lace shawl from France.

"The girls are next door making sure the boys get ready," she says. "They will meet us downstairs." I nod and offer her my arm, and she curls her hand around it. "I am ready to go home, Louis," she says, and I give her a brief hug.

"I think we all are," I say in a moment of candor.

We go back to my room to meet Henriette. My beautiful wife wears a dark blue tailored gown with white gloves and a blue silk paisley shawl. I escort both ladies into the hallway, up the stairs, past the lounge, and down another hallway that eventually opens onto the grand staircase. Since we have paid for first class tickets, we get to descend the grand staircase. I hold onto my mother's arm and she holds the railing, and I escort her down first. Once at the bottom, a purser shows me the seating chart and guides my mother to our table while I return up the stairs to escort Henriette down.

"I feel like a queen," Henriette whispers in my ear.

"You are one, my darling," I say back, smiling.

We make our way to the table, for which I paid the porter, earlier, a small bribe to make sure we secured a spot away from the windows. The rolling view of the sea makes my mother uncomfortable.

We sit, and as I settle in, I look around the room. I see Brits, Germans, and Americans, Japanese, Chinese, East Indians, and Australians. The couple from Bombay particularly catch my eye. As opposed to the Europeans, they are dressed in the most vibrantly exquisite colors. The gentleman wears blue and green silk with golden embroidery, and the woman wears a red and yellow sari. All together we bring an elaborate rainbow of colors, fashion, and language into the dining room.

I hear my girls and their brothers and look to the top of the stairs. I watch them walk down the Victorian staircase, quickening their pace to reach our table.

"Papa, do you know how many people there are on the boat?" Georges asks, his curious 13-year-old mind already at play.

"About 700, all together. I heard most of the 450 in steerage are soldiers from England and Australia, on their way home."

"That's a lot of soldiers!" says little Louis, who is not so little anymore. He has expressed interest in joining the military one day. "Some Middlesex Army Regiments are on board, Papa. They will be setting up a boxing ring on the upper deck tomorrow for all of us to watch! Several regiments will be competing. They call themselves The Die Hards. It should be great. Can you come to the boxing match with us, Papa?"

Before I can answer, Edith adds, "Paule and I met a few soldiers from Australia. They are on their way from Vladivstok to Vancouver and are very interested in the match tomorrow. One named Harry Russell asked if I wanted to watch." I see her cheeks blush. "But I told him that I preferred to go to the concert in the grand salon."

"We have three weeks on the ship. I'm sure you'll be able to see him another time if you want," teases Paule.

I see a waiter taking orders from the table next to ours and I tell my family to look at the fans on the table. Everyone is delighted to see a French menu printed on the inside of the beautiful Japanese silk fans with two orange and white *koi* carp swimming in the background.

The first course offered is *aspic de foie gras* and *caviar frais de Russe Volga*. Filet of *Sole a la Normande*, asparagus *a la Nicoise* and salad *Orientale* finishes the meal. For dessert, we have ice cream, fruit, salted almonds, and coffee or tea. After we finish our feast, Edith and Paule keep their menus as souvenirs, put them in their purses, and take another one from an empty place setting as a gift for Andrée.

After dinner we return to our cabins. The day has been long, and we are ready for the *Empress* to gently rock us to sleep.


Two weeks go by quickly on the boat. Our family settles into a daily routine. We eat wonderful meals, visit, and play games. I enjoy the extended time with all of them, and our voyage across the ocean feels like a vacation. In Yokohama I rarely had this much time with my children. Henriette and I watch the girls make new friends with people they will likely never see again, but probably will keep in touch by postcards for a while. The boys visit with the soldiers, watch boxing matches, and play shuffleboard and deck tennis. Even my mother makes some friends, chatting with French and British women from a charity group in Yokohama over tea in the upstairs salon.

Henriette and I have reserved deck chairs for today at three o'clock. Comfortably seated in a quiet alcove, the ocean breezes blow a cool hint of fall across the sun deck. Henriette has her cashmere throw draped across her knees, ready when she needs it to keep warm.

"So, Louis. What have you decided about building your new investment houses? Will you let go of the automobile business?" asks Henriette, curious. She has seen me through so many business ventures.

"Well. There are many automobiles available in Japan now. Kaishinsha Motorcar Works is having success in Japan, and some Japanese companies are partnering with European brands, making it easier for them to license and sell the cars. I'll keep the garage and the Michelin Tire business, but I have decided not to import cars anymore. This will simplify things for us."

She nods. "Less paperwork for you, and more time with you for me," she says, smiling.

"As far as building homes," I say, smiling back, "I already leased six lots for building. I have ordered the wood and bricks and left detailed instructions with the builders before we left. It's an expensive project, but a safe gamble this time. Many Europeans want to live on the Bluff, so I will build six houses in the Western style to sell or rent to the growing International community."

"Six!?" Henriette exclaims.

"Yes, six! They are popular now, and the rent we get from them will be our money to save for when we get older and no longer want to work. We can't go wrong. I've decided to use lots of bricks to lower the incidences of fire, as we know too well that a wooden home in Yokohama is dangerous."

Henriette covers her legs with the blanket. "Louis, that is a lot of money. This sounds risky to me."

"Oh Henriette, I've become more careful over time, as you know, and keep to safer, more traditional projects and investments. And I have spent many weeks coming to this solution, *ma chérie*, and I know it is the best. What could happen to six houses?" She is too cautious sometimes.

"So, you will not own the land, but you will own the houses?" Henriette asks.

"Yes, *Chérie*. Remember?" I say, helping her pull her shawl around her shoulders against the cold. "In Japan, we cannot own the land. I purchased a one-hundred-year lease on the land. I don't think we will live longer than a hundred more years and the rent will help pay for our home in France."

"Louis, you always think so big. Maybe you are right. I seem to worry more as I get older," she says, shaking her head. "Ah. Here comes Paule!"

Paule approaches our chairs, dressed in a stylish nautical navy-blue hat and middy blouse with a pleated white skirt. She looks serious as she places a teakwood deck chair next to ours and sits.

"Paule, why are you not with Edith? Are you all right?" Henriette asks.

"Edith is visiting with our new friends on the deck. I thought it would be a good time to talk in private with you. I've been feeling quite anxious and nervous, and I haven't been able to sleep for several nights. It's Maurice. He is probably already in Paris since he left four weeks ago on business for the silk company." I bring my attention more into focus as she says this—I have not noticed that she has been lacking sleep. "I want everything to go well in Paris when we meet Maurice's family."

"I'm sure it will go well, *Cherie*," I say.

"Tell me what you think about him, Papa?" begs Paule, and I realize that she is feeling uncertain, not unusual for a 19-year-old looking at marriage.

I try to assure her. "I like Maurice and I know he is a good businessman and he has a good character. When the war started in France in 1914, he volunteered right away in the army. I remember him telling me that he drove the first tank of the French army into war—that is certainly a reflection of his strength and integrity."

"Did he also tell you that he was decorated with the Legion of Honor and the *Croix de Guerre avec Palme*, an honor given for heroic combat with the enemy? His friends told me this, too. They say he was a war hero. But Maurice doesn't talk much about the war, and he always remains quiet about the fighting. He says it is painful to talk about it."

"Paule, don't worry about this," says Henriette. "I think it is just his nature."

"I heard that at the end of the war he was offered a position as a silk buyer by Jardines Mathesons in Yokohama. It's a very reputable firm," I add. "I have been in written contact with his family, and I can assure you things will be fine. Be patient, my dear, and go find your sister for dinner. We should hear the bell soon."

Paule walks away slowly. "She clearly misses Maurice," Henriette says, watching her with that keen look mothers have.

"I hope she sleeps well tonight." The dinner gong sounds. As I stand, I can see over the railing.

"Look, Henriette!"

She rises, and we watch several dolphins riding on the wake from water being pushed by the ship.

"I'm ready to be on solid ground again," Henriette says. "This has been a long trip. I am looking forward to our vacation in America, but I will be especially happy to be in Paris. I'm so happy you rented the townhouse on Rue Dumont d'Urville. Such a luxurious residence. And Andrée will finally be with us once again. She is already 18, a year older than I when I married you!"

"Do you remember after I finished my military service and proposed to you for the second time?" I ask her. While we watch the dolphins, we reminisce over life together. I scan the skies for sea birds, announcing we are getting close to land.

She takes my arm, and we walk towards the dining room. Our table is already a hub of noisy chatter. The girls and boys have a copy of the miniature newspaper made by the ship's printer. There are articles by passengers, gossip, rumors, and scandals. I ask them to put the papers away until after we eat. Henriette and my mother enjoy the exuberance, but I am feeling tired and would like a quieter meal this evening.

"Edith," Henriette says, "I understand your cousin Gems has offered to help you meet new friends and get acquainted with the city and all the changes that have taken place in Paris in the past 20 years."

"Yes, it is very generous of him," my daughter says.

"Papa, will we live in the city or in the country?" asks Louis.

"After a year or so in Paris, we are going to buy a new house in the countryside, a chateau big enough for all of us and your future families. I think we need a chateau with two kitchens and ten bedrooms rooms, dining halls, and sitting rooms — some with fireplaces, some without. I want a barn and some farm animals with fields of wheat and apple trees."

"Such lofty dreams. A chateau! After living in busy and smoky Yokohama, I'm ready to live in a quiet place far from a town and noise," says Henriette.

The conversation continues, but I take a moment to look through the window to the horizon and imagine this idyllic life in a chateau with Henriette beside me, cows in the pasture and someone to take care of them. I want more time for leisure projects and less business work; invest my time into carving wood and painting. I imagine sitting outside at the end of the day with my family and a glass of brandy and breathing the fresh country air.

Could it really happen? *Bien sûr!* But, of course.

# Chapter Twenty

Namazu the Earth Shaker.
Unknown artist. 1855 woodblock print shows Namazu,
the catfish in Japanese mythology.
In the chaos that is left, wealth is redistributed.
*Ancient History Encyclopedia*

# Chapter Twenty
## Nice, France, 1955
### — Paule Speaks —

The southern coast of France has been hit with terrible southerly winds. This is not unusual for autumn, but it means we must stay inside with my son, Jacques, and his wife and their three young children, Guillaume, Blandine, and Frederic. My husband, Maurice, was not able to come because he is in Japan on a business trip.

We are visiting my parents at their home in Nice. Jacques and his wife were expecting to spend time on the beach with the little children, but the weather has had different plans.

Instead, we gather in the drawing room watching the children try to build a castle with wooden blocks. Blandine brings a block to her grandfather and grandmother who are sitting together on the velvet sofa. I smile to see her playing and getting to know her great-grandparents.

"Paule. Did you bring the story for me?" asks my father as he hands a wooden block back to my daughter.

"Yes, of course, Papa. If the typewriter is out, I will type it for you tonight after the children are in bed," I reply. My father asked me to help him with a chapter for his memoirs. He wanted me to write the story because I was in Japan at the time of the great event. Jacques was with me when it happened, but he was only two — too young to remember.

As we talk, Frederic brings his older brother, Guillaume — who is six years old — a book and sits down next to him on the red and gold oriental carpet. Blandine joins them, and Guillaume shows his younger siblings the cover of the book. "It's about an old fisherman and a golden fish with special powers." I smile as I see in their eyes how much they love their big brother. Guillaume is still learning to read, but he has this story memorized, so he can recite the story to the younger children while acting like he is reading.

A clap of thunder gets everyone's attention. The children look to the adults for assurance that the walls of the house are not caving in.

Sitting in an armchair, Jacques closes his newspaper and says to his son, "Don't worry. It is just angels making their beds. The storm will pass soon." But the littles get distracted and wander off. Guillaume looks disheartened.

"Come here, Guillaume," says his great-grandmother, Henriette. "Finish the story with me." He goes over to her and scrambles up onto the couch between his great-grandparents.

"Ok, little ones, it's bedtime," Jacques says. "Mama, will you bring Guillaume upstairs when he is finished reading to you?"

"Yes, of course," says my mother.

"Tell us a story?" little Blandine asks her father.

"Alright," answers Jacques. "While I put you to bed, I will tell you Guillaume's story of the fisherman who was lucky and the golden fish was kind — unlike the giant catfish Namazu," Jacques says, looking back at me.

"Do you remember that day? Or do you remember what I have told you about it?" I ask him.

"I remember both. And the sound of thunder shaking the house still makes me shudder to this day." He scoops up his children and carries them upstairs.

I leave my parents to take care of Guillaume, while I make my way into my father's study to write.

*Namazu, the Earth Shaker*
**Yokohama, Japan, September 1, 1923**
**Paule Speaks --**

My father, Louis, and the rest of the family returned to Paris four years ago. After my mother and father met Maurice's parents, they gave us their blessing to get married. In 1920 we had a lovely ceremony in a beautiful old church in Paris followed by an elaborate party for family and friends.

We quickly returned to Yokohama for Maurice's business. We have lived here now for three years and have a lovely home with a garden for our two-year-old son, Jacques, and his baby sister, Malou. The offices of Jardine Matheson and Co. where Maurice is a silk buyer are not far away, and he usually comes home for a few hours for lunch each day. I like living in Japan; however, I will never get used to the unpredictable shakes underground.

*Tremblements de terre.* Earthquakes. Japan is a land of nearly one hundred volcanos that tremble at will. Just this morning, amah Shigne-san told little Jacques that the earth shakes when Namazu, a giant catfish twists and shakes his tail under the island. I watch my son run around the dining room table, pretending to be that catfish.

Amah teases and says, "*So.* I am god Kashima. I will hold you, so you will not run away and make trouble. I will put cushion on you, so you cannot move!" Jacques laughs and runs faster around the table, delighted when he is caught by his amah.

"Let's move the games outside, please," I say. "The table is set for lunch and I don't want it getting messed up before Maurice comes home." I can't help but smile, though as I watch them play. I remember hearing funny traditional Japanese folktales from Papa when I was little. He showed me pictures of Kashima holding the huge catfish under a gigantic stone; Kashima had to control Namazu all the time or he would get away. Papa told me the story that in 1855 Kashima was distracted one day, maybe even went away for a while, and Namazu escaped, causing the horrible Edo earthquake. Edo is the old name for Tokyo, so the quake was very close to Yokohama. Kashima must get distracted easily since there are smaller earthquakes almost every week in Japan.

I hear Malou crying in our bedroom. "I will go change her and bring her down," says Amah. "And I'll meet you—" she points at Jacques, "in the front garden!" He squeals with delight.

I hear a breeze nudge a window shut. While she goes upstairs, I go to Jacques' bedroom and take his brown corduroy jacket off a hook on the wall. He comes to me and I help him put his arms in the sleeves and button up the front.

It is a Saturday morning. Jacques toddles over to the Michelin tire swing hanging from an elm tree in the garden near the road. My father put it together the last time he was in Japan. It is sunny, but a chilly fall wind is sweeping up the bluff from the harbor. While my boy is swinging, I take a postcard out of my pocket and re-read the message from my parents in France. Papa says he will be coming back to Japan soon for his business. I miss him, but I am happy here with my handsome husband, Maurice, and our two children.

I put the postcard back in my pocket. Jacques sits happily on the swing, teasing his little dog by swinging his legs just out of the dog's reach. I take the moment to walk to a planter at the end of the garden row to pick off some dead flowers. Jacques calls, "Mama? I'm hungry!"

Sambe, our little terrier, begins running away from Jacques and around the yard, barking, seemingly for no reason. "Sambe, quiet down!" I call out to him, thinking he is barking at the neighbor's gardener. The homes are close, so I don't want the dog to disturb the neighbors.

Jacques waves his arms, wanting to get out of his swing and play with the dog. Sambe continues to bark and run back and forth across the garden.

Without warning, the earth starts to shake. I feel momentarily dizzy and shift my footing as I try to comprehend what is happening. The first quake seems to last forever. My instincts send me running to my son. Just as I take a step, another violent spasm shakes the ground beneath me, and I fall. I get up, take another step and get thrown off balance once again by the jarring earth around me. The intense cycles keep coming. Finally, I make it across the yard to the elm tree. Jacques is screaming as he clutches the tire swing with all his might. I quickly lift him out and hold him close, taking a second to breathe. The heaving and buckling jolts continue and I hear a crash behind me. I turn towards our house.

In the few seconds it took to gather Jacques, our house transformed into a mountain of rubble. Beams protrude from what used to be walls. Heavy dust permeates the air and I begin to cough. I hear more crashes around me, and I look down the main street to see the other houses, built so closely together, drop into devastation.

I force my head to clear and fight the panic that threatens to overtake me—my baby, Malou! Shigne-san! Where are they? Carrying Jacques, I run to the demolished house but am overcome with anguish. I hold Jacques closer to try to calm myself. He wiggles and I put him down and hold his hand tightly. I look around me and see neighbors' faces sharing our common terror and dread. I must do something. But what? I bend over and place both hands under a beam to lift it, but the effort proves futile. The beams are too heavy to move by myself. Fighting for self-control and holding back tears, I beg a sympathetic Japanese man for help, explaining how my infant is in the rubble. I have spoken with him before when he was tending our neighbor's garden.

He calls to a few others, and the group goes to work, cautiously trying to remove the treacherous rafters and timbers one plank at a time. I take Jacques' hand again, walk him over to the elm tree, and lean against it for support. I watch the men work and feel helpless. Sambe sits with us and leans against Jacques. I hold onto his collar, so he won't run away in the confusion. The oppressive land tremors continue as the men brave the risky work. Each beam removed fills me with hope, and then terror when Malou is not seen.

For a while I try to hold both Jacques and Sambe, but the dog pulls out of his collar and escapes. He runs, jumping over beams and directly into the rubble, stops, and starts barking. I pray to God he has found them. The neighbors follow his lead, and work with renewed energy at an almost reckless pace. Time is passing and Malou and her amah are in immediate danger.

A British neighbor approaches me and offers to watch Jacques. I nod and move towards the rubble. I hear other people crying as they try to grasp what has happened. Some families are huddled together and watch in shock at the broken homes and lives in front of them. The wind from the harbor brings the smell of smoke to our street.

The Japanese gardener calls to me and signals with his arms they have found Shigne-san and my baby. Hope pushes me as I run desperately into the dusty wreckage tearing my stockings and scraping my skin with splintered debris. I carefully walk over several timbers and see a wooden beam from the collapsed roof on top of our amah, who is face down on her hands and knees above the bassinette. Three men working together remove the offending beam and add it to the rubble. The kind gardener reaches under Shigne-san and gently pulls out and cradles a screaming Malou, and then brings her to me. I unwrap Malou's blanket and inspect her arms and legs. She appears untouched by the disaster. I don't have time to cry with relief. Instead, I rewrap her and hold her close to my chest with one arm, and with the other I take Amah's hand as the men lift her off the cradle. They lie her gently on the ground.

She does not respond. Fighting against what must be immense pain, she appears to have gone into in shock. Her legs are twitching, and her arms are cold and damp. And her skin looks gray. When I talk to her, she doesn't respond to my voice and she hasn't opened her eyes. I put my face next to her and look at her chest, and I can see her breathing is not regular. She takes a deep breath and then there is nothing for what seems like minutes.

I hold Malou close and feel helpless. I try to make Shigne-san comfortable, gently holding her hand and encouraging her to be strong, while suppressing my own tears. Jacques comes over to me holding my British neighbor's hand. She lets his hand go and says she needs to return to what used to be her home. I thank her and Jacques sits in my lap.

Dispirited, I stay on the ground, cradling my children in my arms, rocking back and forth like the earth itself. I hear buildings crash and people screaming and wailing as the land continues to rock. I can't do a thing to stop the trembling earth and chaos or to save our beloved Amah. Holding my children close, tears come freely. I don't even know where my husband is or if he is safe. I can feel despair taking over.

After some time, I hear Maurice calling my name. I look up as he runs up from behind me, takes Malou tenderly and holds her in in his arms for a moment. He gives her back to me and then hugs his son close. I stand up and look at him, never so grateful to see, and hold, someone. He looks at Amah, and shakes his head, not quite able to comprehend what has happened.

"Paule, we must get out of here right away. We will go towards the high bamboo forest in Hokokuji. It is the only place where the earth is stable in an earthquake. We need to hurry. The road to the forest may be damaged, and carrying the children will slow us down." When the ground is more stable, we will make our way to the harbor."

I try to tell him what has happened to Shigne-san, but I can barely get the words out through my tears. Without a word, he crouches down to our brave Shigne-san still laying on the ground. A neighbor found a blanket and covered her, but she is barely conscious.

"We can't leave her, Maurice."

"We must, we have no choice. Fires are ripping through the city. We are not safe here, Paule."

I turn to the Japanese gardener for help. He agrees that we are all in danger if we stay and we cannot take her with us. But he insists on taking over caring for Shigne-san. She cannot travel in her condition, and he thinks he knows and will be able to contact her family. He says the hospitals are likely destroyed, so she will stay here or with his family until help is available.

Maurice tells Amah how grateful we are for her sacrifice and kisses her on the cheek. Words cannot capture the gratitude we are feeling, and the cruelty of the moment that is forcing us to leave her in such a state.

"Sambe!" squeals Jacques, afraid we will leave him behind, too.

"Yes, Jacques, of course we will take Sambe," I say. I am grateful for his sake for the distraction of our dog. We have too much to worry about, so I let the dog run without a leash. I hope he will stay with us.

We turn and leave everything behind. We don't have time to cry over what we have lost. Our home, our furniture, family heirlooms, and perhaps Maurice's business. And our Amah. We need to find the strength to look ahead and keep our family safe.

After a just a few minutes of walking, we witness that the road cracked open during the quake and, to my horror, I see several bodies covered in dirt. People fell inside this giant fissure and became trapped when the earth closed over them. The arms and legs, partially covered in the cracked road, do not move. Maurice, carrying Jacques, forces me to look away and continue. I hold Malou close, as I pass by horrible situation after horrible situation. I don't know how much more misery I can take.

We make it part of the way to the bamboo forest, and as we ascend the path towards higher ground, Maurice stops for a rest and tells me what happened in the center of town.

I am grateful to catch my breath. Maurice puts Jacques on the ground so he can run around a bit, and I sit down with Malou, sleeping and comfortable, on a moss-covered mound to rest and listen to Maurice, who also sits next to us.

"We were in the silk company office and the walls started to oscillate. We are used to smaller tremors, but nothing this big. My brother Leon was thrown from one room to another, then into the hall. He got up and we both ran out of the building."

"So, where is your brother?"

Maurice starts to shake and covers his face, but his voice comes out quiet and clear. "He said he forgot his cigarette case, and before I could stop him, he rushed back into the building. Before I could do anything, the building collapsed on him and immediately caught fire, flames spreading everywhere, fueled by the winds from the bay. Paule." He shakes his head and looks away. "It was horrifying to know there was nothing I could do to save him." He is silent for a moment, before continuing in a low voice. "There was so much chaos everywhere I looked. And a hideous fire was spreading through town, chasing everyone out. I knew I had to come home and find you."

I put my free arm around him, but he stands up quickly and says, "Paule. We must outrun the fire. I will carry Jacques. And Sambe can take care of himself."

"Just for a moment longer, Maurice, can't we collect ourselves?"

"We must deal with the immediate danger. I cannot cope with my brother's death now. I can't talk about it," He is as quiet as always about pain. That is how he took care of himself during the war. "Paule, the town is being destroyed. When I was running home, I watched a five-story building collapse. A woman in her bath fell from the upper floors, landing in the wreckage below. To my astonishment, she crawled out unhurt from the tub, probably protected by the water, but nude and helpless. I gave her my jacket and kept running away."

"Maurice, I'm not ready to go. I have to feed the baby." Only this makes him pause. He calls Jacques over.

I begin feeding Malou. I hear some voices and turn around. We are faced with three angry men in prison clothes, coming towards us, speaking in Japanese, motioning for whatever we are carrying that is of value. The prisons have apparently been destroyed, and the inmates have escaped, and are taking the advantage of their new freedom.

"Here, take my watch and chain. That is all I have," says Maurice, fumbling to retrieve any silver coins he might have from underneath where Jacques is clutching him. The men grab his offering and push him and my son aside and continue running. They will become rich from the frightened people in the woods today, I am sure. Chaos breeds chaos.

We sit down, shaking, to collect our thoughts and devise a safe plan. The wind shifts, and suddenly the forest is full of smoke. We cough and gasp as we inhale the soot-filled air.

Strong southwest winds blow from the harbor and add to the destruction. From our vantage point we can hear the crackling fire below us, too, a patchwork of charred homes and red burning timbers.

Then, just as swiftly, the wind shifts again, and we can see trees and land in front of us.

"It will be dusk in several hours. We need to turn back and get to the harbor before dark." Maurice says. "Going downhill will be easier for us. The Empress of Australia Steamship is in the harbor. We can go there for help."

He picks up Jacques and places him on his strong shoulders. We move as fast as possible with two children and a dog. I finally feel some hope.

Yet, as we go across a ridge towards the city, I see for the first time the damage below us. What used to be a business district and homes is a field of glowing rubble covered with white dust. I look toward the sea and the sun going down; a smoky red ball in a sky of somber grey smoke. I am looking at the unimaginable.

As we look to the harbor, we can see lines of people, probably locals, Europeans and Americans, looking to take refuge there. From our vantage point, we can see the destruction of a tidal wave. Whole oceanside villages have been washed away.

We plod down the road and join other survivors. Sambe is the only one with any energy left. We cannot keep up the quick pace after such a long walk up to the bamboo forest, only to turn around and start back. No one speaks as we are consumed by fatigue and our own tragedies. Some children cry, but most are too weary to complain. We arrive at the harbor dock, exhausted, tired, and hungry. Jacques has been sleeping on his father's shoulders, worn out from our plight. Malou is asleep again, thank goodness.

Maurice talks to Jacques to wake him up. Our son opens his eyes and reaches for me. "Paule. Can you stay here with the children? I need to go quickly to speak with someone on a ship. This line is moving too slowly. I can make some arrangements for us."

"Yes. Hand me Jacques, and we will wait here for you." I find a log to sit on, in front of a wooden railing.

Jacques plays with his dog and another young child comes across the dock to meet Sambe. I start a conversation with his parents and find out they are British and looking to get on a ship as well. A man with a wooden barrel on a cart filled with water comes by and offers us a drink from a metal cup. Jacques and I take a long drink. The man tells me to cup my hands and pours a cup of water into my palms to give Sambe a drink. Tears of gratitude blur my eyes, and I don't know Maurice has returned until I hear his voice.

"I have good news for us," he says, picking up Jacques. "We will be on an Australian ship until the French ship, the *André Le Bon*, is ready to accept people. But we must wait in line with the others on the dock." I nod, and we return to the line to wait.

As we stand and talk, Maurice speaks to me quietly, so others cannot hear, and so Jacques will not be frightened. "Paule, I spoke with an Australian friend and heard horrible stories. This morning at eleven o'clock, crowds of people were at the docks to see their friends off," he tells me. "The earthquake hit and people on the boat watched in horror as their friends and their automobiles fell into the water. Then the fire came, rampaging down the hillside. The captain of the ship organized a fire brigade among his crew and willing passengers, and he kept the ship safe until it got to the outer harbor. Miraculously, the oil on the water and the tsunami didn't affect the ship."

I don't know how I can bear to take in anymore, and I lean my head against his shoulder, to simply rest.

We finally make it to the front of the line and are assigned a cabin in which to stay with our family. It is small, but we are safe. The food, we come to find, is basic: oatmeal or toast for breakfast, toast and soup for lunch, and rice and a small piece of fish or meat for dinner.

After several days, we move to the French liner and settle into our new cabin. We are on a lower deck and, for the first time in my life, I experience a room that is not a first-class cabin. Food is severely rationed on the boat since so many are in need. Fortunately, we have enough even for Sambe, who is a small dog with a little appetite.

Another French family has been given a cabin next to ours. They have small children as well, so Jacques has some new friends with whom to play. He doesn't understand what has happened and seems content. Malou is just a baby, so she is happy to eat and be carried. I am starting to feel anxious being in such a small room day after day and being around so many people I don't know. I invited our French neighbor, Francoise, and her children over for the afternoon, but feel embarrassed that I don't have anything to offer them. They understand, but it still bothers me. We visit for a few hours, until Jacques and his new friend, Antoine, begin to squabble over one of the few toys available, a small wooden cart with wheels and a carved horse from the children's play area upstairs. Finally, it is bedtime for them. Both of our husbands spend their time talking with other men on the ship, and the evenings are lonely.

After they leave, and we have had our early dinner of bread and cheese and a watered-down onion soup, I lie on our bed with Malou, trying to nap. Jacques is already asleep. Since coming onto the boat, he has developed into a deep sleeper, and can sleep through just about anything.

Suddenly the door flies open and Maurice barges into our cabin. He slams the door behind him. I sit up and can see in his face how his exhaustion and fatigue is bringing out the worst in him.

"Quiet, Maurice, you woke the baby," I say sharply, before he can say anything.

"I am going to speak with the French Ambassador!" he hisses. "I hear the captain has barricaded the top bridge and some of the higher-ups are having champagne and large meals!" He paces through the tiny room. "I am going to form a delegation and ask to be received by the captain. I am taking Paul Claudel with me."

"Claudel? Do you think that is a good idea? He is more dramatist than diplomat. Perhaps he will make things worse."

"I don't think things could get worse," he says, looking at me. "I must go now and find some more members for my delegation." He leaves as abruptly as he came, and I take a breath to collect myself. I rock Malou back to sleep. Hours span in front of me.

I reach behind me and pick up the Jules Verne book I found in the hallway, earlier today: *Twenty Thousand Leagues Under the Sea*. Turning to the first page, I read 'For some time past, vessels had been met by an 'enormous thing,' a long object, spindle shape, occasionally phosphorescent, and infinitely larger and more rapid in its movement than a whale.' I read in the dim light for several hours, fighting my own exhaustion, but waiting for Maurice to return.

My imagination is interrupted when I hear some voices coming down the hall. I gladly close the book. My husband comes in, having had a few glasses of wine with his delegation, the captain; the French Ambassador, and Monsieur Claudel. He looks grim, but he moves fluidly, and I know he is satisfied. He even closes the door softly so as not to wake the children. He sits in a chair across from me and removes his jacket, the same one he wore in the earthquake.

"Ah! Jules Verne? A good book to have on a ship. I remember reading it as a child."

I hand the book to Maurice and say, "Perhaps this isn't the best book for me to be reading now. Why don't you put Mr. Verne on the shelf behind you?"

He smiles, takes the book and says, "Paule, I have good news. From now on, the captain has promised he will stop this circus of pitiless behavior. He assured us that rations will be equal, including a bottle of wine now and then."

"Oh Maurice. You are courageous and fearless," I say, shaking my head. "That is a relief." Malou is asleep again, and I put her down on the bed behind me. Sambe sleeps at Jacques's feet. "Maurice, I feel so restless and distraught. I want to return to land. And I want to start our life again in Yokohama."

"You want to stay, Paule? After this?"

"We have some good friends here and it is the center for buying silk, which is good for you. I have lived here all my life, and Yokohama feels like home. I just want to get off the boat."

"In time, Paule. In time," Maurice says, putting the book on the shelf behind him. "First, we need a home. I found out a lot more about the earthquake at dinner with the captain. He said that after the first tremors, people ran from their homes, leaving their lunch time meals on the burners. Fuel for business and industrial use was left to burn out of control as well. And ruptured gas mains and the wind fed the flames."

"Oh, so that's how the fires started?"

"Yes. And people thought Tokyo's Sumida River would be a safe place and hundreds ran there, only to face a scalding death by fire, a 'dragon twist'—a fire tornado that must have been 500-meters wide, blazing across the city, joining fires in other locations."

"Oh, that's horrible. The city lost so much," I say, rising to him.

"Paule. Every day I hear something more terrifying than the day before. But I also hear stories of heroism on the land," he says as he gets ready for bed. He moves the children to the center of the bed, climbs over them, and lies down between them and the wall. He adjusts the wool blanket over them all. "We must be hopeful. This is all we have," he says and turns on his side. He is asleep in a moment.

I don't say it to him, as I don't want to open his scars, but I know Maurice still burns with grief and regret at how his brother died, and right in front of him. A terrifying moment over which he had no control. I look at my children asleep in the bed and can only imagine how his parents will take the news when they learn what happened.

Before I join Maurice, I cross the room and rest my hands on the brass framed porthole window and look through the glass. Is it tears again or fatigue that blur my vision? I blink trying to clear my eyes. Golden-green waves ripple in the water and remind me how peaceful the harbor used to be. The smoky burnt-orange sun has fallen below the horizon leaving just enough light to see something menacing on the waves. Is it a reflection of the light from another ship? Or something else? I look closer. Jules Verne's monster? Or did I just see the tail of Namazu the catfish indignantly leaving the harbor, pursued from behind by god Kashima?

# Chapter Twenty-One

Office ruins after the quake and dragon-twist fire.
*Suzor Collection*

# Chapter Twenty-One
*Aftershocks*
Yokohama, Japan, October 1923

I have read accounts from Paris newspapers and telegrams, but I need to see the devastation with my own eyes to understand what has happened in Yokohama. I also want to claim whatever remains of my business and homes. And I am most anxious to see my daughter and her family. By some miracle they were spared, sending us a letter with news about the earthquake six weeks ago.

My ship drops anchor in the deep outer bay, joining many steamers that have come to help with humanitarian aid. Even the Red Cross is here on an American ship. My daughter and her family are staying on the French steamer *Andre Le Bon* until they decide what to do next. I hope they will come to France with their children.

I think I have prepared myself for the reality of the earthquake and am hopeful that the port and city planners are working to help people with businesses and residences. I step aboard a smaller boat that brings me towards a makeshift dock in Yokohama harbor. Pools of blue and silver oil reflect off the waves on our way to shore. As I look towards the wharf, I am stunned by what I see. The destruction looks like a war zone, or worse. The smell of oil on the water and the smoke is caustic, and the acrid air hurts my lungs and leads to coughing spells. I cover my nose and mouth with a kerchief, but my eyes burn, and tears appear. How have people lived in this?

People gather at the dock with various agendas, like always. But this time they are looking for work or lost friends and family. Those who became sudden refugees are leaving for other cities in Japan, or back to their home countries. I read in the *Figaro*, our newspaper in Paris, that Kobe has been very welcoming and is set up to help and receive as many people as the city can accommodate.

I get off the boat and see a familiar face—Maurice, my son-in-law. Usually I would greet him with the traditional kiss on each cheek, but instead I hug and hold him, expressing my sorrow at the loss of his brother in the fire.

Looking around, I am almost speechless. So many questions to ask and I don't know where to start. My throat tightens, and I hold back tears.

Maurice points to where there used to be a village near the beach. "Look, Louis. A tidal wave took all the homes and left only one house—with a boat on top of it. This is just the beginning of the horrible nightmares you'll see today, and every day. We'll walk through parts of what used to be our city and discuss what the future may hold."

"Tell me what happened to you and Paule and the children? Are they doing better now?"

As we walk, he tells me their perils, their run from their house through the bamboo forests and to the harbor. I am amazed and so grateful they are alive.

"What happened to Shigne-san, your Amah? I know she was like family."

"We haven't been able to find out anything about her. We don't know if she made it to the hospital or not. Some roads are impassable, and there is very little transportation available. Even if she did make it, many hospitals were damaged in the quake, or burned down since. Along with their records. So, we can't trace if she was admitted or—" he leaves the sentence unfinished. "Many foreigners have been saved by their Japanese servants and friends, like our baby, Malou. We'll never forget Shigne-san's self-sacrifice. How quickly life changes, Louis."

"Maybe I can help you find out what happened now that I'm here," I say, nodding. "I'd also like to know if our cook and little Mariko survived the quake. I will do what I can to learn anything about them."

"There is so much to address," says Maurice. "But let me take you to the Bluff where you built your new houses."

I have been putting off thinking about the houses. As we turn onto what used to be a row of European style homes, only three partially-collapsed homes remain standing—and they are not mine. The rest burned or crumbled to the ground.

Walking clumsily along the former road, we stand in front of where I built my investment houses. "All four gone, as well as the two that were still under construction," I say. "I knew about it, but this is painful to see. I thought it was the perfect plan for a responsible father and husband. They were only two years old! I never even got a single rent payment." I shake my head. "Twenty-three years of work, Maurice, swallowed by an earthquake in one afternoon."

"Yes, and there are so many more of us in the same situation," Maurice says in a quiet voice. "Louis, you sell insurance. Will you not get money for your homes?"

"No, Maurice. I spoke with my company and the houses were not insured for a natural disaster or a vicious act of God. On top of that, I don't own the land. You know the Japanese let foreigners lease the land, but only Japanese citizens can own land. So no, Maurice. I have nothing except what is in the bank in France."

I look up and see groups of people walking by in thin ragged clothes on their way to get water from relief shelters, carrying what few containers they can find. It will take time to get clean city water flowing again. Some people are carefully carrying valuable bags of rice, also distributed by the city. There are no buses and few cars, and only the main roads have been cleared. Great fissures in the earth have appeared where some road used to be.

We sit on cement blocks for a rest. I feel overwhelmed, and I can only shake my head and look around in silence. After a few minutes I look up and see a familiar face across the road — my former employee, Daisuke.

"Monsieur Suzor! So good to see you!" He calls out. I rise as he comes towards me and we bow, and then shake hands.

"Daisuke-san! What are you doing here?"

"I'm so sorry your buildings burned, and your business office is gone," he says. "I have relatives in Yokohama and my brother had a photography studio that used to be on this street. I am here to help him and his family."

"Thank you, Daisuke-san. Maurice tells me all that is left is cinders."

"Perhaps you can rebuild a small office for now with building materials found in the rubble?"

"I don't know how or where to start to rebuild," I say, bowing my head.

Daisuke and Maurice understand. They have had time to acclimate to the new reality.

"I have saved money," says Daisuke. "If you need it, I can let you borrow to help start again. You will see the bank is gone and it is almost impossible to borrow money."

I look up, heartened by his generosity, a trait that I find so often in my Japanese friends and workers. "Thank you. I will be all right. I am not sure if I will rebuild. But that is a decision for later," I tell Daisuke.

"I will be in Tokyo if you need me. And I am so sorry your employees died in the fire. Some were my friends, too. So sorry," Daisuke says as we shake hands and bow to each other. We say goodbye for now.

As he picks his way through the rubble, away from us, Maurice says, "Louis, there is some hope here. The silk merchants have worked together, and we are leading some recovery efforts. The Yokohama government wants the silk buildings repaired and running again as soon as possible. The city has agreed to build twenty-nine houses for businessmen, and our family is on the list. Most international families, at least for now, have moved home or to Kobe, but we want to stay here."

I take this in to ponder. Somehow, businesses always go on. "Shall we go back to the ship? I'd like to see Paule and the children."

We slowly walk back to the new dock, each of us enmeshed in our own thoughts. I can feel emotion growing, full, in my chest, but I am still in too much shock to do anything with it. I don't know what to do. My mind is at a loss, with nothing to clutch. At least my family is alive and unharmed — that is a miracle. We don't speak much on our walk back to the docks, but I feel comforted at least to be with Maurice, a companion in this surreal environment.

As we walk, I decide to meet with Adhemar Ronvaux within the next few days to discuss business options. Adhemar has worked for me since he was fourteen years old, for almost twenty years, and I trust him to help and give me some guidance. Maurice said earlier that he is on the ship.

At the dock, we board the smaller boat to meet the French ship in the outer harbor. I read in the newspapers in Paris that the ship was almost burned from balls of oil on fire in the harbor. The crew of the boat saved the ship and the passengers. I look towards the ship, anxious to see my family.

The boat ties up to the ship and I climb the stairs to the ship's deck. Paule and the children meet me, and Sambe runs in circles and barks a welcome greeting. Jacques hasn't seen me in a long time, so he hides behind his mother's skirt. Paule hands baby Malou to me. I cradle her in my arms, careful to support her head of soft curls and admire her serene face. Not willing to give up this bundle yet, I hug Paule with my free arm. I can finally rest — I have been worried about her and the children, I realize. Holding the baby gives me a renewed sense of hope. I kiss her forehead and then give her back to her mother.

Maurice takes me by the arm and says, "Many people who sought refuge on the ship right after the earthquake have gone to other cities in Japan or to their home countries in Europe and America, so there's room on the ship. I have arranged for a cabin for you while you are here. And we will meet up with Adhemar later this evening — he and his family are on the ship as well. Come. It is not far from our cabin." Jacques, warming up, comes up to me and takes my hand as we walk down the wood paneled halls towards my room.

The next week is spent focusing on one thing at a time. What has happened to the people I knew? How do I rebuild a business without years of documents and records? How can I help the local community when I have nothing? So many questions without answers. My restless head pounds with ideas and questions, and I cannot sleep.

The next day, Adhemar and I board a smaller boat from our ship to the inner harbor. After a short ride, we tie up to the dock, and then step up to the walkway and start into town. We walk up Main Street to what used to be the Royal Hotel and many other businesses.

"Louis, people stopped to help get others out of the hotel before the fire came, but some did not get out before flames engulfed what was left of the brick building. And look," he says pointing to more unrecognizable bricks and debris. "The Yokohama United Club, a favorite meeting place for your automobile club. The concrete building used to be over here. Twenty people from our international community died when that building fell. The bodies have been removed, and all that is left is this white dust," Adhemar says, running his hand over a stack of stones and then brushing the powder off with his other hand.

"And then there was the tidal wave. Did you hear about it?"

"Yes, Maurice told me."

"Over 300 people died from the damage in Kamakura. If you walk to the village you can see boats on top of houses and the remains of homes under hills of sand that slid around and through the buildings and into the sea."

"Adhemar, this is too much. And we haven't even seen our business office. Do you think there is anything to save?" I ask him. The way the city looks, I really don't expect an encouraging answer.

"Let's keep walking down this road. I'm not even sure exactly where the office was, but I think we are close." The only things still standing are some streetlights on burnt poles.

"Wait, Adhemar," I say, "I think that two-story cement structure with the pointed roof was a city office. It was just three buildings down from our building." We stand and look at a pile of stones, broken beams, and crushed glass. Only the entryway arch remains. "Everything is burned and unrecognizable," I say. I have no words, and frustrated and overwhelmed, I kick the remains. Then, I stand and look for anything that might prove this was my office. But no luck—not even a stapler. Anything that could have been saved after the quake was then destroyed by the fire.

"What do you know about our employees? Who died in the wreckage?"

"Right now," Adhemar answers, his voice quiet, "the city has lists of people missing and they are trying to match it with people who survived or are known to have died. I check it once a week, but 14 of your employees are still missing. I am so sorry. What a nightmare."

I rub my eyes to stop the tears that are rising. Twenty-five years of work, gone. In an instant. Now, standing here at the ruins of our office, I know there is nothing that can be done. My shoulders start to shake, and I cry silently, finally.

Adhemar stands in silence with me until I can speak again.

"I don't know how I would have handled the situation if I had been here," I say as we look around us. Only the contours of the land remain.

"Let's go, Louis. Let's get back to our families as it is getting close to lunch." I am relieved to go, and to follow someone else's direction for a few moments.

When we get to the docks, we sit on a low wooden rail overlooking the new makeshift pier while we wait for a smaller boat to ferry us across the harbor. Bobbing like a pod of large gray whales, relief warships anchor in the bay with their precious cargo.

"Adhemar," I say after a long silence. "I want to thank you first and foremost for everything you have done for our company in Yokohama these past two years. We barely survived that dishonest thief of a priest we put in charge, and now the earthquake has swallowed even more. I don't know what I would have done if you hadn't been here."

"Oh, Louis," he says, looking at me. "It is my pleasure. I have been working hard and am proud to be part of the business. Now we will work together and do what we can to restart the company. First, we need a building!"

"Bah, no. First, we need money to buy materials," I reply.

"Look, Louis. There is our boat. Let's go."

We step into a completely open boat. The fall air and marine breezes feel refreshing on my face. Since the current is going out and the wind is blowing against us, we get occasional splashes from the blue-green waves. Adhemar's enthusiasm and the winds have restored my energy a bit.

Once aboard, I join Maurice, Adhemar, and their families for lunch. We share bread, butter, and canned roast beef—clearly relief food from some other ships. The children eat quickly and are ready to play. Adhemar's wife offers to take care of Jacques and Malou, so Paule can spend some time with me so we can catch up on the last few months.

We sit on teakwood chairs on the deck. Warm blankets draped over our legs, we watch a colony of sea gulls hover and glide above us. Paule asks, "Papa. Did you hear that Karuizawa and Kose Hot Springs were not in the path of the earthquake?"

"Really?"

"The roads and bridges were repaired and widened before the earthquake, and from what I understand, the homes are undamaged. I've been thinking—our summer home and our belongings should still there, unharmed. If Kose wasn't so far away, and if it were summer, not fall, we could live there."

"It's too far away from business, Paule. But it is comforting to think that there is a house still standing for us, somewhere."

"Papa, could we go up there just to visit? I'm so tired of being in a small cabin on a ship, I think I'm going crazy. And the children are turning into wild animals, always climbing and getting into trouble."

"I'm sorry, Paule, but there are too many loose ends to tie up here in town. And after what Maurice told me about being robbed, I wouldn't take you and the children to the mountain anyways. You heard that the roads are safe, but who knows about the forests around the roads. I can't risk anything happening to you and the family. Not after I almost lost all of you, and Maurice already lost his brother. And we don't have an automobile."

"Yes, Papa, you are probably right. But," I ask, slowly. "Do you know anyone with an automobile? Maybe in a few weeks we could go, before the cold weather arrives?"

I can't help but chuckle. She is as persuasive as her mother. "Maybe, Paule. Maybe. We will have to see."

Maurice and Adhemar approach us from the outer decks, where they were talking with business friends. Paule pats my hand. "I'll leave you and these gentlemen to solve the rest of our problems," Paule says, excusing herself from the table to look after the children.

Maurice takes Paule's chair, and Adhemar brings a third over to join us. I sit back in my chair and ask, "Well, gentlemen, I have a question. How can we rebuild without bricks and lumber? How do people recover from such devastation? I can't figure it out. Whatever we do must be done quickly. I need money and materials to build an office, and I need small living quarters that I can stay in when I return to Yokohama to check in on the business."

"What if we gather materials from other buildings that have fallen?" asks Adhemar. "We could clear the rubble and remake a building."

"That is a good idea," Maurice responds, "but it would take too long, and getting workers now would be difficult. The city is still in shock. I think we would have to build in a new location."

"I don't have enough money to buy materials," I say. "But Paule just gave me a new idea. What about our family's summer home? I could sell it and use the money to buy the new materials." Adhemar wrinkles his brow, and Maruice leans in. "We aren't using it anymore, and I was planning on selling it at some point in the future, anyways. It won't sell for as much as it would have before the quake, since no one has money right now, but maybe someone would have enough."

"That's a good idea," says Maurice.

"I agree," says Adhemar. "Now all you need is a way to get to Kose."

"Adhemar, would you go up the pass with me, if I can find a vehicle? It might be a bit risky."

"Yes, of course I will. Let's go back into town early tomorrow morning and see if we can borrow a truck from a garage, if any survived. Some have been coming in on the main roads from Kose, so there is a possibility. If we are lucky, we might be able to start right away."

The next morning, we find a garage with a truck that works, most of the time. We rent it for several days and start our ascent up 3,200 feet to Karuizawa. The main roads to the pass were cleared promptly after the earthquake to allow people, carts, and vehicles to move in and out of the city. The journey is only ten miles, but the roads are narrow and steep. The going is slow.

Finally, around noon, we park in front of my two-story summer home. We jump down from the truck and go to the covered entryway. I look up and see all the curtains are closed and windows shut. I get out my key, slide it into the lock, and open the door. The air smells musty, but I see the furniture still covered with linen sheets, just like we left it over a year ago. I have missed coming here, and today is probably the last time I will see it before it is sold.

"Well, Adhemar," I say, returning to the porch, "with a little paint the place should look great. Selling this house should be easy, I predict. Let's go see if the owners of the hot springs and hotel would like to buy it." I take one last look inside, and then close and lock the door. Investments are paying off, even if not as I expected.

We hop back into the truck for a short drive this time, up and down a few roads, and then onto the dirt road behind Kose Hot Springs and Bath. Young pine trees line strangely quiet streets. I am surprised at the lack of children playing in the pools with their families. I park the noisy truck, and Adhemar and I disembark.

Before we get to the door, the odor of sulfur greets us. I open the tall sandalwood gate and we enter a spacious steam filled hall. Inside are hefty cisterns made of thick wood. The rims of the tubs are level with the floor, and the baths sink deep in the ground. Each bath can accommodate four adults, comfortably seated. Usually the tubs are all occupied, but not today. There are only a few bathers this morning.

Adhemar and I go through two more doors to the front desk. To our surprise, we are not greeted as we have been in the past. I don't recognize the people at the front desk of the Hotel and Baths. A man steps forward, dispensing of usual pleasantries. No bows or offers of tea. Instead, he appears detached and unsociable. He won't even look at me. The atmosphere in the room is tense.

"*Konnichi wa.* I am here on business. I would like to sell my summer home at a very low cost, and I thought it may be a good investment for you and your business."

"I am sorry, but I cannot buy your house. We have many families we are helping in Yokohama, and we cannot afford it now. No one can afford a summer home."

"It is much lower than the usual price, as I said," I counter-offer.

"Thank you for opportunity," the owner says, turning, and leaving the room.

Adhemar and I turn and look at each other, surprised not only by the uncustomary treatment, but also because we are not sure what to do next.

"What do we do now?" I ask Adhemar, as we leave the building.

"It looks like we turn around and go back to Yokohama."

"No, no. Not yet. We clearly can't sell the house. This simply calls for a new strategy!" After the drive, and the change in setting, my business wheels are turning again. "I won't despair yet."

Adhemar laughs. "There is the Louis I know! We are on the quest again! You have that look in your eye. What is your idea, business partner?"

"Well," I respond. "Do you remember how the villagers relocated their houses on the way to Nikko, all those years ago?"

"How could I forget? It was an amazing moving village!"

"Do you think we can put the two-story summer home on logs and roll it down the mountain?"

"Louis! What? Are you serious?"

"No, of course not. But I have an idea that might get us a small building in Yokohama," I say, trying to sound hopeful. "Since we don't own any land, but we do have a house that no one will buy, we really have only one possibility. I believe we must disassemble the house and take it all down the mountain on a train car."

"This is absurd, Louis."

"I know it sounds crazy, but I think we can do it if we can get enough help. Adhemar, let's find some strong men who would like a job for several days or more."

The next day the work begins. I send two of the ten workers Adhemar has hired through the Kaurisawa local authorities up our ladder and onto the roof to remove the shingles. While he is doing that, I travel back to the train station and speak with the station master who rents us a train car for three days.

"Adhemar!" I call over the pounding of hammers. "Tell the rest of the men to remove the doors when they are ready. And watch out for flying shingles outside."

"I will, Louis!" I look up from inside the house and see blue sky between the beams above me. We are making progress.

"And Adhemar," I add. "How many doors and windows do we need in Yokohama?"

"I think we should take as many as we can, even if we don't need them all. People can use the materials in town. And if there is too much for the train, we will leave the rest here. Someone will put it to good use."

We work side-by-side with our crew for several days, and when we run out of light each night, the men who live out of town find places to sleep on top of and under blankets all around the property. I get to sleep in my old bed inside the house—what remains of it—looking up at the stars through where the roof used to be.

The second and third days we take numerous trips to the train station, bringing everything from the house, including beds, chairs, and other furniture, to the flat-bed train car, and send them all down the mountain. The final morning, we take the supporting beams and cut them into reasonable lengths, so we can move them easily.


On the afternoon of the third day, we drive the rest of the household goods that did not fit in the train-car down the mountain in the rental truck. As we wind left and right down the switchbacks, I feel hopeful doing something useful instead of dwelling on my own problems in the city.

I reminisce over those weekends spent with family and with members of the automobile club. And even before that, I remember my first automobile trip driving up into the mountains to meet the mayor and motoring down, one flat tire filled with roadside grasses. I remember the people, too: the villagers rolling their homes to a new location, the farmer trying to control his frightened horse and cart filled with packages of salt back when the road was narrow and only one lane. I fondly remember bringing friends and family up to our mountain retreat and raising our children here in the summers. Our life here was good. And as I descend into the city, I wonder to myself, how much longer will I stay? Is it time to go home?

Over the next few weeks, I work on building a small business office. The city managers rent me a spot that has been cleared of debris, not far from the harbor. With the help of another crew of workers, we assemble the building materials from the mountain onto the property. I hire and supervise a small crew to build a makeshift hut in town as our new office, complete with a desk and chairs from our summer home.

Once it is finished, I feel a modicum of comfort. The business has a place from which to regrow, like a lesser phoenix from the ashes. And I have a small yet thoroughly adequate place from which to work and live when I return for business in the future.

While the new construction is happening, I spend the nights in my cabin on the *Andre Le Bon*. The time with my family and friends is a warm distraction on this challenging trip. I am getting older, I can feel it, and my body is tired from the physical work. But my heart is full, and I feel through and through how much I love this place, the Japanese people, and the international way of life that my business provides.

After dinner the night before I leave, I go above deck to relax and sit in a comfortable lounge chair. The months have turned their wheel of time to October, and the sea offers her cool evening breeze to the deck. The stars sprinkle the sky, and a persimmon-orange crescent moon emerges over a cloud bank in the east. Its reflection on the shimmering water adds to the natural masterpiece equal to any in a Paris museum.

Paule comes to join me on the deck. She sits down in a chair next to me and puts a cashmere blanket over her lap, just like her mother would do. I notice she has changed from a funny young girl who always followed her sister's cues, to a woman with her own mind, a serious wife, and devoted mother in just a few years.

"Beautiful stars tonight, aren't they, Papa?"

"Yes, Paule. As beautiful as ever."

"So, Papa, what will you do?" she asks, tucking the blanket in under her skirt. "Will you rebuild a big house in town again? Will you continue your business?"

"*Chérie*, I don't know, but I have been thinking very seriously about all of the complications and difficulties in front of us. You and Maurice are young, and he has a bright future in the silk industry. But do you want to stay in Yokohama?"

"Yes, Papa. Maurice is convinced we can rebuild and live here, or maybe Australia. Right now, Yokohama is the center of silk in Asia, so it would be advantageous for us to stay. He loves the business and sees opportunities for advancement in his future."

"Well, Paule, I am downhearted, as are many people I see every day in Yokohama. I want you to have a good, full, and joyous life, and if you feel that can be done here, then this is where you should be." She nods and smiles a half-smile, acknowledging the distance there will be between us in the years to come. "However, your mother and I talked extensively before I left Paris about what our future holds. From a business point of view, motorcars are now being made in Japan. Buses are replacing streetcars. Tires will soon be made in Japan, and the people will support their own country's products. Many people blame the earthquake on foreigners, and a new nationalism seems to be brewing," I say.

Paule puts her arm in mine and says, "I am so glad you are here, Papa, and I think it is also time for you to spend more time at home at the chateau in France. You have worked hard and gave us a wonderful life in this city. You spend much of your time away from *Maman*, between your time here in Yokohama and the months it takes to travel from there to here."

"Perhaps that is so, Paule."

"You could turn to your wood carving and gardening if you were in one place. You have been wanting that for years. And I think I hear you saying that you might believe it is time to go home, too."

"Yes, perhaps, Paule. But I will continue to work from Paris for a few years. I can't leave Adhemar and the business the way things are now. We will get the business moving again, but on a much smaller scale. I'll have to take a few more trips, still, and it will be a good excuse to come see you and the grandchildren when I am here on business."

"Oh, Papa, you do love this country and the people! Even under these miserable conditions you are finding it hard to leave!"

"Yes, Paule. You are very observant. When I was young, I was always eager to try new things and visit far-away places. But the earthquake has changed Yokohama, as Japan has changed me. My affection for this country will always be a part of me. I'm not fully French anymore. When I was your age, I didn't know where my travels would take me. But I think they have taken me far enough. Your mother and I had our chance to be young, and now it is your family's turn. Christmas is in two months, so it is time I go back to Henriette in Paris. She is my home."

"That is wise, Papa. And I promise, we will be okay here. Maurice will take care of us."

The next morning, I step down from a ladder on the *André Le Bon* into a small passenger boat in order to transfer to a different ship. Marseilles is my destination, and my ship leaves today. As two men untie the large ropes between the ship and our boat, I look up to the passenger deck above me. Paule and her family are at the steel railing to see me off. Paule, carrying Malou, leans in toward Maurice. He bends down and lifts Jacques up to the rail. They all wave and blow kisses, and I put on the face of the happy traveler, waving back with gusto.

I am leaving another daughter behind. My heart aches as it did each time we had to leave Andree behind. But this time is different—I know we will not permanently reunite, as we have done with Andree. Instead, Paule and her family survived the devastation of their city and will create and follow their own new path. I trust they will do well.

My family becomes smaller as the transport boat navigates between relief ships and merchant vessels. After a bumpy ride, we tie up to the ocean liner. I grab my leather bag, climb the ladder, and transfer to the steps that lead to the passenger deck. From there I climb more steps to the front deck. I'm not ready to go inside, not quite yet.

Leaning once again on the iron rails, I look back at Yokohama Harbor. The salty breeze feels cold and fresh. I watch clouds separate as they travel across the skyline and I feel a golden warmth when the sun breaks through. Looking down, a kaleidoscope of colors and shapes reflects off the surface of the waves. My imagination plays games with my memories. On the crest of one wave I see the first automobile I brought to Japan. The chrome headlights glitter on the water. I can almost feel the smooth leather upholstery. I hear the rumble of the ship mimic the noise of my newly assembled motorcar. A whiff of oil from ship's black coiled lines brings me back to the mechanics disassembling the postal trucks. Another reflection reveals my silver coach clock oscillating on the waves below me.

The complaints of a flock of sea gulls interrupt my reverie. I walk across the deck to a teakwood chair and sit down, out of the wind. When I left France to come to Yokohama after the earthquake, my intent was to see my daughter and her family. Now I am satisfied they will be able to rebuild their lives.

But I was also looking to reclaim whatever had been left of my business, homes, and automobiles. Instead, the dragon twist took all of those away, its tail leaving a horrid path of destruction. There was nothing left for me to claim beyond a summer home in the mountains pieced for parts to rebuild my business.

I look back at Yokohama, and I say goodbye to the place into which I invested my time, passion, and imagination. I say goodbye to the risks I took that weren't meant to fail. And I say goodbye to the friends I met and the friendships I cultivated, and to the spirits of those who died in the earthquake.

The country I have known as home for twenty years has changed me and my family. The memories I am taking home in my heart cannot be packed into an automobile or an ocean liner. And they cannot be taken away.

# Chapter Twenty-Two

# Memories Held Close
## Nice, France, 1955

I take a deep breath and look out the library window. Champagne rain from the Mediterranean Sea mists the glass as droplets meet each other and pool on the bottom sill.

That's it! We need champagne to celebrate! *Finalement!* I have finished writing my memoir. The omniscient silent words of my intuition tell me that at long last my work is done.

I pull the last piece of paper from the typewriter and place it face down on the top of the stack. I turn the pages over, and see my manuscript, 100 pages long, looking back up at me. I must go and get Henriette to show her my finished work!

I push my chair away from my typewriter and pick up my cane from where it leans against my desk. I move more slowly than when I started this memoir, and I must be careful not to fall. No broken hips for me.

I leave the library and walk past the carp swimming on their silk *kakejiku.* On an oval marble table next to a family portrait, a porcelain statue of a Shinto fertility god holds a child in his arms and smiles at me. I come to the doorway of the drawing room, and Henriette rises from her chair to meet me.

"Henriette! Do we still have the bottle of champagne Gilbert gave us? We must have some tonight to celebrate! I can't wait to tell you—I finished my stories from Japan!"

"Louis, that is wonderful news," she says, taking my hand and giving me a kiss. "Come, my handsome husband, and sit with me on the sofa while I finish my tea."

She takes my free arm to help me stay balanced and hands me my cane so I can walk as best I can. I sit on the sofa and she settles in next to me, handing me my lap blanket. My knees and hands get cold these days, so I need the extra warmth. The coffee table in front of us has her latest embroidery project laid to the side. She is making dinner napkins with little blue pagodas on the corners. Next to her sewing project is an automobile magazine and her half-full teacup.

"Henriette. I wrote about our lives before and during our time in Japan. I would like to write about our lives after Japan, but I am 82 years old. My eyesight is not what it was, and I have a hard time hitting the right keys on the typewriter. Thank goodness I had the pictures and postcards to help me remember the years in Yokohama. Everything is getting as foggy as that city's harbor air. I'm afraid I'm too tired to write anymore."

"Louis, what an accomplishment. Ten years of work? I think that is enough, my love. This is something our grandchildren can read when they get older, and I think the pictures will be a great help sharing our extraordinary life in Japan." She smiles at me and pats my hand. "And we have certainly continued to have a remarkable life together."

"Indeed, we have," I say. "But I'm not sure what I'll do now without this project."

She smiles, but instead of answering, she asks, "Would you like me to help you pack up the pictures and papers in your office? Then, you can show me your finished manuscript."

"Yes, of course. But first, I want to show you something in this automobile magazine. My reading glasses are in the office. Maybe you can find the article. There is a picture of Maurice Trintignant and his red Ferrari! He won first place at the Monaco Grand Prix in May of this year."

"Louis, is his car another Red Devil? Do you remember that?" She laughs. "Sometimes when I am in the garden, I can hear the Formula One racers in Monaco all the way over here in Nice, 13 miles away. They are so much noisier than the street racers we saw in Paris in 1900."

"Lucky for me, Henriette, the noise doesn't bother me because my hearing is almost gone," I say as I watch her fan through the pages.

"I'm glad they have barriers on the streets, but I hope dogs understand what barriers are for. I still remember the dog we lost to The Red Devil and his friends," she sighs.

I decide not to tell her about the article I read last week, about one driver in this Monaco race who miscalculated a turn coming out of a tunnel and crashed through the barriers into the harbor. He had to swim to safety. No, no. I'll keep this one to myself.

"Yes, yes. I think this is the picture here," she says handing me the magazine.

I marvel at the fearless racecar driver. "Look. He has sparkling daredevil eyes, but he doesn't have Jenatzy's red devil hair. In fact, Trintignant is going bald! Henriette," I say, getting excited. "Do you know those cars can go 185 miles per hour? And to think I was excited when the

Red Devil went 26 miles per hour!" I can't help but laugh. "I wonder what cars will be like in another 50 years."

"Well, Louis, I don't think we will ever know. Now let's go to the library and I will help tidy things up," she says, standing. "I would like to have things put away before we go to see Malou and her family for the holidays. I can't wait to see our great-grandchildren again."

I stand up slowly, stiffly, and she hands me my cane. I choose my steps one by one as I pass by the sofa end tables with their Japanese blue and orange floral cloisonné lamps. A round wooden carved tray adorns the wall facing the kitchen. The inside of the tray has black lacquer crows perched on gold-leaf elm tree branches.

We walk together back to my library. When we enter, I can see my room from Henriette's perspective. She is right—it has become a bit cluttered.

I stand next to my desk chair and I feel a sense of relief to have finished this arduous task. I place the finished manuscript on the top shelf over my desk and sit down. At times I was afraid I wouldn't live long enough to see this day.

"Louis, look at the tea crate next to the desk. The paper covering has been wearing away slowly for years. The chrysanthemums on the front are faded, and the wooden sides show signs of some water damage," Henriette says as she rubs the corners with her hand where paper has worn through to bare wood. She opens the box, leans the wooden cover against a chair, and makes room for the remaining photos and cards.

Henriette brings the small ornate green brocade chair from under the window closer to the tea crate and sits down. I start to pick up small stacks of assorted postcards with Japanese postal stamps. I hand them to Henriette, and she places them neatly on top of other papers. She gets up and walks the several steps across the small room to gather pictures from the silver tea tray in the corner, some from the windowsill and still others from a shoe box under the sofa.

"Lucky for us the tea crate has a strong tin lining," she says, raising her eyebrow, and placing photographs and postcards into the crate. "Our paper memories have been well kept by the wooden chest. Thank goodness it was in the guest house during the fire, remember? Here, hand me some more."

"There you go. I think that is it," I say. "We can arrange them in order by date some other time. Oh. And one more thing. I almost forgot," I say. I get up, shuffle to the windowsill and pick up my coach clock from Yokohama.

"Look, Henriette. This clock was in my first order of automobiles from France to Yokohama. I remember opening this tea crate, and inside was a smaller wooden box. I took the coach clock out and felt so proud to see *Yokohama Automobile Garage* printed on the face. We even had some made for the Automobile Club."

I hold the clock in my hands for a moment. The hands haven't worked for several years, but the memories are strong and clear.

Henriette sits back down in the brocade chair next to the crate and watches as I bring the time piece to the box. She hands me a cotton doily from the armchair, and I wrap the clock up and place it gingerly on top of our photos, postcards, letters, and other memorabilia in the box. I sit down in my oak chair and look at her, and notice tears welling in her eyes, too. She gets up and brings me the worn wooden lid, and together we cover, and hold close, our memories.

# Epilogue

Chateau de Bel Air purchased in the Loire Valley, 1921

# Epilogue

The Kanto earthquake changed the Suzor family's lives forever. Louis closed his business in Japan in 1937 for several reasons. He was getting older and it was difficult to run a business from so far away with others in charge. There were financial problems and the international community felt nationalistic tremors coming from Japan. Foreigners were no longer welcome.

Fortunately, in 1921, two years before the earthquake, Louis bought the Chateau de Bel Air in the Loire valley. After the earthquake, he had to mortgage Bel Air to save his business.

In 1930, Louis and Henriette's youngest child, Georges, died at 24 after a terrible glider crash in an airfield in Tours, France. He used a rope instead of a safety belt, and the injuries from impact proved fatal a week after the crash. They were overwhelmed with grief at their loss, always feeling his absence.

Activities on the farm were a welcome distraction. There were 7 hectares of park, 30 of farm, and 50 of forest. It was a wonderful place to spend time with family, especially grandchildren. However, Louis started feeling restless and ready to move.

In 1938, he decided the Chateau de Bel Air was too big and too much work for a man of 65, even though he had maids and farmers hired to help. He bought the Chateau de Rilly from the Comte de Chauvelin. It was smaller and more manageable. They even rented rooms out to the clergy for their vacations.

They had been at Rilly only two years when German Panzer divisions invaded France in 1940.

Henriette and Louis went to Millery to stay with their daughter, Paule, and her growing family. He clearly remembered Luftwaffe planes shooting at cars and people as they tried to escape to the south.

In 1943, before Hitler and Petain signed an armistice making peace with Germany, the Gestapo discovered that Louis' daughter's family were secretly stowing a great stock of arms and they all fled into hiding. They escaped back to the Chateau de Rilly, but it wasn't safe. Louis arranged for them to hide at the farm of a generous and kind American with help from the caretaker of his property.

As the end of the German occupation approached, the younger men in the family went most nights to join a resistance movement. One captain spent the war in a big dugout in the middle of a cultivated field covered by a corrugated iron roof, then covered with dirt. He stayed there all day, only to come out at night. He was in daily contact with London by radio, receiving their instructions about actions to take and sending news of German movements.

At last, the great day came, and the other side of the Loire River was liberated. It took several weeks for the Americans to come to his side of the river. They didn't know who was at the chateau and shot at Louis' family sporadically. Louis had everyone settle in the corridor at the back of the chateau to keep his family safe.

Louis decided to get a local fisherman to help him get to the other side and let them know his family was not German. He met with an American officer and the shooting stopped.

A few days later, five American commandos crossed the river to check on what they thought was a canon. They all laughed when they saw it was the handle of an abandoned cart.

On their way back, the same soldiers came to Louis' chateau where a crowd from the village, together with his family, showered them with food, wine, and gifts.

From then on, they never saw any Germans except prisoners.

On August 16, 1947, Louis and Henriette celebrated their fiftieth wedding anniversary at the chateau with their growing family. The next year, at age 75, Louis felt restless again, and decided to sell Rilly and move to a smaller home in Notre Dame d'Oe, in the Manor of La Noue. He spent his time carving fish using Julius Bien lithographs to guide his hands and eyes. He painted them in natural colors revealing his innate ability as an artist. He even carved a carp freehand by watching it swim in their bathtub, and he had the carving bronzed when it was finished. It is easy for to see the influence of his time in Japan in the fish's graceful curves and twists.

In 1953 he moved again. Their new home was in Nice, France on the Avenue de la Corniche Fleuri. They stayed there for 4 years, then moved again to 71 Boulevard du Mont Boron, enjoying the warm climate by the water.

In these later years, he started to lose his hearing and his sight. Henriette was always kind and patient with him when he struggled. One of his joys, even though he couldn't see well, was to go around the table and hold her chair out for her to sit down for dinner. He wouldn't have wanted her to think that his age was keeping him from being a gentleman.

In 1967, at the age of 94, my great-grandfather passed away from natural causes. Henriette moved in with her grand-daughter Marie Louise. My great-grandmother, Henriette, died in 1976 at the age of 96 of natural causes as well.

Like Louis and Henriette, I hold their memories close. This book is a tribute to their words, family stories and photographs that guided me through their museum of memories.

Chateau de Rilly-sur Loire in Loire et Cher purchased 1938
in central France.

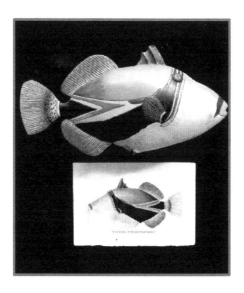

One of the many fish Louis carved for his aquarium in the wall. The picture
he used shows how he used a pencil to grid out the colors and shapes on the
wood. The original drawing was by A.H. Baldwin, and the lithographer
Julius Bien created the pictures for the US Fish Commission Bulletin *The Reef
Fish of the Hawaiian Islands* 1903. This carving is 9"x 4".

# Appendices

An oil painting of fiancée Henriette at 16
in 1896. Paris, France

An early proposal led to the wedding of Louis and Henriette.
Married August 1, 1897. Paris, France

From the left: Louis born 1903, Paule born 1900, and Edith born 1898.
Yokohama, Japan

Maneuvering a narrow road on a mountain
outside of Yokohama, Japan

A dinner with family and friends at home in Japan. The painting on the
wall on the left was by a cousin, Sir John Everett Millais (1829-1896). It was
a portrait of Louis' mother's brother, Laurence Malet de Graville. and was
later lost in a fire

Edith got her Japanese driver's license several years after her father on
April 7, 1918. Louis' journal states her license was the first granted
in Japan to a person of the fairer sex.

Postcard of Motomachi Street in Yokoham

Beibendum advertisement for Michelin tires. "*Nunc est bibendum*", means "Now it is time to drink." He was created to look like a stack of tires. He says, "Here's to your health. The Michelin tire drinks up obstacles."

New home in Honmoku built in the Japanese style,
constructed to withstand typhoons.

The new home after a typhoon. It took a bit of work,
but it was reconstructed and remained a wonderful summer home.

Postcard of Chuzenji Lake, Nikko.

Postcard of Mizusawa Temple, Ikano.

Postcard of Bishamen Hall at Misen, Itsukushima with postal stamp.

Family portrait from left: Paule, Henriette, Edith, Louis and Georges. A framed picture of Andree is on the table because she could not live in Yokohama or in the high mountains because of asthma.
She remained in Paris with grandmothers.

Louis and Henriette are on the balcony of their family summer home in Karuizawa. The resort was popular for westerners as a welcome escape from summer heat and humidity in the coastal lowlands. It was dismantled and brought down from the mountain board by board to build a small office in Yokohama after the earthquake.

Andree in chiffon dress in Paris circa 1915.

Edith with Mariko. Yokohama.

Mariko finds a new family with Amah.

Dressed for the Armistice Day Parade from the left: Family friend Aubree, Edith, Paule, Georges, Henriette, son Louis, and Louis Suzor.

Paule graduated from Sacred Heart Convent in Tokyo. Third row down from the top and seven students from the left. She graduated and went back with the family to Paris, but returned to Yokohama, unaware of what lay ahead for her and her family.

Homeward bound on the Empress of Japan.
Edith posing for a photo 1919.

Paule and Maurice Viel wedding. 1920 Paris, France.

Shigne-san. The Suzor family remains grateful for her courage
and sacrifice for baby Malou.
Photo taken by F. Fukuda Studio, Yokohama. Suzor Collection.

Craters in the road in Yokohama. Suzor Collection.

Young man walks among the ruins of Yokohama. Suzor Collection.

Kanto earthquake aftermath. Tokyo and Yokohama in ruin. Getty Images.

# Family Tree

Louis Pierre Theodore Suzor married
Edith Villeneuve Malet de Graville

They had three sons
**Louis Marie,**
Paul, and Georges William

Marie Eugene Boutard married
Fanny Laure Boutard

They had two daughters
**Henriette Adrienne,**
and Adrienne

**Louis and Henriette were married August 1,1897**
They had five children

**Edith** Henriette Fanny Eugenie Marie was born May 26, 1898
**Paule** Henriette Marie was born July 18, 1900
**Andree** Marie was born August 16, 1901
**Louis** Philippe Jean was born January 7, 1903
**Georges** was born September 26, 1906

Letters from Grandson Gilbert 1952

In Chapter 15, Louis and Henriette receive letters from their grand-son Gilbert. Born in 1931, he would have been 21 years old at the time. I asked Gilbert if he would write a few letters imagining himself 21 years old and writing to them about his travels. Gilbert welcomed the opportunity and wrote these three letters.

*Dear Daddy and Manyette,*

*You will be quite thrilled I have arrived in Hong Kong. The trip on the cargo ship Le Tournay has taken one month. I left Marseille late June 1952 and we stopped first in Genoa for one day.*

*Then the ship took the direction of the Strait of Messina and reached the Stromboli Volcano at midnight. It was in eruption, and as the sea was calm, the spectacle was a pure miracle with jets of lava illuminating the sea for miles. The next day we reached Port Said and crossed the Suez Canal, and I thought of all the times you travelled there. In Suez, 4 Yemenites from Nasser Military School boarded the ship. We became quite friendly, and they explained they were on their way to help with a revolt against Sudan, and would I be interested in joining them?*

*They disembarked in Aden, Yemen, without me! However, when I arrived in Colombo, Sri Lanka the newspapers showed photos of the brother of a Sultan parading on his horse with the head of his brother at the tip of his sword. I was happy to leave to our next stop.*

*After, we stopped in Penang and Singapore where I had lunch at the Raffles Hotel.*

*With all my love,*
*Gilbert*

*Dear Daddy and Manyette,*
*I have spent a marvelous 2 months in Hong Kong with Vera and her family.*
*They own a magnificent 60 ft. sailing yacht, dark blue with white sails. A*
*winner of the Sydney Hobart race. Every weekend we go sailing around the*
*many islands of Hong Kong territory.*
*During the week, I try to sell the fabrics produced by my parents' firm in*
*Lyon. I want to go to Japan, but I cannot afford to stay there because it is*
*too expensive. So, I applied with Jardines Matheson to be a passenger on*
*one of their old cargo ships that has sailed for the last 50 years (except dur-*
*ing the war) between Calcutta and Yokohama and back with many stops.*
*The ship was about to leave for Japan, so I boarded it and saw there was*
*only one passenger, a French woman who was a journalist, and the ship*
*staff. The bottom deck was full of Chinese passengers who had no communi-*
*cation with the top deck!*
*I look out the window at the grey weather with a forecast of a possible ty-*
*phoon. We reach Hsinchu port, Taiwan, and the journalist very kindly ar-*
*ranges for a one-day visa for me so I can take a bus and quickly visit Taipei.*
*When I return to the ship, we leave the harbor and the typhoon strikes us*
*and follows the ship until we enter the inland sea. Tremendous waves make*
*the ship's bow plunge down, picking up great quantities of water that gush*
*to the back of the ship. On the way, it fills my cabin with one foot of water,*
*but I manage to keep on the top bed with my luggage.*
*The typhoon passes and we stop in Moji (Kitakiushu). After we sail through*
*the inland sea, a magnificent scenery appears like a garden of Bosai trees*
*floating on a blue sea. Kobe is a short stop and finally Yokohama.*
*I tried to find 31 Bluff, your old neighborhood in Yokohama. The taxi driver*
*said it was all rebuilt after the earthquake. Then I took a tour bus to the 5*
*Fuji Lakes, but it rained all the way and I never saw the volcano. Next, I*
*took a train to Kamakura and admired the Buddha. Last, I took a train from*
*Yokohama to Kobe to catch up with the ship returning to Hong Kong, and at*
*last I saw Mount Fuji from the train.*
*With all of my love,*
*Gilbert*

*Dear Daddy and Manyette,*

*I left Hong Kong shortly after returning from Japan. I was booked on a P&O passenger ship. I slept on the bottom of a ships cabin with eight beds. A lot of snoring men! Daddy, I am reminded that your father travelled in third class on trains, even though he was reasonably wealthy. His friends would ask, "Mr. Suzor. Why do you travel 3$^{rd}$ class?" and he would answer," Because there is no 4$^{th}$!"*

*Most of my fellow travelers have dark skin and they are not at all friendly. I would like to talk to them, but I can feel their dislike of me because I am white. Luckily, I have found a friend, an Irishman. Unfortunately, he starts drinking whiskey at 10am, followed by a beer chaser (as he says), and by mid-day he is quite drunk.*

*We are bound for Bombay, India, via Singapore and Colombo. I went to visit a tea plantation and had a ride on an elephant with the mahout guiding the elephant on foot while I rode on the neck. A question of balance!*

*I arrived in Bombay, not in my smartest appearance, welcomed by Dabeh and Sylla in their brand new luxurious white Buick convertible with a chauffeur in white uniform. My small luggage promptly disappeared on the large boot and I was seated between my Godmother and Sylla, driven through Bombay to Petit Hall. Arriving there, I saw their magnificent estate, a copy of the White House, in the very best residential area of Bombay, complete with a park going down to the sea. I walked inside and I was given a suite with a bathroom and a boy whose job it is to serve me while I am here. My godmother explains that they are short of staff, having reduced from 600 before the war to only 40 servants and workers now, a service unknown to me in France. When I go out for a walk and come back sweating, I take a shower, throwing all my underwear and shirt to the ground. Two hours later, I find everything washed, ironed, and placed in the cupboards.*

*My Godmother Dabeh, inspecting my wardrobe, decided it was insufficient, took me to the best taylor in Bombay and ordered, after measurements were taken, a dinner suit and a number of fashionable bush shirts. Obviously, my life was going to change radically for my 6-month visit. I will keep you informed!*

*Your loving son,*

*Gilbert*

# Reference List by Chapter

## The Suzor Collection

This heart of this collection is a journal Louis Suzor completed in Nice, France, 1955 titled Souvenirs des Débuts de l'Automobile au Japon. The collection includes letters and postcards written to and from Louis and Henriette and their children. There is also a stunning photographic account spanning Louis and his family's 20 years in Japan and Paris. There is an audio interview with Philippe, one of Paule's children. Gilbert Viel, another grandson, provided me with his written stories and memories of Louis. My grandmother, Edith, saved pictures and postcards and diligently wrote little anecdotes by some pictures and on the back of others. Newspaper articles and records of births and marriages are included in the collection.

## Chapter 1 Le Diable Rouge

"Camille Jenatzy (1865-1913)." uniquecarsandarts.com.au/history
Suzor Collection « Souvenirs des Débuts de l'Automobile au Japon.
1 :1-2)

## Chapter 2 Soupe du Jour and a Marriage Proposal

Suzor Collection Oral history

## Chapter 3 A Zouave, A Gentleman, and Cabaret Pasha

Calatayud, Jesus. Gonzalez, Angel; "History of the Development and Evolution of Local Anesthesia Since the Coca Leaf." Anesthesiology 2003; 98(6);1503-1508. anesthesiology.pubs.asahq.org

Editor. Military History Now. "Meet the Zouaves. A Brief History of the 19th Century's Most Colorful Soldiers." May 27, 2013 MilitaryHistoryNow.com

Heggoy, Alf Andrew. "Education in French Algeria: An Essay on Cultural Conflict." Comparative Education Review, vol. 17, no. 2, 1973, pp. 180–197. JSTOR, www.jstor.org/stable/1186812

Suzor Collection. Oral history, photographs, and written accounts.

## Chapter 4 Tragedy at the Bazaar de la Charité

Alister. « Le Bazar de la Charite. » September 9, 2014 France-PUB.com

Watch the Films of the Lumiere Brothers and the Birth of Cinema 1985." Culture and Educational Media on the Web. www.openculture.com. Aug. 201

Suzor Collection. Oral history and written account

## Chapter 5   Henriette's Intuition

McCullagh, Francis. "The Story Tellers in Japan." Pp.214, 215. East of Asia Magazine. Volume 1. Shanghai. North China Herald Office. 1902

Suzor Collection. Oral history and written account

## Chapter 6   Precious Cargo

Kato, Yuzo. Yokohama Then and Now. Yokohama City University. 1990

Suzor, Louis. « Souvenirs des Débuts de l'Automobile au Japon. ». (1 :2-3)

Suzor Collection. Oral history and written account

Kato, Yuzo. Yokohama Then and Now. Yokohama City University. 1990

## Chapter 7   The Mayor on the Mountain

Kato, Yuzo. Yokohama Then and Now. Yokohama City University. 1990

Suzor, Louis. « Souvenirs des Débuts de l'Automobile au Japon». (2:5-8)

## Chapter 8   Siberian Roulette

De Windt, Harry Paris to New York by Land Thomas Nelson and Sons ca.1904

Martin, Janet. Treasure of the Land of Darkness. Cambridge University Press. December 11, 1986.

Suzor Collection. Oral history and written account by family.

## Chapter 9   Pulling Strings

Kato, Yuzo. Yokohama Then and Now. Yokohama City University. 1990

Strelavina, Daria. Russia Beyond the Headlines. "Caviar: Russia's Original Black Gold." rbth.com/longreads/black_caviar. 2016

Suzor Collection. Oral history and written account by family.

Suzor, Louis. « Souvenirs des Débuts de l'Automobile au Japon». (3:14-16)

## Chapter 10  Ocean in a Box

Association French Lines. "Association French Lines: History and Heritage."

Le Havre, France. Eric Giuily, Publishing Department. February 2016

Suzor Collection. Oral history and written account by family.

Suzor, Louis. « Souvenirs des Débuts de l'Automobile au Japon. ». (2:12-13)

## Chapter 11  Mechanical Marvels

Kato, Yuzo. Yokohama Then and Now. Yokohama City University. 1990

Suzor Collection. Oral history and written accounts

Suzor, Louis. « Souvenirs des Débuts de l'Automobile au Japon». (3:17-18)

## Chapter 12 Something given, Something Taken Away

Suzor Collection. Oral history and written accounts

Suzor, Louis. « Souvenirs des Débuts de l'Automobile au Japon». (5:30-31)

Wanczura, Dieter. "Fires and Firemen. Ukiyo-E Collection of Japanese Art Prints from the 18th Century." Icking, Germany. Artelino.com

## Chapter 13 Rules of the Road

Kato, Yuzo. Yokohama Then and Now. Yokohama City University. 1990

Suzor Collection. Oral history and written accounts

Suzor, Louis. « Souvenirs des Débuts de l'Automobile au Japon». (4:20-23)

## Chapter 14 Three Geishas and the Michelin Man

Suzor Collection. Oral history, photographs, and written accounts

Suzor, Louis. « Souvenirs des Débuts de l'Automobile au Japon. (4:23-24)

Bardsley, Jan "The New Woman Meets the Geisha: The Politics of Pleasure in 1910's Japan." Intersections: Gender and Sexuality in Asia and the Pacific. Issue 29. May 7, 2012.

## Chapter 15 The High Road to Nikko

Kato, Yuzo. Yokohama Then and Now. Yokohama City University. 1990

Suzor Collection. Postcards and written account by family.

Suzor, Louis. « Souvenirs des Débuts de l'Automobile au Japon. (4:23-24)

## Chapter 16 Midori Bird Gets a Ticket to Ride

Kato, Yuzo. Yokohama Then and Now. Yokohama City University. 1990

## Chapter 17 Mariko

Suzor Collection. Oral history, photographs, and written account by family.

## Chapter 18 The Yokohama Armistice Day Parade

Kato, Yuzo. Yokohama Then and Now. Yokohama City University. 1990

Suzor Collection. Oral history, photographs, and written account by family.

## Chapter 19 Homeward Bound

Association French Lines. "Association French Lines: History and Heritage."

Le Havre, France. Eric Giuily, Publishing Department. February 2016

Suzor Collection. Oral history, photographs, and written accounts

Suzor, Louis. « Souvenirs des Débuts de l'Automobile au Japon. » Journal.

## Chapter 20 Namazu the Earth Shaker

Hammer, Joshua. "Aftershocks. The Powerful Earthquake that struck Yokohama and Tokyo on    September 1, 1923, traumatized a nation and unleashed historic consequences." Smithsonian. May 2011

Kato, Yuzo. Yokohama Then and Now. Yokohama City University. 1990

Suzor Collection. Oral history, photographs, and written accounts

Suzor, Louis. « Souvenirs des Débuts de l'Automobile au Japon. » Journal.

Viel, Paule. Gilbert Viel, her son, shared a written record she wrote about her experiences during and after the earthquake.

## Chapter 21 Aftershocks

Hammer, Joshua. "Aftershocks. The Powerful Earthquake that struck Yokohama and Tokyo on September 1, 1923, traumatized a nation and unleashed historic consequences." Smithsonian. May 2011

Kato, Yuzo. Yokohama Then and Now. Yokohama City University. 1990

Suzor Collection. Oral history, photographs, and written accounts

Suzor, Louis. « Souvenirs des Débuts de l'Automobile au Japon. (5:31-32)

Viel, Paule. Gilbert Viel, her son, shared a written record she wrote about her experiences during and after the earthquake.

Grace, Michael L. "Line History: Messageries Maritimes." www.cruisehistory.com. Feb.1, 2011

## Additional Resources

www.oldtokyo.com . Vintage Japanese Postcard Museum is a virtual collection of postcards from 1900-1960.

The Japan Weekly Mail. This newspaper began in 1870. It became The Japan Daily Mail and was written in English for foreigners in Yokohama. Archives are available and gave me a window into daily life and commerce in Yokohama at the turn of the century.

# Acknowledgements

I am so grateful to the following: My great-grandfather for taking the time when he was 82 to write his memories of his family's journeys in Japan. My grandmother Edith Suzor for keeping scrapbook upon scrapbook of postcards, photographs, letters, and even pressed flowers artfully placed on the pages chronicling her family's years in Yokohama. My mother Nicky Suzor Plath and her passion for our French family roots. My cousin Gilbert Viel in France, Louis' grandson, who was an endless source of stories passed on to him by his grandfather, historical dates, and positive encouragement as I shared chapters with him. Gilbert's mother, Paule, who wrote of her experiences on the day of the Kanto Earthquake and shared it with Gilbert. Anni Kamola who helped me with the structure and details of the stories brought youth to the character. Janet Bergstrom who gave me support and critical feedback when I needed it. Linda Kolody for her insight and honesty. Vickie Farmer for her encouragement and attention to detail, especially commas. My sister Sylvia Plath Moore (not that one) for tolerantly reading each chapter and her positive feedback. Quicksilver Photo Lab for their outstanding work in restoring vintage photographs. Hamilton Hayes for his discriminating photographic eye for the cover of this book. Norman L. Green's positive influence and patience in formatting and creating this book. Richard Pearce Moses for his expert guidance in referencing materials. Kate Batten for clarifying the mysteries of technology and helping me create a website. My family and relatives for urging me to persist, and most of all my husband, Doug, for patiently listening to these  stories for the three years it took bring this book to fruition.

Made in the USA
Middletown, DE
20 November 2020